MW00903876

Success

By Hilary Masters

NOVELS

The Harlem Valley Trio:
STRICKLAND
COOPER
CLEMMONS

PALACE OF STRANGERS
AN AMERICAN MARRIAGE
THE COMMON PASTURE

SHORT FICTION

HAMMERTOWN TALES
SUCCESS

BIOGRAPHY

LAST STANDS: NOTES FROM MEMORY

Success

New and Selected Stories

Hilary Masters

Foreword by George Garrett

ST. MARTIN'S PRESS
NEW YORK

SUCCESS. Copyright © 1992 by Hilary Masters. All rights reserved. Printed in the United States of America. No part of this book may be used or reproduced in any manner whatsoever without written permission except in the case of brief quotations embodied in critical articles or reviews. For information, address St. Martin's Press, 175 Fifth Avenue, New York, N.Y. 10010.

Design by DAWN NILES

Library of Congress Cataloging-in-Publication Data
Masters, Hilary.
    Success : new and selected stories / Hilary Masters : introduction by George Garrett.
        p. cm.
    ISBN 0-312-07090-X
    I. Title.
PS3563.A82S83   1992
813'.54—dc20   91-36384
                                        CIP

First Edition: February 1992

10 9 8 7 6 5 4 3 2 1

KATHLEEN

Yo me fío a
su fluir sosegado.

—*Octavio Paz*

Contents

Acknowledgments

These stories have appeared in different versions in these publications, which have my thanks for their permission to use them in this collection.

"Hall of Mirrors," *The Kenyon Review;* "The Foundation" and "Trotsky's House," *The Ohio Review;* "His Father's Garden," *The New England Review* and *Breadloaf Quarterly;* "A Mechanic's Life" and "On Silver Skates," *The Virginia Quarterly Review;* "Grace Peck's Dog" and "Success" from *Hammertown Tales,* published by Stuart Wright; "Touching Down," *Sewanee Review;* "Blues for Solitaire," *The Texas Review;* "Ohm's Law," *Provincetown Arts;* "The Moving Finger," *The Massachusetts Review;* "The Sound of Pines," *The Missouri Review;* "The Catch," *The North American Review;* "How the Indians Buried Their Dead," *The Georgia Review.*

Also, my gratitude to Carnegie-Mellon University for the support and community tendered me while most of these stories were written.

Foreword

The sixteen stories brought together in *Success* offer an ample and various representation of the short fiction of Hilary Masters. For some readers, meeting the author and his work for the first time, and at the prime of his professional career, this gathering may prove to be, among other things, a surprising experience in the sense that Keats had in mind when he argued that poetry must surprise "with a fine excess." Readers new to the writing of Hilary Masters are bound to be surprised they have not found him before now. For others, readers familiar with his six novels, his earlier collection of stories, *Hammertown Tales* (from which two of these stories are carried over), and from his perhaps best known single work so far, the autobiographical *Last Stands: Notes From Memory*, the stories of *Success* will serve to satisfy earned expectations and to confirm the sense of literary professionalism and excellence the other works of Hilary Masters have established.

There are, inevitably, some shared qualities in all of Masters's work, matters of the author's interests and concerns as well as choices, technical and rhetorical, that help to shape the identifiable characteristics of his fiction. Like our good artists and good athletes, our best writers develop some habits and cultivate them to advantage. In some cases a writer goes too far, permits habit to become the deliberate embrace of inhibitions at best, uncontrolled obsession at worst. The irony is that it is so much easier to market and to sell (therefore to publish) the former—the easily recognizable work of a writer with limited, even idiosyncratic means, focusing attention on certain specific (habitual) subject matter; and it is easier, sometimes more fun, to *talk about* (literary journalism becoming at once the source and fuel of other kinds of serious attention) those obsessive writers whose work can often be examined more as case studies of this and that than as exemplary literary experience.

Masters certainly has his habits as a story writer, but they are neither inhibited nor obsessive. His stories are accessible, written in an easy, graceful, and fluent language, very often quite close to the spoken American vernacular in rhythms, idiom, and vocabulary, though not limited to the range of talking voices, as the actual talking voices, the dialogue in these stories (and he has a fine-tuned ear for all kinds and nuances of dialogue) makes clear in contrast to the style of narration. That style is clean, clear, and almost always unmarked by any winks or buck-and-wing showboating of self-conscious virtuosity. One sign of this is the extremely sparing use of comparative images to divert or distract attention from the perceived and felt thing in itself. He is almost as sparing as Hemingway was in his use of similes. And when he does depend on the impact of comparison, it suddenly illuminates rather than diverting or distracting attention. See the smile of Bargello, "like a computer screen clicking on," in "Face in the Window." See also, in the same story, Professor Cantwell's perception of the dull and boring style of his son's letter from home: "But the prose ran on evenly like a suburban lawn; flat and neat with nothing untoward left carelessly in the context." There is nothing "flat and neat" about the prose style of Hilary Masters.

A highly regarded photographer himself, Masters has a firm sense of precise and evocative visual details. His interior settings (see "Trotsky's House") are exactly described but with something more, an awareness of how the *things* of our lives at once reflect and conceal the truth of ourselves. Similarly, his landscapes are splendidly lit, alive and allusive (see especially the example of his poetic rendering of the Tuscan countryside in "Face in the Window"). Speaking of landscape, it should be noted, with pleasure, how in the stories of *Success* Masters is himself at home and makes the reader feel perfectly at home in a variety of places, both city and country, rural Ohio and upstate New York, Mexico, Colorado, and sophisticated California, a villa in Tuscany, an expensive inn in Ireland, O'Hare airport in Chicago.

Not unlike another writer-photographer, his friend Wright Morris, Masters does not send prose on photographic errands. He uses all five senses freely and more or less equally to create the sensory affective surfaces that first capture our physical attention, then allow us intellectually and emotionally to participate in the creation of the alternative (and no less real and valid) world of fiction. More unusual, Masters makes full use of the consciousness of his characters, not merely in their perception of the outward and visible, but in imagination, memory, dream, even idle fancy, all the things we are in our simultaneous mystery (the dancer and the dance), managing seamlessly to join the inner and outer lives and visions of his characters without breaking the spell.

His characters are diverse, also, of all ages and backgrounds, uniformly lively and dimensional. His women characters are especially interesting and well realized. "Blues For Solitaire" gives us an authoritative first-person story as told by a complex, decent, troubled woman. "The Moving Finger" proves a woman can be as big a nutcase as any man and just as mean, also. Lonely as they may sometimes appear to be, Masters's characters are seldom all alone. They are intricately bound to each other in the subtle bondage of family network, in intense relationships, often in love, sometimes spurred by desire. They often have trouble communicating with and understanding each other, face to face or (a lot) on the phone; but they are, for better and for worse, like "real" people, on each other's hands.

Readers familiar with *Last Stands* will notice, here and there, in several stories, characters who bear a resemblance to and seem to be shadowy versions of Masters's grandfather, the Irish immigrant and U.S. Cavalry trooper in the Indian Wars; of his famous father, his mother, his half-brothers. This is a legitimate and deliberate use of autobiographical material in a fictional context to transform the factual and thus to create a resonance of authenticity for the reality of a fable. Both the factual and the fictional are changed by connection to each other. It is not necessary to have read *Last Stands*, or other works by Masters, to experience the individual stories deeply, but there is no denying that these fictions are often haunted by personal facts that are neither secret nor camouflaged.

There is nothing minimal about these stories, far from it. They are efficient, spare in the sense that there is nothing idle or wasted in them. Accessible, ample, controlled without being self-conscious, witty and funny (see "Grace Peck's Dog" for some good laughter) without being cute, these stories might conceivably be called old fashioned, if it were not for the several signs and clues that Masters is fully aware of literary fashions and willing to use them effectively when they suit his needs and purposes. For instance, time and the tenses. Since Masters is very often concerned with the constant process of change, time (the catalytic fire in which change is to be found and takes place) is urgently important to him. Moreover, since one of his habits, as you will see, is a kind of double story, taking place simultaneously to the reader, but at two or more distinct times as far as the characters and events are concerned, he is almost compelled to move about, free and easy, present and past, in the narrative sequence of tenses. He is as good at this and as graceful (I almost said as clever, maybe as cunning) as anybody alive.

Masters is also very contemporary in his magical sleight of hand with point of view. He can handle, as he here demonstrates, several forms of first-person narration (he puts on voices as easily as hats), third-person limited, and, more rare these days, classical omniscient narration. Does all this sound too technical, like some kind of an owner's manual? Never mind. The point is that he is the kind of performer who can do anything that is called for, but in such a way that whatever he does with a story and its parts seems not only natural, but also inevitable.

The endings of Masters's stories have something in common—a very quick curtain. This, too, is highly contemporary; though I feel that the reason for the habit is deeper than any matter of trends or technique. It seems to me that one of the points involved in the fiction of Hilary Masters, a *view* more than any kind of "message," is that in our world and in our times things don't get settled. Resolutions are seldom final. Note that in several stories a central figure in the family has died, but life goes on and the impact of the dead person's life continues. A Masters story is more a matter of discovery than resolution. We and the characters learn things. Sometimes the same things, sometimes not. Often we are surprised; the "fine excess" is there. At which point the lights do not dim gradually. Curtain falls. Blackout.

I am here as an open admirer of the stories of Hilary Masters, but I am not writing a blurb or any kind of flap copy. And this is no kind of a book review. Far from it. Call it, instead, a reader's report, an accounting of some of the things I find delightful and instructive in the stories of *Success.* The attentive reader will find a good many others.

One thing more. Usually the Acknowledgments don't tell us a whole lot. In this case they do. Not surprising that the stories were first published, in different versions, in literary magazines. Literary magazines are where the majority of the good stories are published in this rich and various age of the short story. What is surprising is the particular magazines that, in recent years, have been publishing these stories by Hilary Masters. Much of the literary world, especially the highly competitive world of the good quarterlies and literary magazines, is a nasty little battlefield. (The urban model for the American literary world is someplace like Beirut.) Many of the magazines (see for yourself) in the Acknowledgments list aren't even speaking to each other, let alone publishing the same writers. I doubt very much that any other American writer has managed to publish work in *all* of these particular magazines. It speaks directly to the quality and independence of the fiction of Hilary Masters that he has been able to write stories wholly his own, in his own voice and focusing on his own concerns, stories that then found a place in an astonishing variety of places, each distinctly different from the other. *Success* is more than the sum of its parts, but those magazine editors are to be congratulated and may take some measure of honest pride in their part of it.

—George Garrett

Success

Hall of Mirrors

All this happened a long time ago. The Palace of Versailles and it is Sunday. Several of us, all students, have taken the train out from Paris to see the palace, the Hall of Mirrors. It is June and we have just arrived in France. A girl on the plane over and I had become lovers the night before. But it was a mistake. I mean she wasn't the one I had been watching but the girl who had sat next to her. All the way over the Atlantic I had watched this other girl; she had been the one who attracted me.

It was one of those student package tours, and four of us had casually teamed up, the two girls and another guy and I—we had all taken adjoining rooms when we finally got to Paris. We were exhausted. No jets as you have now, but grinding engines that landed us in Gander, in Shannon, in Zurich. Then we took a night train to Paris, rented the rooms and fell into bed. The bathroom was in the girls' room. All through these travels, I had been watching this other girl, dark and exotic, and never noticed the rather plain girl sitting beside her. She was a senior at some kind of female seminary. Mousy.

Her name was Anne. So, we all fell into our beds and sound asleep. Later, I was awakened by someone stroking my hair.

1

Moonlight coming through the windows. It was the other guy, saying he had been watching me all the way over the Atlantic and had fallen in love with me. Serves me right, you say, but I told him to go back to bed. I wasn't interested but it was okay. He mustn't be upset. It was okay. He was very apologetic and I had to spend a lot of time assuring him that it was okay. An honest mistake. Okay.

But then, I couldn't go back to sleep. I got up and went to the bathroom, passing through the girls' room. On the return, I pause. The moonlight through the open windows highlights the curve of their hips beneath the comforters. Their pillows are tangled depressions. It was like a negative but printed in the Paris air and just then, one of them—the dark one, I was certain of that—sighed in her sleep. It was a child's sound, moist and faintly sweet, and I could almost taste it. I walk to the bed by the open window, lift the covers and slip in beside her. She must have been having an erotic dream, for she turned and opened herself to me.

Before you say anything, let me remind you that this was the wrong girl. I had made a mistake. Yes, Anne, the girl at Versailles. Anyway, this is not what this story is about. It's about the Hall of Mirrors and why I never got to see it. Remember, it's a Sunday in June, a long time ago.

The next morning, the four of us have taken the suburban train out from Paris. Anne holds my hand most of the trip. At Versailles we join other tourists, mostly French, in a guided tour of the palace. Anne is small, slight, and there is a faint line of perspiration above her upper lip. The day has already become hot and muggy. She has dressed as if she were about to attend chapel at her Catholic college. I think she probably dressed like that all the time. Our companions walk ahead of us. The dark girl wears shorts and a sleeveless blouse and she has idly taken my roommate's hand who talks to her with great animation. He seems to know a great deal about the palace and its history.

You'll remember that the Hall of Mirrors, the Galérie des Glaces, was created by Mansart for Louis XIV in 1678. It is situated at the end of one wing on the second floor. Inside, the old palace is cool and smells of floor wax, dusty fabric, masonry.

Anne and I bring up the rear as our group ascends the wide circular stairway. The marble along the walls is curiously stained here and there, as if leaks had sprung through the wainscoting, and the treads of the stairs are worn and uneven. Waiting rooms, antechambers, boudoirs, pantries—one after the other and each augmenting the next, making for an array of deference, a fealty of rooms, as it were, to the large chamber of reflections resplendently waiting for us at the very end. The walls are painted with pastoral idylls: shepherdesses in swings, shepherds playing lutes. A few sheep.

Where's the bathroom? A good question, better than you know, but there were no bathrooms. The guide shows us porcelain bowls discreetly set within painted cabinets, and then there are those stains on the marble walls of the staircase. Anne and I have just followed the group into some sort of a recital room—the royal rustics on the walls are playing musical instruments in silent harmony. Pianofortes set up beneath willows, that sort of thing. It's a small room and our group squeezes through the doorway into the next. Over their heads, several doorways down, I can see flashes of light against the ornate ceiling, like luminous fish darting in a mirrored pond. Our companions have disappeared into the crowd. The last I saw of them, the boy had slipped his arm around the brunette's waist. Anne let go my hand and took my arm firmly. "Something terrible has happened," she says.

"And that's a terrible mirror," Aunt Bess said yesterday. We had just come back from lunch and she caught me looking into the Federal-style mirror that hangs in the hallway of her apartment. "Of course, at my age all mirrors are terrible, but that one in particular. The glass is malformed and the coating has become dark. Your mother sent me that from Boston, when she was with that company of *Oklahoma!*"

All through the meal at the Faculty Club, she had reviewed my mother's career, so her reference to this gift from Boston and the touring company of the old musical was one more point where my mother's vagrant rush through life had briefly struck a visible object to make an impression. Increasingly, my aunt has talked about her younger sister. "Your mother was always on tour," she said, and not for the first time; the judgment has become familiar and tiresome, along with the petulant tone with which it is sometimes rendered.

But yesterday she was also in a boastful mood, an alternative that sometimes companioned her attitude to make for an ambivalence that has confused me since boyhood. She recounted my mother's triumphs as she looked about the dining room, as if these triumphs, to which she was related, set her apart from the other widows of professors emeriti who tasted their lobster bisque. I have heard it all before, many times. How Harold Arlen had written two songs for my mother. The compliments paid her by Danny Kaye and Bob Hope and other such stars she had worked with. What Dinah Shore had said to her one time after a TV special. I used to think my aunt repeated these items to impress me with my mother's accomplishments, but I've also wondered if she summed this account to remind herself as well.

So, when we returned to her apartment, I knew Aunt Bess would direct me toward the bathroom at the end of the hallway where the Federal mirror hung—not just direct me toward the bathroom but to its usage as well, for she is of that age where consequences are of an abiding interest; whether those of a meal or of a life's work. And, while I was so occupied, she would be setting up the albums and memorabilia that would endow our afternoon and give my visit its mission.

Yes, I was interested in turning these brittle pages again, for I had been thinking of this collection of pictures and programs, page after page of them, thinking how they presented only one version of my mother's life and that somewhere just off the page, just outside the boundary of the album lay another account, if not the explanation.

Like the frontispiece of an old biography, my father's photograph takes up the first page, and the brownish eight-by-ten print shows the young airman I never knew. A white silk scarf is tucked into his leather jacket and his cap is set rakishly over rather solemn eyes. His smile is a little forced, perhaps put on to appease the studio photographer's exasperation with his natural gravity. "He never made it into combat." My aunt delivered the

4

familiar eulogy, a statement whose pathos has been perfected over the years. "He was killed in Pensacola. Someone ran into him as he was taking off."

Nor did he make it into the rest of the album, but I've been thinking that his large image on the first page does propel all that follows; he might even be somewhere between the other pictures, still trying to take off from those narrow, black strips between the photographs; or maybe he had already flown off the page. Because my mother's history, as represented here, seems to start at the point of his solo appearance on the first page. For there are no pictures of her as a young child, in high school or growing up on the family farm near Ava, Ohio, and if there are such albums, my aunt has never shown them to me. I suspect they might have been destroyed, so as to eliminate the modest genesis of her brilliant career. On the other hand, it was a family that never considered any of its gestures worthy of memorial, except for my mother's, and then only after she had begun to turn in that spectacular light of show business, an illumination that was to set her apart from every one of us.

Pert would be the one word that would describe her as she appeared in those first pages of the album, for it was a time of pertness, an ideal established by such actresses as Veronica Lake and June Allyson and Joan Leslie. It was a time for childlike women, cheerfully giving over themselves and their defense to men—even men who never got off the ground in Pensacola. In this early photograph she is one of a group, slim-legged and with her arms comradely linked with those of other chorus members in a road show of *Hellzapoppin*. In some of the first USO tours, she stares out at the camera with a fierce determination that singles her out in this crowd of hopefuls—a rather gawky Jeff Corey one of these. Her expression is a mix of gaiety and fury; a persona that a press agent was later to inadequately describe as a "bundle of energy."

"She wrote you such wonderful letters from North Africa," Aunt Bess said and, as if to give a setting for these letters, she had turned the page to a world of sand and palm trees, even a camel or two. It's a strange bivouac and the Hollywood stars in these snapshots seem much at home, as if they had just taken

5

their places on a back lot only recently given over to the filming of *Beau Geste*. But the musicians in the troupe are clearly ill at ease, their Broadway references of no use to them in the sands of Africa. My mother sits on the lap of one these men, a trombone player by the name of Chuck Martin. "Isn't he cute?" her roundish script asks in the margin of one picture.

"How old was I about this time?" I asked my aunt.

"If you're wondering about the letters—I had to read them to you. But they were wonderful letters and she went to some effort so that you would have a record." Her look should have been accompanied by the removal of pince-nez glasses, a sternness that unpeeled the years as well, and I saw my mother's green eyes. For an instant, I had a Walker Evans picture of the two of them as children, standing, arms linked, on the sagging wood porch of the farmhouse in Ohio, barefoot and shy, and one of them holding her breath, expectant and not to be denied.

"I know you read them to me," I said. "But I must have been about two when she was in North Africa with this USO bunch. That was about a year after she parked me with you and Uncle Harold."

"You were well taken care of, cared for and loved. Harold and I were not going to have children," she begins the story I know by heart, but the narration is more for her own benefit than for my information. In the same way, she turns over the anecdotes of my mother's career, over and over, to make them by this constant handling into events that could have happened to her, and I sometimes wonder if there is not another album in this small apartment, on the edge of this bucolic college campus, another album that features pictures of Aunt Bess sitting on the lap of a trombone player in Morocco.

What I'm saying is that her stories, her adoption of these stories, if you will, have had a doubling effect upon me, even as they were accompanied, as yesterday, by her arthritic, age-spotted hands turning the album pages between us. "You were just a year old when Glo auditioned for Earl White and got that part in the *Scandals*," she said, and recreated the dialogue between the famous producer and this nervous, wisecracking kid from Ohio, all elbows and knees. If I had wished, I could have

6

repeated the exchange over the footlights with her, word, for pause, for word.

Just now, I caught you looking at the image in the mirror: the man fixing his tie and the woman, flushed from the shower, witnessing this adjustment. We are both the picture and the observers of that picture. This isn't the first time. You often spy on us as we embrace before the mirror but not, I think, from any voyeur impulse but rather to make a happy verification of the two of us as one. Then you turn away, leave me for some genial task, and the image in the misted mirror is halved. Abruptly, I am alone, though I know you are somewhere outside the frame. Even now, you are somewhere in the room behind me. If I were to reach out beyond the glass, I could touch you, take your hand and perhaps pull you back for another group picture.

I have taken Anne by both hands and we stand alone in this music room of Versailles, for the other tourists are already clustering around the guide in the next chamber. I am wondering what was the terrible event that could have overtaken her here on the second floor of this seventeenth-century palace. A sudden, full-term pregnancy after our one sexual encounter the night before? Surely not even the Sun King could boast of such potency. As I watch her plain face darken with embarrassment, I begin to realize what has happened—yes, you've guessed it— she has suddenly become *indisposée,* as these shepherdesses in the murals might have said, if indeed such mortal tides ever concerned them. Moreover, her face has become a sort of magenta hue; she is unprepared for the occasion, and she whispers this information into my ear even though there is no one nearby. Except for a guard who is approaching to shoo us toward the ongoing group. He finally understands my imperfect French but shakes his head gravely. No one is allowed to backtrack, for obvious reasons, monsieur—these empty rooms are priceless— we must continue, must finish the tour through the entire palace. We must go all the way through to the Hall of Mirrors.
Anne becomes frantic. She is holding on to me with both hands and the strength of her grip surprises me. I try to comfort

7

her, saying that I remember seeing in a Michelin guide something about another grand staircase leading down from the Hall of Mirrors, though how much I assist the architect Mansart by sketching in this feature, I cannot be sure. In any event, the rooms between us and the final gallery seem to have multiplied; no doubt some trick of the refracted light coming through that last doorway.

You must remember that I was even more unknowing than she, don't forget the time I'm talking about, so my desperation and anxiety matched hers. At any moment, I fully expected to see red rivulets creeping down the pale skin of her legs and into her Mary Janes. I wondered if we should walk slowly, take small steps or fast long strides, but to where? There are no bathrooms, if you remember. You do not realize how convenient the world has been made for you—bathrooms around every corner and all of your needs handily dispensed from machines for a few coins. None of that at the Palace of Versailles. I suppose if you were a woman in those days, you had to get off the swing, forsake the shepherds for a little bit, and retire to some attic in the palace. Look, I'm not to blame for all that; I am only trying to find my way out of this museum.

Two rooms later, I see an eccentric black line drawn on the scene of the continuous pastoral party that decorates the walls. It is located in an inside corner, and instinctively I know that it marks a passageway back to the real world. Anne and I dawdle as I keep my eye on the guard behind us. Something calls his attention and he disappears around the corner. The tourist group has moved into a royal dressing room. Quickly, I push Anne toward the corner and pry open the secret panel with my fingers. It is like a movie. A dark, narrow staircase spiraling down into obscurity. Anne balks and, suddenly angry with her, I push her forward and pull the panel shut behind us. She is crying softly as we feel our way along the damp, curved walls, one step at a time, down, down, down. After several turns, a glow spreads out below us which gradually becomes stronger and then takes on the shape of an arched doorway that frames an entry into light. We emerge into a paved courtyard, momentarily blinded by the brilliance of the day.

8

* * *

"It was all that lighting they had," Aunt Bess had been saying. "It made Glo's hair seem like it had been electrified, though I guess I've told you she wasn't a natural blonde." The studio still of my mother is almost like a formal portrait, something like a senior picture for a rather exotic high school yearbook, because the strapless gown leaves her shoulders bare and offers the tops of her breasts. Her hair is like a burnished helmet, and her eyebrows have been plucked and drawn, two elegant arches that raise sly, sophisticated questions in the elliptical eyes below.

This is how I remember her, or how I first began to remember her. The commotion of her visits became extravaganzas of furs, clack of jewelry, silky sounds and the pungent aromas of perfumes and lotions, all of which enfolded and smothered me in that first embrace, and I can remember struggling in her arms, not to escape, but to reach through the layers of softnesses to grab on to something. Anything. Her route to the den-study my aunt and uncle used as a guest room could be tracked by the pieces of her entrance dropped along the way: a snakeskin high-heeled shoe kicked off here, there a gold bangle, the silver-fox cape tossed over the back of a chair, a crisp leather purse dropped on the telephone table, and so on, so that the small apartment near the University of Chicago campus took on the appearance of one of those thrift-exchange shops for upper-middle-class women, sponsored and supplied by the luxury of their boredom.

One time, I caught my uncle taking inventory. He had returned from his lab at school just after one of my mother's arrivals, and I spied him from where I sat in the corner of the living room, still a little dazed—drugged, you might say, by the opiate of that arrival. He looked amused as he pieced together the being that had left behind a scarf, sandals, beads, a cigarette case—half open—one pearl earring, a satchel purse, and a jacket lined in orange silk, and, just in that moment, I had a flash of how he must look in his laboratory as he fitted together the old bones and fossilized remnants of the huge animals that were his preoccupation and, ultimately, would be his fame. But my mother was very small, almost birdlike; for some years I used to

9

think we were the same size, brother and sister even, the illusion spelled by those nights we slept together on the convertible couch, when I would be encased within her diminutive, bony frame and feel the caress of her breathing upon my neck. Her breath would be minted, a sugary scent over something more harsh and faintly rancid. Sometimes, she would tell me stories before she drifted into sleep.

"Like what?" Aunt Bess asked.

"About growing up on the farm." We had come to the end of the first album and my aunt had just hefted another one upon her knees. She paused and looked out the window. Students strolled across the small green campus. The white trim of the Georgian buildings sparkled against the red brick. The amplified sounds of a carillon played a pleasant melody.

"How she hated Ava, the farm," she said with half-closed eyes, as if the view outside were too bright. "I think all that perfume, all those baths she took were meant to wash off the Ohio dirt she felt had become ingrained in her skin, under her nails."

"You never felt that way?"

"No, I didn't, but I was just different." She shrugged. "We just responded differently to things." She laughed at a sudden thought. "I sometimes think it might have been that dirigible that did it. It was so startling, so huge and frightening." And she opened the next album.

The gigantic shape of the palace looms over us, and I am wondering if I should carry Anne into the village of Versailles and to the pharmacy that I had noted on our walk from the railroad station. I am more distressed than she is now. You are laughing at this, but you must remember that this all happened a long time ago, only a couple of years after Hiroshima, and long before all the sophisticated techniques and attitudes you take for granted today.

Even as I look back over my shoulder at the palace, I get this sense of passing from an ancient time into another era. The huge building, an apparition from the seventeenth century, remains

10

in place, as if moored to its formal gardens by the spray of the fountains where nymphs and satyrs slip and sport. Anne and I continue to walk away from it, through dusty streets that doze in a postprandial somnolence which alarms me.

What if the pharmacy has closed up for the usual two or three hours at midday? What would I do then? For the notion has already occurred to me that Anne has entrusted herself to me. Meanwhile, I take one last look at the palace, and at the large open windows on the second floor where the Hall of Mirrors is located. Shadows and the shapes of shadows move within, just teasingly beyond the range of definition, but it is clear that our group has finally entered the historic chamber, the tight knot of them suddenly come unraveled in the great hall and frayed by the ricocheting reflections of the mirrors. I try to place the brunette there, all of her sultry attractions multiplied by a factor postulated three hundred years ago, but Anne has just given me her hand once more, and we turn the corner.

I can't tell you what we said to each other on that walk through the village, or even if we talked at all. Her simple decorum, the way she puts her hand out to me, is a gesture of the same trust with which she had given herself to me the night before. Something in the curl of fingers suggests more than a mere acquiescence. Her acceptance of our unexpected intimacy, initiated in error, you'll remember, startles and then amuses me, for she is unaware that a mistake has been made.

On the other hand, with each step I wonder if her manner is not a kind of docility; no doubt a behavior learned in the conventlike atmosphere of her college. I ask her several times how she feels—how is the emergency going, as it were—and she gives me cheerful reports. All will be well, she says, and squeezes my hand. But for the language barrier and the small camera that gently nudges her shoulder purse, we could be taken for a young French couple, lovers ambling toward a pleasant lunch at a little bistro where the tables are crisply covered with white paper, the bread is crusty, and the mirrors above the banquettes somehow amplify the aromas of burgundy and cassoulet and fruit tarts. No one would know, to look at us, that something terrible had happened, to use her earlier expression.

11

Yet it is not a bistro but a pharmacy that is our destination, and, as we round a last corner, I note with relief that the store is open and ready to do business. We pause before the large display window to locate the article she requires, for neither of us can speak French very well and such particular fluency is way beyond us. "There." I point against the glass. "See. There are some to the left. They call them serviettes hygiéniques." I read the title off the package label and begin to drill her on the proper phrase when I notice a stricken look in her eyes. "What's the matter?"

"Oh, I can't possibly buy them," she says. "I would be too embarrassed."

"What do you mean, you'd be embarrassed? You buy them at home?"

"No. My mother buys them for me at home."

"But this is France," I say. "No one knows you over here."

My reasoning falls not only on deaf ears but on deaf ears turning crimson, and I wonder if her deepening blush extends below the collar of her prim blouse to color the small breasts whose perfection by moonlight had caused my wonder. Both her hands take mine, and her grip is painful. So I go into the store and make the purchase. The pharmacist—obviously a man of the world as all Frenchmen are supposed to be—wraps the package and makes change with an insouciance that flatters me. I could just as easily have been buying a package of mints, and I remember tossing in, for good measure, a comment about the weather, "Il fait beau," to which he agreed, and returned to his accounts. Outside, Anne and I faced each other. Now to find a place where the *serviette* could be applied.

All of this must sound very quaint to you, even ridiculous in its formality, but if you could have seen that *Life* magazine cover yesterday you might get some sense of what I'm talking about. The photograph featured my mother leaning against a kind of Doric column, gowned appropriately in Attic folds that implied the depth of her bosom while exposing her slender arms and delicate shoulders. If my father's photograph had dedicated and set going the pictorial narrative of the first volume, this

12

professional studio shot, reproduced on the mass magazine, prologued the success in these pages.

"I think this is my favorite picture of Glo," Aunt Bess said, and made the heavy album comfortable on the hassock of her knees. "She was just on top. Everything was going just right for her. And, here you are." She turned the page; even I shared in the glory. "This was one time you visited her in Hollywood and she took you to that famous restaurant. Romanov's Restaurant. He was related to the last czar, I think."

"Not really," I told her. The clipping from a fan magazine showed the two of us smiling from behind an array of long-stemmed glassware; the restaurateur leaned between us, a pose as impersonal as his smile was distracted. Aunt Bess looked disappointed. "Well, maybe he was a distant cousin," I said.

I've reconsidered this whole period also, but find it no better than the one memorialized in the other album. The only difference is that I would be the one coming to visit and then the one leaving; so that it seemed better at first, because I had begun to hate my mother's magical apparitions, since they always foretold her departures. However, my going to see her was to enter the spare studio apartment with a balcony that overlooked Wilshire Boulevard and to pass behind the scrim she had dropped around her persona. In the hours I would spend there alone—for she would leave me to work at the studio or meet with agents and producers—I made an inventory of her wardrobe and accessories. It was very surprising. None of it compared with the treasures that had spilled from those suitcases which seemed ready to burst apart in Chicago, their fastenings giving way to the dazzling contents. Nor did I find any of the jewelry so carelessly strewn about my aunt's and uncle's apartment and whose glittering crumbs I would follow, as if in a fairy tale, into the fateful trance of her embrace. Only after my trips west had ceased did I guess the answer to the enigma. All of that stuff had been borrowed.

"What good times you had together," Aunt Bess said. "Glo always wrote me such wonderful letters about your visits, your daily adventures, so that I would know, because you never said anything. Even then, you kept things to yourself," she chided me, and turned the page. "I've never liked this picture, but I suppose she had to do it."

The obligatory pinup pose of that period had placed my mother with her back to the camera, looking over her shoulder with a coy expression that was, at once, both invitation and censure for anyone who might have been looking. The tight, brief swimming suit seemed to lengthen her legs and swell the curve of her hips. It was a pose made famous by an earlier actress named Betty Grable and which the studio publicity photographer probably had in mind when he arranged my mother. In fact, the gimmick of that *Life* magazine cover story was the half-dozen young actresses, starlets, who were being readied to take over the roles of actresses who had grown into more serious parts.

"I always hated that word," Aunt Bess said. "Starlets. It sounds like something not quite formed, like an uncooked muffin, something dependent on another source. Glo didn't need any of that."

"What was the source?" I asked her. The last dozen pages of this album I know to be blank, and, like a sightless person, Aunt Bess's fingers moved over the clippings and pictures pasted to the two leaves spread out on her knees. Stills from motion pictures in which my mother was featured, the promotion piece for a musical and the number she danced with Donald O'Connor, still excerpted for film retrospectives, some more tours with Bob Hope—this time the early days of Vietnam—and, as if my aunt wished to keep the professional life separate and somehow inviolate, one page given over to the pictures of wedding couples cutting the nuptial pastry—three different cakes and three different grooms but all the same bride. I remember one of these men, an all-pro tackle for the Los Angeles Rams, who had a high voice and rather gentle ways. I liked him very much.

We must have sat through a whole chorus of "Moon River" amplified from the carillon tower across campus, and we might still be sitting there, half hearing the rowdy hilarity of the college's spring carnival, if I hadn't repeated my question. Because Aunt Bess seemed stuck, unwilling to close the book and abandon her sister to the limbo of blank pages. "What about all that light and energy?" I asked her. "Where did it come from?" And where did it go, I wondered as I stared at the black, empty pages. Did she take it with her in that final departure—the messy finale on that highway outside of Palm Springs—leaving, as she always had, the darkness even darker by taking all the light with her; light drawn to light, as the headlights of that semi may have drawn her into them.

"The *Shenandoah*," Aunt Bess said, and set the album to one side. "Don't ask me why, but I think that had something to do with that dirigible. The crash of the *Shenandoah*."

"The dirigible coming down?"

"It was so enormous, so unexpected. So unbelievable." She had tried to find the right word but shook her head with dissatisfaction. "Your mother and I were upstairs getting ready for school. She had started kindergarten. Pa yelled up for us to come outside quick. There was this awful noise, like steady thunder, getting louder and louder. It had been storming but this was different . . ." And I hear the story once more, for it is our family story, about an event that was to make our family famous, give a distinction to these plain farm people in Ava, Ohio, that set them apart from all others. That is, until my mother came along, and that's funny, because I just thought of that. The two are somehow connected, as Aunt Bess claimed; one set the other off.

Unreal. It must have been unreal to run out on the porch and see this gigantic silver shape looming over the meadow, so close it could almost be touched, swinging this way and then the other like a huge projectile out of control; so close that—and here's a favorite detail—they could see the white faces of the men in the gondola, peering out; one even waved to them, as they swept by to their doom. It wasn't meant to be there, that was the scary part. It had come out of—not nowhere—but from an alter world where such enormous constructions were commonplace; to fall through the frame that separates the two worlds and come apart over our family's meadow in Ava, Ohio.

"We could read the words painted on its sides," Aunt Bess said yesterday. "Like a school lesson on the board." US NAVY SHENANDOAH. The motors roared, the propellers were turning

15

crazily, out of synchronization, and the dirigible began to break up into three pieces right over their heads. It was like something drawn in a nightmare but there it was. Then it thundered over the back garden, the privy, the barnyard and barn to disappear over the rise of a corn lot. The collision with the earth shook the porch under their feet and rattled pans in the kitchen. The cats jumped off their chairs; one never came back.

"It was like one of Harold's big lizards," Aunt Bess mused. She had smiled with remembrance but whether for my late uncle, the dinosaur, or his obsession with its fossils, I cannot say. "I think he was forever stunned by the size of those beasts—his wonder kept fresh by the first time he came on one of their bones. He was driven to put them back together, all that bigness put together bone by bone. I think Glo was shocked the same way that morning the *Shenandoah* came down. It was like she had seen one of Harold's monsters suddenly poking its nose up over the orchard. It didn't belong there, but there it was. She had to get away from Ava, she had to run. I was scared, too, but she never got over it. She kept running to fix up something just as big ever after."

I catch glimpses of you busy with your impatience, putting your own life back together as you pick up the litter of our weekend, but whether you are waiting for me to go on or just to go, I cannot tell. You pass in and out of the mirror that currently features me slipping on my jacket and sometimes you look, not at me, but at the other image of me, to gauge his progress, the nearness of this man's disappearance from the glass and your life. My bag is packed; he's ready to go.

Maybe someday, the two of us will go to Versailles, and I can finally see the Hall of Mirrors, walk back through those rooms, but this time all the way to the very last salon. I'm told the mercury coating has cracked and become dull, and the images are distorted. We can walk back through the town and I'll point out other historic sites, such as the pharmacy, and then on to the railroad station where Anne and I hurry this day in June.

We need to find a private place she can use for a few minutes and this seems to be our best choice. Public facilities for women were not all that available then. Don't blame me, like I said before, I didn't make any of this up. Even in the railroad station, we discover to our dismay that there is only one W.C. and this for men only. So, I reconnoiter the premises, find them empty, and Anne steps inside, holding her purse, her camera and the package of *serviettes* in her arms as a schoolgirl might hold her books at the end of the day. I post myself outside at the door, putting together in some kind of French a phrase that would stall, if not discourage, anyone from using the facility. If I remember, the literal translation proclaimed that a young girl was being very sick inside at that very moment.

It amazes me, the number of French families who use the railroad on a Sunday afternoon, all of them laden with picnic baskets, folding chairs, various journals and newspapers, children, and all of them waiting for trains back to the city of Paris. Many little boys. Many fathers too, and so far all of them apparently content. Then my mouth goes dry as one of them stands, pulls up his pants and starts toward the toilet. But he walks outside, perhaps assuming that I was waiting my turn and that an alternative—certainly more accessible—was available around the walls of the station.

Anne is taking a lot of time. In fact, the clock on the wall has measured almost ten minutes. In my mind, I construct the unfamiliar procedure, judging it to be a simple matter, practical and uncomplicated, so why is she taking so long? Surely, she is no stranger to the method. Does her mother do more than just buy the things for her, I wonder? Coming up on fifteen minutes.

Perhaps her embarrassment has imprisoned her inside and she has been made a hostage to this phenomenon. She is afraid to come out, to face me, now that I have shared this "terrible" happening, as she called it. But, if I entered to comfort her, what if I came upon her only partway through the business—wouldn't that embarrass her even more?

Then it occurs to me that when she comes back through the door we will be a different couple. We will have shared this unique event, this fantastic accident that overtook us on our way to the Hall of Mirrors, and we will be together indefinitely because of it. Fifteen minutes and more; she must be thinking

17

the same thing inside and doesn't want to come out for that reason. And, I remind myself, it had all been a mistake in the first place.

As if to give a volume to my thoughts, a deafening roar seizes the quiet Sunday outside. An express rushes by, its horn screaming, and the drilling racket of steel running against steel pierces my eardrums. The train has come out of nowhere, its noise at full blast, and then, just as quickly, is gone, leaving in its wake, as if shyly put down during all the commotion, a local train, stopped and waiting to take on passengers through its open doors.

If you will accompany me to Versailles, we will go back to the station and I'll use the W.C. No doubt, separate facilities have been created for women by now. I'll find nothing inside, I know that, but I want to look anyway; not for a clue to Anne's whereabouts or what happened to her after I got on that local train but to go over the mere measurements of the place, the logistics of the fittings, the placement of the washbowl, the mirror above it—to survey this enclosure and get a sense of her contending with the emergency within this room as I prepared to abandon her outside it. Perhaps I can recreate her by her very absence, by the dimensions of abandonment she left behind.

I want to believe that small room, redolent of disinfectant and its light diffused through pebbled glass in the ceiling, contains something overlooked by the cleaning crews, an innocuous scrap that might explain to me the fascination of that terror long ago in Ava, Ohio, when the sky seemed to break open with the birth of a monster from another planet: a terrible thing that was to happen over and over and over.

The Foundation

He got out the Jeep and they drove up into the field behind the house. She had packed a small picnic basket and held it on her lap. It was warm but the pastures were empty, since the farmer who rented the land had already moved his cows back to barns, for it was that time of year. The maple trees that grew along the fence lines had turned, the leaves of the oaks were already brown, and the birch forest on their left had become a golden net that vainly gathered sunlight. Chickweed blazed their course with blue stars along the cowpath.

When they had driven through three fields, he left the trail to steer the Jeep up a steep hill and stopped at the top beside the trunk of a tree that looked as if it might have been struck by lightning. They could see in all directions, a panorama hardly changed from the first time it had been viewed, save for the white verticals of silos that thrust from the tanning landscape like the spires of village churches.

"It's over there, I think." She pointed.

"The old orchard is in that direction."

"Yes, there were apple trees about. We cut long branches of blossoms one time. Remember?" She looked at him but he had been watching the hawks circle above them. The atmosphere was so pure that he could almost count the ruffled feathers about their necks as the birds' heads turned from right to left, from left to right, and once he met a killing glance suspended between the great wings.

"Don't you remember?" she repeated.

"Yes, but it wasn't there—in that direction."

"Let's see," she urged. He put the Jeep in low gear and eased it over the crown of the hill and down the other side. The ground here contained large shale deposits, and he had to handle the wheel carefully.

It was slow progress through the thick brush, some of it above the Jeep's windshield, and saplings sprang meanly, like whips, through the open sides of the vehicle. She put the basket on the car floor and stood up, hands on top of the windshield frame, to better direct their advance. The front end of the powerful machine pushed through the dense screen of vegetation; the wheels turned without pause.

Suddenly they were in a clearing. It was unexpected and strangely wonderful, like a park of fair weather within the fierce province of a storm. The grass was still green and short, almost as if they had driven onto someone's lawn, an abandoned lawn that was still somehow cared for. But the unpicked fruit on the trees had been frost pied and the treefalls on the ground fermented in a sodden mash that gave off a husky odor.

"We could get drunk from just the smell," he said, and smiled. He had stopped the Jeep but let the engine idle. She still stood in her seat, her hands gripping the windshield, a militant posture almost.

"It wasn't here," he continued. "These old orchards all look alike, grown wild, unpruned. It did not look like this, I agree, but there's no foundation here." He shut off the engine and slipped out of the Jeep to walk to a low branch with several apples. Two came off easily into his hand while the rest, disconnected by the slight vibration, plopped on the ground. He came back to her side of the car, polishing the apples on his sweater sleeve, and handed one up to her. "Have an appetizer," he said.

"It might be over there, behind that stand of sumac."

"What kind of apples are these, do you suppose?" he asked, and took a bite. "Northern Spy? Could they be Northern Spy?"

"There were lilacs growing around what might have been the front door."

"You know"—he spoke gently—"I'm not even sure that foundation was on our property. When was the last time we were there?" She looked down at him, her eyes deep and a little dazed, as if caught by a sudden light. "If I remember," he continued, "we used to walk into the place on that old farm road above us, before we had the survey done."

"It's here. I know it's around here someplace," she said, and sat down to dangle her legs over the side of the Jeep. The patina of perspiration on her cheeks caught the light and illuminated the hair that fell around her eyes, the gray hairs transformed by the sun's alchemy. The flesh of her neck was full and smooth and pink. He thought she looked extraordinarily attractive. "Maybe if I walk and you drive, we could find it."

"It's not on our property, I'm sure of it," he said and threw the apple core into the weeds. "Those times we were there"—he took one of her hands—"those times we went there, we thought it was part of our land. That was before the survey was done. Remember? The foundation, it turned out, was in a field on the place above us."

"The roses had gone wild, but the herb garden was still there. Chives and rosemary and tarragon, thyme. All planted long ago and still growing."

"Yes," he said. He moved around the front of the Jeep and got behind the wheel. It had become very hot all of a sudden in the clearing, as if they were in a parlor, windows closed, and the heat had been turned up. "Let's find some nice place for our picnic." He started the motor.

"Not yet," she replied. "I want to look some more."

"All right." He nodded and put the car into gear. "Which direction should we go?"

"Don't be testy."

"I'm not testy," he replied evenly.

"After all, there's not much else to do around here, is there?" They drove slowly through the overgrown byways of the

21

old orchard and, from time to time, their senses were assaulted by the pungent odor of manure, mixed with the scent of rotting apples, for cows had stood in the shade of these old trees all summer. He also noted signs of deer. "Of course," she continued, "I'm used to doing nothing on Sundays, or whenever. But I thought this might be a change for you—fun."

"Now, don't start that," he replied carefully.

"Go over by that big oak tree." She pointed. "Doesn't that mark some sort of a corner of a boundary or something?"

"Yes, I believe so." He shifted gears, and they passed over a slight knoll, leaving the orchard, and drove toward the oak. The remains of an old stone wall formed a near right angle at the tree's base, and on the other side of this line lay a clean-picked cornfield, the property of the farmer who rented the pastures.

"Let's follow the wall, going that way," she said. "Do you think we can?"

"We can give it a try," he told her. "At least as far as the scrub will let us."

"It's too bad we never did anything with this orchard, bring it back," she said. They were bumped and rolled together as the Jeep made its way over the uneven terrain.

"Well, if I remember, you made an awful lot of apple butter."

"Yes, I did," she agreed. She braced one foot against the car's frame. "By the way, the children say they would like to hear from you."

"Would they?"

"Do you have their address? When was the last time you wrote them?"

"I'm sure I wrote them from London."

"At their new address?"

"Yes. Yes, I have it."

"Stop here." She got out and walked off to the right through a thick screen of sumac. He could hear her moving through the brush, stop, then move off in another direction. "Go ahead. Follow the wall." Her voice came from yet another direction. "I'll walk a bit. We'll meet at the other corner."

A fallen tree forced him to detour, and he had to make

several passes in different gears to pull up over a rather steep ledge of rock. He enjoyed the Jeep, liked to shift its multiple gear ratios and to feel the bite of the four-wheel drive as it pulled him over obstacles, the difficult ground. Ash trees as large as two or three inches in diameter were easily pushed over and he grew more daring on the steeper slopes, though he laughed nervously.

A regal sycamore with an escort of birch secured the other corner of the plot line, and he pulled up behind the slender white trees and stopped. From this vantage, he could review the old orchard, everywhere they had been. Farther on, he could see the opposite hillside with its deft parallel lines of birch, straws about to fall and tangle. There was not a sound, the engine turned off; nor could he hear her moving anywhere below, as if she had become absorbed by the vegetation.

The hawks had circled higher, though still in tandem, perhaps connected by an invisible line, and, over on the hillside, just below the treeline, a groundhog worked methodically around the entrance to its lodge. The animal's fur glistened luxuriously in the sunlight, flowing and undulating as it moved like a miniature bear. Abruptly, the groundhog sat up, head cocked and its small front paws pressed to its breast. Then it was gone, down the hole, as if it had never been there. It had simply disappeared, but what had startled it, he could not see. The hawks still played in the lifting currents. Something only the groundhog had been aware of and had reason to fear had alarmed it; maybe his looking at it.

He let a long breath pass slowly from his lungs. This field going back to brush and woods with its citizenry of hawk and woodchuck, deer and transient cow was all at once unreal to him; unimaginable and outside the ken of his life beyond its unkempt borders, though the wild hawthorn spikes that pricked his shirt material were authentic enough, sharp.

Moreover, if he tried to tell someone next week about this moment, he would be unable to do so, and his listener's attention would lapse because the language once used to describe such scenes was no longer spoken; the patience to hear such words had ceased. It was all going back, from sumac to birch to ash to oak and maple. Everything was going back, and his life outside this old orchard sent out shoots as ubiquitous, as common, as those of the sumac. Even now, and he suddenly jumped up on the Jeep's seat, he might catch a glimpse of it slipping through the old fence lines.

Something had flashed below, like the turn of a trout in a streambed. It was the silvery crown of her hair as she walked through the autumnal palette of the field. She had picked up a stout stick along the way to use as a walking staff and advanced with a graceful pace, near silently, though she seemed a bit winded as she spoke.

"I guess you're right." She stood by the Jeep. "It's not anywhere down there."

"I'm pretty sure it was over behind that pine woods." He pointed over his shoulder, behind them, to the area on the other side of a wire fence that put down this leg of the boundary. It was an unusual fence for these parts, where two or three strands of barbed wire were the rule, because it was about five feet high and constructed of a web of heavy-gauge wire. This kind of fence was more suitable for keeping sheep rather than dairy cattle, and none of the natives had known who had put it up or for what reason. "This fence wouldn't give us much trouble," he continued. "We could step over it like a ladder almost. Leave the Jeep here and hike in."

"No, let's forget it," she said. She was already in the Jeep and adjusting the collar of her blouse. He took her hand in his and, after a moment, she turned toward him and he kissed her. "We can find it," he said. Her eyes became wide and dark. "I'm pretty sure I know where it is. I think it's in the field just beyond those pines."

"No, let's go," she said, sitting squarely on her seat. "I really only wanted to get some slips from those old lilacs. There was a white one, planted at the front door—what must have been the front door. I remember they were white because we went there once in the spring and they were in bloom."

"Yes." He nodded his head and then started the Jeep. For a time, her eyes followed the fence line as they made their departure from it, but when the vehicle turned away, back toward the fields, her attention went with it, indifferently. The return trip seemed easier, faster, and halfway through the second pasture he made a sharp turn toward the hillside topped by the birch forest.

"Well, you brought me out here for a picnic." He spoke to her questioning look.

At the edge of the wood was a pretty clearing carpeted with moss, and the sunlight filtered through the birch leaves to pollinate everything with a fine glow. The remains of an old wall were strewn among the white trunks of the trees, and the stones resembled the vertebrae of a huge serpent that had perished, confounded and entwined within the shimmering maze. The couple felt awkward, almost formal, as if they were the first guests, perhaps the only guests, to arrive at an unusual garden party.

As she unpacked the lunch basket, unfolding and spreading a checkered cloth on a table of moss, he picked over the rocks of the ruined wall. "The quartz they used in these old walls." He held up a large piece of it. "Strange that they found no gold in it around here. A different sort of quartz, I guess."

" 'A Quartz contentment,' " she said, placing a small bottle of wine beside the corkscrew.

"What's that? That's familiar."

" 'The Feet, mechanical, go round— . . . A Wooden way' / of something, something, something"—she laughed over her lapse of memory—"then, 'a Quartz contentment, like a stone.' That's Emily . . . Emily Dickinson."

"Dear Emily," he sighed. She had completed the picnic arrangement and looked toward him. For several moments she sat by the edge of the cloth, a handsome woman with young eyes under heavy brows, her hands clasped in her lap and her torso leaning slightly into the hill. She watched him lay out the rocks from the ruined wall into a square pattern; an open space on one side.

"What on earth are you doing?" she finally asked.

"Only one room right now," he replied. He started a second course. "But it can always be added onto."

"Oh, don't be silly." She flushed, but her tone was not angry. "Come, open the wine."

25

Trotsky's House

The surburb of Coyoacán stretched out forever in the midday heat, and the Mexican light put a knife's edge to leaf and stone. Every flower, every wall and house roof looked cut out, she thought, as in a picture book, and set off from its background, yet somehow cleverly attached to the page by a hidden flap. The walls of the villas on either side of the Avenida Viena had closed up behind exotic draperies of bougainvilleas, and the whole neighborhood seemed to her particularly smug, as if its seclusion was a distinction quite apart from its distance from the central frenzy of Mexico City. They had got here by subway ride—all the way to the end of the line, in fact—and then a taxi ride, and now were on foot in the noon-hour brilliance.

"Why didn't we have the taxi bring us to the door?" she asked. Her face had become pink and glistened with perspiration, which gave her a very youthful look, he thought. Like a student. "What if it's not open?" The side streets were empty too, but from over the high abode-and-brick walls, and the tall purple jacaranda trees within them, came the sounds of traffic two blocks away. A continuous spill, like a mountain stream in spring, as cars and buses and trucks poured through the complex network of highways around the city, and some of this noise spilled over into the stillness of Coyoacán.

"I think it means coyote, something like that," he said. He had already told her this at the hotel before they left. "Well, I just wanted to get a feel of the place on foot." She looked at him. "Also, I didn't think it was a good idea for the taxi driver to know where we're going." This time her look made him laugh a little and he added, "It didn't happen all that long ago. They take politics seriously down here. Even to murder."

But she wasn't impressed, and broke their clasp of hands to fetch a tissue from the small shoulder purse he had bought her in Mérida. After she wiped her face, she continued to hold the tissue in a fist. She was not sure that he knew the way or that the place would be open if they got there. Such side trips always marked their travels and often became the main excursion, as if all the intricate hotel and airline reservations, all the brochures reviewed and assembled, all that effort and energy to plan a vacation had really been to afford an abrupt detour to a crossroad of history, to a small house by the side of that road where some character had lived or was murdered.

"It's along here somewhere," he had just said, with stiff encouragement.

Sometimes, she wondered if he sought out these minor points on the route to show his contempt for the pyramids and palaces, the great masters and royal treasures—all the usual fare of the ordinary tourist itinerary. Sometimes, he seemed to her like a perverse reader, ignoring the main text for the footnotes below. But actually these changes of plan took him by surprise as well.

Only yesterday, as they drowsed toward a siesta, he recalled something in the Diego Rivera mural they had seen that morning. The great assembly of faces crowded into the curtained radiance of their hotel room. This jumble of figures and animals had advanced upon them from the museum's wall like a pitiless vanguard of history that threatened as much as it inspired. In one corner of the painting, the Mexican master had limned a group of faces quite different in their European pallor from the others. Almost like a solemn cheering section, the ponderous

27

miens of Marx and Engels, Lenin and Stalin, and a half-dozen more observed the passing parade. But his attention had fixed on one face, someone as important as Stalin or Lenin, at least given equal rank by Rivera's brush; yet he did not recognize him. The man's countenance was a comical contrast to the forbidding scowls of the other revolutionaries. Coarse black hair stuck straight out from his head, a thick mustache, horn-rimmed glasses behind which the eyes seemed ready to roll around in their sockets like loose marbles. It was as if one of the Marx Brothers had wandered onto the set of a Cecil B. deMille extravaganza: *The Story of Jesus* or *The Conquest of the World*.

Leon Trotsky. One of the several brochures he had purchased at the museum had a diagram of the mural that numbered the actual personages Rivera had put into his masterpiece. Heroes and villains, Aztec martyrs and Spanish conquerors, all marched shoulder to shoulder down the crowded road of Mexico's centuries. Number 46 was Leon Trotsky, a founder of the Bolshevik revolution, it said, and the first chief of staff of the Red Army. Assassinated—he had caught his breath and read the information again—assassinated in Mexico City, August 20, 1940. The word had taken on a particularly exotic turn in his mind. But where? Where did the act happen? On a street corner? During a public ceremony? In a restaurant? Contemporary assassins have favored such sites for their work. That Trotsky had stepped from the security of this cartoon of Mexican history, replete with its own betrayals and murders, only to be then killed in the actuality of that history, and recently besides, suggested a paradox—he thought that was the term—which could not be ignored. The place had to be visited.

"He was killed right here," he had said. His wife looked around the hotel room with mock horror. "I mean here in Mexico City, in a suburb called Coyoacán. I think it means coyote." She nodded and hung up her skirt, but did not remove her underwear, which was a disappointment to him.

"That last quesadilla was too much," she said and stretched out on the bed beside him. Too much for what, he automatically asked himself and looked up at the ceiling, though he knew the

28

answer. It was another one of those explanations he had learned not to ask for. On the ceiling near the casement window the faint residue of a brown stain spread out like the coastline of a continent on an old map. An unexplored continent.

With a drowsing fancy, he poked into the different coves and inlets of the stain to finally anchor in a harbor where the natives seemed friendly. Their colorful canoes were flower-laden and the ship was encircled by Indians who held up thick strands of shells, baskets of plump fruits, and wedges of corn cake that glistened with honey and nuts. His men raged to go ashore, to plunge into the ambrosial stew that awaited them. The voyage had been long and arduous, with many perils, and he was keenly aware of their needs, but other things must come first.

We will go ashore tomorrow, gentlemen, he would tell their disappointed faces. *Meantime, the ship is to be given a clean sweep down; all decks, all ladders. And tomorrow every man shall wear his best uniform ashore, all linens clean and pressed.* They grumbled among themselves. *Standards, gentlemen, standards.* He'd have to keep his eye on that one fellow with the glasses—a foreign type who had signed on at the last minute. Obviously an exile and a rabble-rouser. Leon Something-or-Other.

"Are you sure this is the right street?" she said. Such questions had been ironed into flat statements by the frequency of their posting. Music faintly played behind the walls of a house. A dog barked in the garden of another. She was accustomed to neighborhoods noisy with children and lawnmowers, the rise and fall of conversations on porches and sidewalks. But the blank emptiness that closed them in on every side was creepy, as if they were walking between rows of mausoleums in an elaborate necropolis and the two of them set out like offerings for the fierce and indifferent sun.

But it had been enough of a question to make him stop and fuss over a tourist map to check their bearings. The heat rose up her legs from the pavement and beneath her skirt. He had turned the map several times as if to coordinate it with a compass in his head and then he squinted up at the sun to find its position. He adjusted the map once again.

"It's right down here," he said, and pointed straight ahead. "Just as I figured," he added—unnecessarily, she thought. On the other hand, he understood that to question him was one of the prerogatives to be endured in a successful relationship. The well-adjusted couple exercised these privileges without fear of invading each other's space. Yet it always rankled him a little. Their travels had been successful because of his careful preparations, because he had researched every turn and step of the way, reviewed all the possibilities. Even spontaneous side trips, like this morning's, were not taken haphazardly and without some planning.

During the several minutes he had waited for her to come down for breakfast, he had been able to get directions from the desk clerk, even enlisting the opinion of the switchboard operator. The three of them had traced the route on the map he had spread out on the hotel's front desk. With a judicious twist of her lips, a queenly moue, the woman had ordained the subway route they would take to Coyoacán. Nor had that been all. In the time left, he dug out a small book purchased at the museum the day before. He remembered seeing something about Trotsky in its back pages. Two brief paragraphs told of how Rivera and his wife, Frida Kahlo, also a painter, had befriended the Trotskys when they arrived in Mexico, in exile and chased by Stalin's agents. The artists had turned over their own house to the Russian couple, and Leon and (the pamphlet did not give her first name) Madame Trotsky had lived there for a time before moving to the place that was their destination this morning. All in all, he thought he had put together a considerable amount of information before she had stepped out of the elevator, eager for breakfast.

"I hope there's a bathroom," she said. They walked down the middle of the empty street.

"It's a house. Of course there's a bathroom."

"I mean one that can be used. Not something roped off with a purple cord."

30

The idea of a respectful viewing of the commode used by the old Bolshevik amused him. Would he have worn his glasses, for instance? Or had he misplaced them? *Madame Trotsky, I cannot find my glasses. . . . Here they are, Leon, and don't forget to flush.*

"What's so funny?" she asked.

"Just something about using the same bathroom used by someone who has shaped our history. You remember what Montaigne said about taking a dump?"

"No, I don't remember what Montaigne said. But there is something I'd like to mention." They had come to a cross street, and they looked both ways down the abandoned pavement before stepping off the curb. The ghostly rush from the unseen boulevards nearby had made them hesitate. "I wish, just one time," she continued, "we could come on the same thing together."

"But we do," he protested. "I've never been here!"

"No, I mean ignorantly, I guess. Unknowing. You do all this homework and I feel sometimes like I'm on a tour."

"But I'm only trying to make it enjoyable for you," he replied. "To give you the full benefit of . . ."

"Yes, yes, I know." She took his arm in both her hands. "I appreciate all that, but don't you think it would be fun if we discovered something all at once? Together." She could see her words had hurt him a little, so she let one hand go to his waist to hug him, then drop lower to cup his left haunch. "And there's something else about it." She wanted to confide in him and put her steps in rhythm with his.

"Here we are," he said, looking at the street diagram again. He matched up the number on the map with the double digits above a narrow steel door set into a blank wall. The arrival at their destination frustrated her a little, though she guessed her disappointment would have weighed even more if she had had the time to tell him that she felt managed sometimes. Was that the right word? Never mind, he would only have misunderstood her and been hurt even more.

No sign or plaque marked the anonymous façade, which reflected the heat and brilliance of the sun full strength into their

31

faces. Yesterday afternoon, he had led her through some narrow back streets in the center of the old city to an ancient chapel on a small piazza where the remains of Cortés had been plastered into a wall near the altar. This too had been unmarked, nothing outside or inside the church to identify this spot as the final occupation of the Grand Conquistador, as if the local populace were too busy with their daily lives, marketing and drinking coffee, even to care where these stations of their history were located. Perhaps they relied on tourists such as they to make the identification for them, to pay their respects for them, and now they were about to enter this place that looked like a small prison, where a man who had murdered many was, in turn, murdered. This much he had demonstrated to her, that most historic sites signified the human addiction to violence. Major tourist attractions were either the birthplaces or the barrows of villains and martyrs, of crucifiers and the crucified. But how important this insight was, she had yet to figure out.

"It says *Ring Bell and Wait*." The hand-printed sign was in both English and Spanish, and the inked letters had faded. One corner of the card had become unattached, and curled out, away from the brass mullion. "Ring bell," he repeated as his finger pressed the button, "and wait." He regarded her as if to measure her patience with this last part of the instruction. "Shouldn't be long." He smiled. But what he read as anxiety in her expression actually came from an eagerness to get into the cool refreshment of the garden that she had learned often lay within such bleak walls, and to meet up with another person, if only a gatekeeper.

They stared at the dime-sized peephole in the middle of the steel panel, but it remained blind. The metal of the door had been painted a pale green like the verdigris that will coat copper. Nothing stirred behind the door, nor could they hear any sound from over the high wall. Jagged pieces of broken glass had been embedded into the cement along the top of the wall, and these shards caught the light like fragments of malevolent sugar candy. Across the street, a mongrel stretched out in the brief shadow of a shallow entry. About a half-dozen blocks down, a small truck passed very slowly through the intersection, then was gone.

"Maybe they're closed," she said.

"Oh, it's just Mexico," he joked. "Slow."

"It's lunchtime," she said.

"Not really." He checked his watch. "For you and me maybe, but not them. It's only a quarter to one. They don't eat lunch down here until around two." Across the street, the dog had turned over, and his muzzle sought for a cooler spot on the hard pavement.

"Maybe the bell doesn't work. I didn't hear it ring inside."

"Not likely." He shrugged. "Probably, it's set inside the house somewhere. Which seems to be at the far end of the garden." He had stretched his height, as if he could look over the high wall. He was sorry about her discomfort. "Maybe we could find a restaurant nearby, have a fruit juice, and you could use the bathroom and then come back."

"Give me a break," she said. She surveyed the deserted streets around them and imagined the long expedition he would mount, agreeably pointing out this or that feature of lifeless architecture as they marched toward the horizon. "Try the bell again."

"Let's give them a little more time," he said. He took out the small Berlitz language book he always carried with him and flipped through its pages for a quick study.

"What does the Spanish part of the notice say? It looks different."

"Just about being closed on certain holidays. Actually, that proves they must be open today. Don't you see? It's not a holiday."

She nodded and studied her feet in sandals. Her toenails were chipped and needed some attention. She hated to expose them but the sandals were so much more comfortable than sneakers. The homogenized slur on the expressway several blocks over was split by the siren of an emergency vehicle, an ambulance or police car. The angry pulse of its alarm vibrated her nerves. When she looked up, she found him watching her as if he were choosing from several possible procedures, all to benefit her. "How about it?" she said. "Try it again?"

"You're like one of those people who come up to an eleva-

33

tor and always ring the bell even though others are already waiting, standing there.''

"That's right. I do that too," she said, and put her finger out and pushed the little button set into the brass cup.

Instantly, the door swung inward. It must have been a coincidence, but the shy smile on the young woman's face suggested she might have been there all along, listening to them talk while waiting for another ring of the bell, a second and more demanding one that would verify their seriousness. He also thought she was a little young for the job, maybe still in high school, but quite pretty. She almost bowed, and entreated them to enter with a gracious gesture of one hand. Immediately inside the door, a plaque mounted on the left wall stopped him short. He turned to it, pointing with a look of discovery on his face.

In Memory
of
Robert Sheldon Harte
1915–1940
Murdered by Stalin.

"Only the beginning," he told her with a curious triumph, then became quickly sober. He turned to the young girl. "Por favor, Señorita, pero la Señora . . . quiera . . . necessita . . . uno baño."

"Feel free to speak in English, if you wish," their guide told them in a delicate voice. "The facilities are down this path and around behind the rabbit hutch."

"Rabbit hutch, no kidding?" she heard him say as she made her way through the garden. The main house was to her right; several outbuildings lay ahead. She almost bathed in the heavy humidity of this walled estate; it had only seemed cooler at first. Once a more formal garden, the planting had been allowed to grow wild and unpruned. A slender marble plinth stood by the path, a gray stone wand trying to conduct the green cacophony. Several large trees, a couple of them palms, kept the place in a perpetual, dripping gloom. "Who keeps rabbits?" she heard him ask as she opened the door to the toilet.

No plaques adorned these unpainted walls, and only the basic items had been installed; one commode, one sink with one faucet, and one small mirror. A tourist site might be evaluated in terms of its plumbing, she thought. She recalled some of the places they had been, and the bathrooms she had used. Some had a half dozen or more neat cubicles surrounded by spotless tiles and large basins with both hot and cold water. Busloads of tourists, of any nationality, could be accommodated efficiently in such places within a few minutes, and perhaps that efficacy was related to the site's importance. The meager facilities she had just used made her wonder how many people came here at all, nor was this a new speculation for her. Not even the water in the one faucet worked, and a spider had set up shop in the sink's drain.

"He kept rabbits," he said when she returned. "Trotsky kept rabbits," he repeated to engage her interest. Apparently, he had been chatting up the young guide, gaining all sorts of information in her absence, because he directed her attention once again to the plaque by the wall.

"That was a young American, a bodyguard, who was killed in the first attempt on Trotsky's life. Yes," he continued to her silence, "there was an earlier attempt, about six months before and planned and led by one of their most famous painters, whose name was Sa . . . que . . . ?" He looked around. The young girl had walked to the house and waited for them by the door.

"Siqueiros." She supplied the name and looked demurely at her feet. She wore black loafers and pink anklets. "David Alfaro Siqueiros."

"Yes, that's right. Siqueiros. Didn't we see one of his murals at the Bellas Artes the other day? Can you imagine that, a painter plotting an assassination? Then trying to do the job himself?" She had not exactly shrugged but had turned to one side to regard the roof of the largish house. A watchtower rose up behind it, to overlook the surrounding wall and the streets beyond. "Well, I mean, can you imagine Norman Rockwell doing something like that?"

A ridiculous example, to be sure, but the extreme seemed

to match the heat and the fervor of this culture, which nourished such anomalies. He thought of the Aztecs cutting out beating hearts while playing flutes, writing poetry. The very vegetation that surrounded them in this garden seemed about to give up violent, unexpected fruits—a last few drops of moisture splashing upon the brick walks, a held-in silence and then: grenades of blossoms, exploding. He thought he remembered the Siqueiros work—an enormous expanse of tortured limbs and torsos, mouths and vulvas stretched wide in the grimaces of some awful agony of Mexico's past. But the artist's passion, as it turned out, had not been confined within the mere dimensions of a huge mural but had stretched out to grab at the very throat and pulse of life, right here in this suburban garden, here in this very house they were about to enter. The idea chilled and excited him in the midst of the midday's damp heat, and he knew he could not find the words to clarify his fascination with this duality; in any event, she became impatient with such abstractions.

Besides, she had gone ahead to stand on the low stoop of the house's entry to talk with their guide. Like half-sisters, say, the older one from a father's earlier marriage, they had commenced an intense discussion about opportunities for women in Mexico. He heard the young girl say she studied "communications" and he immediately had an image of her a few years from now, reading the news or talking of the weather on television, one more enameled and tightly coiffed visage to be turned on or off in a hotel room. The sweetness in the girl's face, the expectant set of her features around her future, made him look quickly at the other countenance, which was both tolerant and amused.

The first room was a kind of entry, and a pair of old work gloves, a blue jacket and some boots collected dust in one corner. Their guide told them of the Russian couple's strange odyssey— the flight from the Soviet Union, their temporary stays in different countries until at last Norway had asked them to leave. Always pursued by Stalin's agents, the two Trotskys had no place to go until President Cárdenas of Mexico, at the recommendation of Diego Rivera, invited them here. This bare room suggested the haste of their arrival, still propelled by the momentum of the chase—just time enough to use the one chair, take off the boots and gloves, sling them into the corner with the jacket, and pass through the armored door into the main house. That's what it looked like to him.

But the next room was different. Their guide had taken up a position by one wall. A scatter of holes punctured the plastered wall just above her head but her pose, hands clasped before her, demonstrated a patience with the two of them, as if a larger group crowded into the bedroom behind them. He noted a band of silver in her chestnut-colored hair, a barrette. Sheets of black iron had been bolted to both sides of all the doors.

"The first attempt took place here on twenty-four of May 1940." One of her hands lifted casually to wave at the bullet holes above her head. "Madame Trotsky hears the commotion at the garden door. It was four o'clocks in the morning. There were shots. She wakes up her husband and make him get under the table, there in the corner. Then she threw herself over the table. Meantime, the party had overwhelmed the guard at the door, Mr. Robert Harte, and have come up to this window."

She points and waits for them to look at the large window that looks out on the garden. It shares the same wall as the table in the corner, opposite to where the girl stands. A plain double bed lies between. Glass-fronted bookcases line the other wall, but the spareness of the place almost duplicates the severity of the outer room. "The mens start shooting through this window. They have submachine guns. But their bullets are harmless, striking only this wall and the empty bed. The Trotskys are just only wounded very little by splinters."

She paused, hands once again clasped in the folds of her skirt, obviously prepared to answer questions. To oblige her, he walked to a narrow doorway set into the inside wall and to the left of the bullet scars. "This was the bathroom?" he asked.

"Yes, this is the bathroom. As you see, the steel plates also put on the door and the window barred and screen. Security was observed. Everyone using the bathroom would take a pistol with them." Indeed, a thin ribbon had been tied across the entrance so he had to lean through to see all of it. Water supplied the old-fashioned commode from a wooden reservoir box set high up on the wall, level with the small barred window. At the far end of the long room, a tub nosed into the wall, almost taking up the entire width of the narrow room.

"*La fortaleza chica*, they called it—the house," the girl said and smiled. "The little fortress. Now, if you will excuse, I have matters I must attend to but be free to take your time and I will rejoin you in the next room." Her step was light, barely making any sound, as she left them, going through a door next to the bed.

"What do you suppose Montaigne would say about that?" She had come up behind him as he stood in the bathroom doorway.

"About what?"

"About going to the toilet with a gun."

"Well, that wasn't his worry, and he was making a different point anyway."

"Like what?" He felt her move close behind, press herself against him as if she might be trying to look over his shoulder at the facilities. And he was about to tell her the essay's thesis, the idea that no matter one's position, monarch or peasant, everyone shared this common throne, but she had moved away and that did not bother him. He wanted to abide the monastic feeling of the place a little longer. The plain, almost primitive aspect appealed to him, reinforced his idea of Leon Trotsky, the revolutionary, the intellectual as a man of action. The barren dimensions of the place, its meager furnishings, conversely suggested a devotion that supplied its own comforts. Such devotion today had become as outmoded as the toilet. Something to be remodeled, he thought, and made more agreeable by modern conveniences.

She had been drawn to the books in the glass-fronted cases. They were all the same volume, lined up in martial order, shelf upon shelf; the same title and author repeated in English. "*Stalin* by Trotsky," "*Stalin* by Trotsky," "*Stalin* by Trotsky" across and back and across again like the same integers being added to themselves over and over but never to increase the sum. The repetition amused her, the two names locked together in a mortal combat, a movie barroom brawl, but he would not see the humor of it. He had not caught her mood a minute before. The

38

idea of the machine guns firing over the double bed, all that commotion in her imagination had brought a sudden heat into the cool room. "I suppose that appeals to you," she said with a laugh. "Mrs. Trotsky throwing herself over the table, protecting the genius."

"It was a different time," he said agreeably. "Her background, a different culture made her think that way." The answer didn't satisfy him either. "Just the way she was, I guess." A silent agreement turned them toward the doorway of the next room. On the way, he idly poked his fingers into three of the bullet holes.

The next room was jammed with tables and chairs, bookcases and files. Through the large window that opened out on the garden, a slight breeze rippled the papers on the top of a very large desk in the center. A pair of wire-framed spectacles had been set down on the open sheets of a Mexican newspaper, as if the exile had just interrupted his reading to answer the phone to the left. A glue pot and an old-fashioned Dictaphone dominated the desk's surface. Also, a small automatic pistol. To one side, an upright standard typewriter was tabled, and clippings and journals in several languages were piled on a wide shelf fixed to the wall behind. Thick bars on the window, and the door, like the others, was sheathed in thick steel plates.

"As you see this was his study." Their guide had begun talking as she appeared through the other doorway; a little distractedly, he thought, as if she had just put down her own schoolwork to meet them. "On that day of August twenty, 1940, a man who called himself Jacson came to visit, bringing an essay for Trotsky to read. They came here, and Trotsky sat at his desk to read the paper." She took up a position behind the vacant chair.

"As Trotsky was reading the paper, Jacson took out a small pickax used for . . . for . . ." Her face had pinked and she wrinkled her nose and shrugged. "With a small handle for hiking . . ."

"Yes, of course," he helped her out, "used for mountain climbing."

39

But she had continued as if in a trance or caught up in the rote of her demonstration: ". . . and standing behind Trotsky hit him two, three times with it in the head but with the flat part of the blade and not the sharp point or else it would have pierced his brain and immediately killing him. You see this small telephone hanging by the desk leg is an alarm system to the guards which Trotsky knocked off as he fell to floor.

"But then he spring up, blood coming down his face and he start struggle with Jacson. The two mens fight. A gun goes off." The young Mexican had come to the center of the room, her arms stretched out as the sunlight put a glaze upon her eyes. "Jacson is wounded. Trotsky has bite him in the hand." She puts her own hand in her mouth. "The guards are running in from the garden. 'Don't kill him,' Trotsky say to them. 'He must talk.' Madame Trotsky is calling police, ambulance. Her husband walk into next room. Blood pouring down from his wounds. 'Look what they have done to me,' he say to her and then fall down here." She had moved to the spot in the doorway. "He lose consciousness."

Immediately, she resumed her patient pose, but her breathing had become rapid. She resembled a successful player in a game of charades, sure of her performance and that it had won the round. Drums beat in the neighborhood's distance, a regular tattoo that marked a parade, or a funeral procession. Someone in the suburb was being buried before lunch, he thought. Afterwards, the family and friends would go to a restaurant for a funeral feast. A *cazuela*. He remembered the word for "casserole" as the drums marched into the midday silence.

Come to think of it, he could detect no smells of cooking in this house. Did no one live here? Did their guide live here? Was she part of the Trotsky family, a great-granddaughter perhaps, whose turn had come to show the occasional tourist around? He didn't know if the old Bolshevik had had children. *Maria, there's the bell. Go down and show them where Great-Grandfather took it in the head. Oh, Momma, do I have to?* The room's inventory begged for hundreds of questions, but the three of them remained silent, immersed in the dense haze of noon at the scene of the crime.

The murder that had happened at this desk before them had erased all of his curiosity about the rest of the room's memorabilia. The profusion of books and papers, framed pictures and documents was enough for a month of questions. Busloads of tourists could pass through the chamber and never exhaust the room's potential for wonder. Yet the slaughter of Stalin's adversary by one of his agents, right here in front of where they stood, monopolized his interest. It was a strange pornography with its own perverse fascination; the shock of it, the actual realization of an act that had only been talked about, read about, until now; but here it was—he could see it. He could put out his hand to the desk and touch it. Almost.

"If you have no questions," their guide said sweetly, "I shall leave you at your deserves. Please feel free to take your times as much as you please. I must excuse myself to attend to something but will meet you later in this house."

"I can't believe it," he said in a low voice. "She leaves us alone in the place. We could take anything in it we want."

"Like what?" she said. The challenge in her voice was no surprise.

"Well, his spectacles, for example. Or that paperweight—looks Aztec. And see this!" He pointed to the small pistol. "Looks like a twenty-five caliber. Or maybe a book." He completed the short list and started reading the old newspaper on the desk, but it was in Spanish. On the shelf were editions of the *New York Herald Tribune* from August of 1940. "It's like stepping into a history book."

"Maybe she's cooking something," she said. "It's getting close to lunch, as you said before. I don't remember seeing any restaurant on the way in here. What were you planning for lunch, by the way?"

"What are you doing?" She had pulled out a drawer of a small table.

"Maybe he left a few crackers. Or gingersnaps even. People like that always have a secret vice of some kind—like gingersnaps."

"Don't do that! Close that drawer." He glanced quickly at

the doorway behind him. It was empty. "This is like a museum."

"You gave me the idea."

"But I was only joking." Sometimes he still didn't understand her. The room was saturated with the blood of history and all she could think of was food. The huge Shakespearean drama of it, giants plotting and scheming against each other, the whole epic climaxing here in this room where they stood: murderous blows, a brief struggle—did the assassin say anything at the end, this Jacson, had he been given any memorable lines? Did he, indeed, talk? Then she introduces something trivial like lunch. He couldn't believe it.

Nor would she ever understand this fascination he had for the apocalyptic, this obsession that dragged her like the captive of a vengeful god through museum after museum and before canvases and murals that glorified the butchery of human beings (most of the carcasses seemed to be female, she had noted some time back) as if to teach her unruly indifference an awful lesson, a lesson that she had never been able to use.

And didn't these rooms house the same kind of mania for hate and killing, a single-minded vindictiveness that sought out sleepers to murder them in their beds? With all the sunlight, the irrepressible Mexican sunlight pouring into the room, she felt as if she were standing in the epitome of darkness, a senseless waste of mind and spirit represented by the dead-end equation of book titles—more of the same in this room—"*Stalin* by Trotsky," "*Stalin* by Trotsky," "*Stalin* by Trotsky." It was a reverse kind of alchemy that went from gold to lead, and the formula seemed to have been boiled down into the residue of a poison so powerful that it never killed its victims but kept them freshly venomed, suspended in fear and paralyzed by hate. All at once she was chilled and she went to the window, closer to the sun and away from this joyless and deadly pedantry. Several large white birds—they looked like cranes—perched in the high purple branches of a jacaranda.

He wished he had brought a notebook, because the old issues of the *New York Herald Tribune* from 1939 contained fascinating articles. He'd have to look them up in a library later.

42

Front-page stories presented Trotsky's predictions of the coming war, America's involvement. The conflict would only hasten the world revolution that was to come, he was quoted as saying. Another piece reviewed his challenge to Stalin, made during the Fourth International the year before, that the Soviet Union had become just another imperialist power. The Soviet pact with Nazi Germany, signed in August of 1939, almost a year to the day before Trotsky's murder, was described by him as one more example of Stalin's "spirit of falsification," his rewriting of history. Strong words, but cause for murder? Last year's presidential election seemed pretty tame.

He turned the brittle pages of the old newspapers carefully, coming on headlines and articles that mentioned Roosevelt and Hitler, Chamberlain and Mussolini—names put to faces he had seen only in old newsreels on television became real personages by their verification in the newspaper, not quasi-fictional characters on the tube, and their day-to-day words and gestures of a half-century before seemed to have occurred only yesterday. It was some kind of magic, this intersection with history, a time warp he felt he had passed through. Earlier editions, from 1937, reported on the Joint Commission of Inquiry that Trotsky had called to answer the charges made against him by the Second Moscow Trials.

The commission had met in the Blue House, the Rivera house just up the street, and John Dewey, the American philosopher, had been one of the panel members. Several of Trotsky's old Bolshevik comrades—their names were unfamiliar to him— had been put on trial in Moscow and had confessed, under Stalin's torture, that he and they had made secret alliances with Hitler and Japan to defeat the Soviet Union. They were executed and contracts were put out to kill Trotsky. The Mexican counter-trial was called to clear Trotsky of the charges, and Dewey and the other panelists voted for acquittal. All this, just two years before Stalin actually signed the same sort of treaty with the Nazis, and the upside-down irony came off the yellowed pages with a freshness that must have stung the exiled revolutionary in 1939.

She heard him chuckling to himself, a little too stagy to be completely self-absorbed. She was supposed to ask him what had amused him, but she continued to look out the window, at the cranes in the tree. One had just spread enormous wings and lifted its emaciated body up and away in incomprehensible flight. Where humor could be found in this mundane play of ego that had ended in millions being butchered was beyond her. The bird had disappeared, and they were together, so she asked, "What's funny?"

"Oh, just something here in this paper." She heard him turn a page and she knew he was searching through the columns for an appropriate item to read to her. "Listen to this," he said finally. "Here's an interview with Trotsky after they had moved to this house. He's talking about the doors, the steel plates on them—'they make the same sound when they close as those in the first prison I was in in Kherson.' "

"Pretty funny," she said.

"And here's something else. His real name was Bronstein. He took his prison guard's name. He stole the man's passport to escape and thereafter used the name, Trotsky. Took his jailer's name," he repeated.

"Let's get out of here." She came around the desk and took his hand. "Haven't we seen enough?"

She pulled him through the doorway and into the next room, which was a kitchen that featured a typical sideboard of a wood-fueled cooking stove running the length of one wall, with spaces for four large ceramic pots—all in line. Everything, including the stove, had been colorfully tiled. A mural was painted on the wall and part of the ceiling, probably by Diego Rivera, but no helpful sheet of information rested on the rough-hewn refectory table. Only a small, gratuitous sign that said COCINA. Nor was their guide around.

They came upon her in the next room, embracing a young man about her own age. Her arms were around his neck and one of her legs was cocked around him so that a pink-stockinged foot spurred his corduroyed buttocks. As she kissed him full on the mouth, he looked wall-eyed at their entrance and, with his back to the wall, he resembled a condemned man receiving his last request. He looked a little apologetic for the whole business, too.

The tourists caught their breath. "What's going on?" the man muttered, and gave half a laugh.

"It's called *Ring Bell and Wait*," she replied, and jabbed him in the ribs with one finger. But their guide had turned from her *novio*, neatly slipped on the one black loafer and checked the silver band in her hair. Her companion smiled sadly, as if he knew the reprieve would be only temporary.

"Here is in this room, they would take their meals," the girl continued. "They ate simply and had many guests sometimes at table. In next room"—she led them out of the dining room, rather precipitately, he thought—"you will find Madame Trotsky's study. Many interesting objects for you to see here. And then the door outside to the garden where I will join you shortly." And once again, the young Mexican turned back and left them alone.

Back to preprandial devotions, she thought. But the charming vignette in the last room apparently had made little impression on him. Earlier, a pistol had provoked more enthusiasm. But was that a fair comparison? He had just come across some familiar books in Madame Trotsky's library and he dutifully read the authors' names out to her. James T. Farrell. Willa Cather. Dreiser. She imagined the young man in the next room fixed to the wall by the girl's ardor, helplessly waiting, during the times she had guided them from room to room, for her to come back and finish the job. "What's so funny?" he asked this time.

"I'll tell you in a minute," she replied, and quickly looked around the room, the roll-top desk and its manuscripts. Madame Trotsky had not only protected her husband with her own body, but she had also been his proofreader; perhaps an even greater sacrifice than the other act. The evidence was piled high on a desk with framed photographs of him and of them both as a young couple. They had posed stiffly, braced against their destiny, as it were, and with a respectable distance between them, as if the photographers had told them their place in history had no room for intimacy. On the other hand, she thought, the unabashed rapture they had just come upon in the last room, if not a part of the exhibit, was surely on the same level of importance with all these papers and books, these manifestos meant to topple governments and shake the foundations of the world. All these mementos of an ancient anger corroding and turning to dust in the Mexican sunlight while an even older fervor refreshed itself; the idea quieted something in her, eased off the urgency to find any item to accompany her laughter. "Nothing," she said finally. "My thoughts were elsewhere."

Now they were both eager to quit the place. He found the house no longer interesting and its contents seemed shabby. The high windows in this room, barred like all the others, admitted an even light that flattened out everything save for the soft curve of her throat where it joined the shoulder. The wide collar of her blouse was open and, as she turned for the door, some of the color of the cotton reflected upon her cheek. It made him aware of a coldness that had crept into him, room by room, a kind of mildew that had been passed on from the moldy artifacts, the yellowing accounts of betrayal and revenge. Something about yesterday's newspaper, he thought, but he couldn't remember the exact idiom as he followed her out the door.

They walked along a narrow path beside the house, past the heavily barred window of Trotsky's study where he had been murdered, past the next window, with its iron picket, which looked in on the bedroom. He could see the punctures of the bullet holes in the opposite wall. And then they rounded the corner of the house, and the garden opened out before them. The young couple stood in fast embrace by the gray stone marker, the girl once again wound around the boy, standing on one leg to firmly lash herself to him with the other. The youth saw them over her shoulder and pulled his lips from hers and grinned. He said something to her.

"This monument is by their friend, the sculptor and painter O'Gorman," their guide commenced her patter. She held her companion by one hand, no doubt to keep him in place so as to waste neither time nor motion once they were alone. "At the base of this monument"—she raised and pointed one polished black loafer, a dancer's pose—"is the ashes of Leon Trotsky and his wife. If you have any questions, I am happy to answer." She seemed to wait a prescribed length of time, again an interval

46

planned for a much larger group. Water ran somewhere behind them, like a garden faucet dripping onto tile. Several dogs barked outside the walls. Then, not surprisingly, she said, "Feel free to show yourselves out. Please close the door behind you and thank you for your interest in coming here."

Across the street, the dog was sitting up and looked about hopefully. She stepped off the sidewalk and waited for him at the curb. He had paused to study the memorial tablet for the slain bodyguard. She heard him pull the steel door shut and test it once or twice to be sure the latch had caught. They were locked out for sure, and to get back in, they would have to ring the bell all over again and wait. But why would they want to do that? Only if they had forgotten something inside, and she trifled with the contents of her shoulder bag, patted the different articles. She stroked her bare arms, which had become pebbled in the heat of the relentless sun. The same pristine light etched his familiar profile to recast its expression, a sharpening of line and contour that made him at one with the roof lines, the walls, the stark reliefs of this neighborhood.

"Well, let's go," he said, and reached for her hand. She looked weary and he knew she must be hungry. Her look tugged at his own fatigue, an ache of more than muscle and bone. They walked down the middle of the brilliant and empty street, hand in hand; companions and each other's defenders. At corners, they stopped and looked both ways down the side streets, into the shadows that darkened doorways.

His Father's Garden

In the forty days since his father's death, Marc Lazor has put many miles on his frequent-flyer account, most of these to service his clients in the southeastern United States, but then he made the flight to Minneapolis, to his mother's, before buckling himself into one last, narrow 737 seat for the trip to Pittsburgh. All these streaks across the eastern half of the country were like lacings that never tied up into any kind of neatness, and he felt as if the cramped space around him, perhaps representing another kind of fitted destiny, might slip off and leave him unattached and free-falling thirty thousand feet above Lake Ontario.

It would be typical of his father, he thought, to be the only fixed point in this landscape of loose ends, nor was it only in death that this distinction had been centered. Joe Lazor had always gone his own way to pursue goals defined and only attainable by him. "Selfish." Lazor's sister had spat the word and looked to their mother for agreement. They sat with her on the side porch of the house they had grown up in. This suburb of Minneapolis never seemed to change, and, on each return visit, Marc Lazor expected to find that one of the large lawns had been subdivided, or one of the rambling homes cut up into condominiums. Their mother had turned her head to look down the drive-way. Whatever her feelings had been, she had never displayed them before her children. At the driveway's entrance several workmen from a nursery were setting a good-sized tree into a large hole. The new tree was replacing an ancient maple that had been split apart by a late winter storm. "I mean," Lili persisted, trying to get her mother's attention, "finding himself, he lost us."

"I wonder how he'd feel about all the walls coming down in Eastern Europe," their mother said. She almost never an-swered anyone directly. "He would talk of that never happen-ing, not in his lifetime, he would say, and well . . ." She let the thought smother in soft laughter. Lazor saw this sort of talk was making his sister uneasy. Lili had stood up and faced the porch screen to look down toward the workmen also, as if to share at least this point of view with her mother.

In fact these reveries the older woman would fall into made them both impatient with her, as they challenged their own angers. The portion of her life she had shared with their father seemed sufficient, and they never understood why. "He used to say that he had been my thesis," she continued. "I was just finishing up my doctorate in sociology, and he had only just arrived from Yugoslavia; a trained and practicing lawyer, a jour-nalist in his own country, but here without a language, friends, connections. Nothing but his mind."

While she spoke, his sister cast a meaningful look at Lazor, as if to remind him of the talk they had had as she drove him in from the airport. The old girl was losing it, she had told him. They had heard this family history so many times. The accounts of courtship and marriage and success had enthralled them as children, but the narrative had become confusing and then dis-agreeable as the absence of its main character became more apparent, more painfully obvious with each telling, so that their mother's stories of their father's history, his supposed heroism and integrity, became a measurement of the depth and volume of his abandonment. Lazor sometimes wondered if these long narratives she used to wind around them as children were also like bandages she wound around her own hurt, a kind of self-

49

healing cocoon of happier memories. But his sister disagreed with him.

"She's even worse," Lili had said to him. Several gold bangles clattered on a thin wrist as she maneuvered the station wagon through rush-hour traffic. "I had hoped the junk dealer's death would free her—free us. You'd think he was some kind of a national hero—leaving us to become what? Some kind of . . . what?" The bracelets clashed as one hand groped the air for the right word. ". . . A goddamn junk dealer."

"That's not exactly what he is . . . or was," Lazor had to say, but the whole discussion was a headache for him. All of his flying in the last month had collected into a large clot that made his head heavy and thick.

"Well, you'll see," Lili had warned. "Why must you go to Pittsburgh, anyway? I don't see why you have to go."

"One of us has to settle the final business. Also, he asked that I attend this church ceremony—this memorial service." He should have let the first reason stand by itself. Never understanding business, Lili would have accepted this reason without question, but she was the sort of person who felt she had a particular insight into moral principles, into duties and obligations, so to accede to their father's invitation made no sense to her.

Actually, on the plane to Minneapolis, Lazor himself wondered why he would fly back to Pittsburgh. Nothing in the will required him to do so. Even the business matters only needed his signature; the probate of the will and all the other details had been arranged by his father's secretary, a woman he had already spoken with on the phone who was, obviously, more than competent. She could mail him the different documents. And if he didn't attend the service, no negative quid pro quo would affect him or the rest of the family. There had been nothing in his father's letter to imply that if the invitation was not accepted then something else would not happen.

> . . . and you might be amused by the ritual, perhaps even interested. It's a curious variation on Rome, studded with rites that celebrate tragedies and

triumphs—more of the former, I'm afraid. We even have a ceremony, performed every year, that marks the slaughter and enslavement of the Slavs by the Turks hundreds of years ago. The priests' robes are studded with cut glass in so many colors. And the food. All kinds of breads and cakes. Especially the bread. Feasts. We eat a lot in this church.

This last gibe was a reference to the plain Presbyterian services his mother's family attended. As the plane made its approach to the Minneapolis–St. Paul airport, and Lazor cinched his seat belt tighter, the disciplined elegance of those church services came to mind: the cream-and-polished-wood tones of their family pew. True, the communion was simple fare, but somehow aristocratic in its plainness, he always thought, to imply the rich sustenance within the individual rather than make an ostentatious show of a supposed spiritual wealth. He never remembered his father going to church; he preferred to spend Sunday mornings reading.

"No, nothing but his mind," his mother had been saying. "Can you imagine what it must have been like to be educated, a professional, an intellectual of some standing and then to, well—overnight, really—be reduced to an immigrant, incoherent and with no way to practice his profession."

"He did well enough," Lili cracked, and took her seat abruptly. Quickly also, she picked up the glass of California fumé blanc their mother served them. She finished the wine as if it were water, and seemed ready to leave. "Uncle Ned did well by him." Her manner was perfunctory, and she looked around her chair for her purse with an assurance that it would be found. Her belongings were always found.

"Yes, that's true," their mother said, surprisingly. "But they didn't get along." It was all they had ever heard about the falling-out of the brothers-in-law. Only that. Then as if some reason might at last be given, she chuckled and said, "One time your uncle came across your father eating a raw onion and one of those sausages he fancied—in his office. He kept such things in a small refrigerator there. Ned opened the door of his office

51

and your father was standing in the corner, wolfing the food down. That was your uncle's word—'wolfing.' " Her gentle laughter reminded Lazor of an earlier time of lawn parties on the sloping lawn just beyond the porch where they sat, of deer carved of ice and the subtle music of small orchestras.

The three of them had been meeting like this once a year for several years, more like a corporation board than a family, and they were a dwindling number of charter members at that— even the charter was barely remembered. At the real board meeting Lazor would attend the next morning, hard-eyed men and women would speak to him with the identical expression, as if the same pattern of a smile had been stenciled on their lips. The annual report on his division would be politely attended to, but with a mannered patience that suggested the more important corporate interest lay elsewhere. He would sometimes tell his wife that when he reached retirement, he wouldn't be surprised if his part of the corporation, the original family lode that had provided a good living for them and from which his father had resigned, would be sold off or simply dissolved, only to be recalled in nostalgic moments in certain boardrooms and clubs or on the screened porches of rambling suburban houses like his mother's.

"Well, I must dash," Lili had been saying, and got up. "I have to pick up the girls at their ballet class. I'll meet you at the bank tomorrow," she told him, "and drive you to the airport."

She let herself out of the house as he poured more wine for his mother. They heard the sound of a car motor and then they observed the station wagon roll slowly down the driveway, pause at the site of the new tree, no doubt for Lili to pass some pleasantry with the workmen—it was her kind of graciousness— and finally coast around the lower curve and out of sight. His mother took a deep breath.

"She's always so angry," she said.

Lazor did not know what to say at this point, but guessed his mother looked for no response. Yet he felt something had to be said, if only to sustain the hours before supper was ready. "He said something very strange to me last time I was there. Last year when I visited him. I had to be in Pittsburgh for that infringement business," he added quickly.

"What was that, I mean, what did he say?"

"Well, he insisted we take this cog railway they have going to the top of a bluff across from the city." His father had led him to a cement platform that cantilevered far out from the face of the cliff, where a splendid view of the three rivers and the city's skyline presented itself. He could look straight up the Monongahela River and, in the opposite direction, down the Ohio—where the Ohio begins. He had felt he could touch the tops of the skyscrapers if he only reached out. Instead, it was his father who spread his arms. "He talked about how it all must have looked before any of that," Lazor told his mother. "With just the Indians and a few fur traders coming down the rivers in their canoes. Like a dream, he said. And then he said, 'I'm trying to tell you about a dream.' "

His mother made a curious noise and folded her hands over her stomach. "That's Conrad," she told him. "Joseph Conrad. His favorite author, he read him all the time. I remember that line. It's from a long story of Conrad's about Africa. He'd read it to me."

"I thought so," Lazor replied, and viewed the fading light through the straw-colored wine in his glass. "I mean it sounded like a line from something. Stagy. It was another of his performances. The way he raised his arms out—like this—as if he wanted to hug the whole skyline, the whole panorama."

"And you," his mother said, and picked up her glass.

The directions to the church his father's secretary had given him over the phone had seemed simple enough, so Lazor had barely noted them down on the telephone pad in his hotel room. The large window beside the bed looked west, out over the Allegheny River and its junction with the Monongahela where the Ohio begins. In the foreground was the huge coliseum of the sports stadium and he was fairly sure that beyond the stadium, and in the general direction of a high hill with a tall radio tower on top, was the fenced-in city block with a large sign raised over sheet-metal doors, the block letters in white paint: LAZORCAK SCRAP.

He had been to the yard several times and had even gone to his father's house, a couple of blocks from the scrap yard; one of many brick rowhouses with back gardens on a street with trees and interesting doorways. One time, his father had taken particular delight cooking pork chops for them on a charcoal brazier set up in the back garden, pinching off various herbs for a salad from a geometric plot meticulously cultivated around the roots of a large ailanthus tree.

"Brought over from Indonesia by some dreamer," his father had said. His broad face looked happy as he flipped the meat. "Thought he'd start a silk industry here, but the worms wouldn't go for it. So the trees grew and propagated. Great city trees, they thrive on pollution. Big weeds is all they are."

It had been another of those annoying performances, Lazor remembered; the older man pulling out a fact or an historical anecdote that had nothing to do with the conversation and which was, usually, unfamiliar information at that. Lili had often accused him of making up this startling trivia, but Marc had checked up on enough of his father's facts to know their truth. Now, sitting on the bed of his hotel room, that evening several years ago permeated his memory, as if the aroma of grilled meat yet rose in the far distance of that modest neighborhood and somehow had filtered into the air-conditioning he breathed. Then, with a snap, he returned to the present, called his wife to assure her he was okay and started off for the memorial service.

The secretary's directions were backed up by the map supplied him by the car-rental agency—it all seemed simplicity itself; yet, after crossing one river and then another a couple of times, he found himself in an unbroken circle of detours and road repairs that turned him down the main streets of small towns with names like Coraopolis, McKees Rocks and Aliquippa. He must have passed the same boarded store windows several times, or else they all looked alike. Even the rusting hulks of steel mills all looked alike—or it was the same one, empty and still at river's edge like the huge husk of an awesome

54

chrysalis, its genus long ago emerged and flown off to extinction.

Finally, Lazor broke out of the pattern by taking a side street that appeared to go nowhere, but immediately became very steep, climbing almost straight up through plain neighborhoods to emerge into the open at the top of the bluff that rose across from downtown Pittsburgh. He had come to the very place his father had brought him before, but from the other side. He saw the cement platform, or one very like it, and Lazor was tempted to stop, to get out and go to the prospect, and to stand there, alone this time, as a kind of personal memorium with the view in case he never got to the church.

"You must understand, Marcus, that I am no rebel," his father had said. "Always, things go backwards from me." The precise English he had learned in night school had relapsed into an immigrant's casual syntax. When they were children, he would amuse them by speaking this way purposely, and it had made him exotic, unique. Later, of course, they would think differently. "Always, I find my own way. In Belgrade as a young lawyer, my lover was the law. Justice was my mother. All that was promised was taken."

"We know all about that, Dad," Lazor remembered saying. "It's part of the family saga. We sit around and tell it by the fire. Your escape from Tito. Your arrival in the land of opportunity, only to be betrayed once again."

"Hush now," his father had said, and raised one large hand, thick with coarse black hairs. But it was not a threatening gesture, but one of comfort, something to soothe a hurt. Joe Lazor had turned to stare at the skyline, the river below, as if to find new thoughts there. How much longer, Marc Lazor thought, were they to be held hostage by these quaint accents, by these tales of betrayal? Even the second emigration, to call it that, was put into the same terms as the first, with the absurd claim that it had been a flight that had benefited them all.

"It is unbecoming for a man to carry such angers." His father had turned to lean against the iron railing fixed around the platform. It was a nonchalant pose with the skyline behind him. "You do well in that life. I could not." He slouched confidently against the railing. The drop below would be hundreds of feet, but the steel and glass and aluminum buildings seemed to embrace him. Pittsburgh was his father's city, Lazor recognized. He belonged here. "Your anger is not with me, Marcus. But if I am a monster, then you must learn to love me. For your own sake."

Lazor had just found a way down off the bluff, and by luck the street came to an intersection that led to the four-lane highway penciled on the map beside him. In minutes, a discreet sign for the Serbian Cathedral directed him to take the next right, and he was immediately impressed by the size of the church that stood out starkly from the hillside. The poured cement of its massive walls looked fresh, as if the forms had just been removed and the concrete had only set up.

The faint singing from within the church was only slightly amplified when he pulled open one of the large aluminum doors, embossed with bas-reliefs of biblical scenes. Inside, the vast parabola of the interior intensified the intimacy of the ceremony already in progress at the front. No more than two dozen people stood together in the front pews on one side of the main aisle. Each held a small candle. Before them, an elaborate screen stretched the width of the nave; it was composed of painted panels that depicted the Christ figure and different saints. Lazor recognized St. George, tentatively holding one foot on the neck of a dog-sized dragon; the whole array was similar to the gold-painted altar screens he and his wife had seen in Siena the previous summer on their way to Zurich for family business.

In the center of this ornate façade, an archway enticed glimpses of a sparkling alcove, an inner sanctum, but its full display was obscured by the scarlet-robed back of a priest. He had been genuflecting before the altar, then lifted his arms to send up a half-sung, half-chanted litany, which was answered by those standing in the pews. Their untrained voices climbed trustingly into the air. Candles in red and green and blue glass holders played upon the facets of cut glass, caressed the sheen of satins and the luster of gold so that the whole affair, the crimson gem of the priest within, resembled a glittering confection, a cake so embedded with citron fruits and sugar crystals that its consumption would be a redundancy.

Just then, a pencil-thin candle was held out to him by an elder, a large man in a plain black suit who had been standing at the rear of the church. Something in his manner suggested that he had been observing Lazor, giving this stranger time to adjust and then to admire the great loft and volume of the interior. The church looked to be all nave, and the stark concrete walls ascended unchecked into immense arches that lifted the dome as high as anything Lazor could remember seeing in Europe. The gray, bare walls set off the encrusted luxuriance of the altar, as the plain skin of an exotic fruit might burst to reveal the rich pulp within.

All the candles had small octagonal cardboard guards at their base to catch the dripping wax, and this feature made them look like tiny rapiers, somehow illuminated and held up by a band of Eastern European musketeers. One of these, a man Lazor recognized as his father's yard foreman, tilted his burning candle at Lazor's fresh wick while responding to the priest's chant in a heavy, rough voice that vibrated the slender taper in his thick fingers. The two flames were harried by a gust of garlic so powerful, of such high octane that, Lazor would tell his sister later, he feared the open flames might cause an explosion that would crack the church apart and thrust the great dome into the sky like a thunderhead.

Lazor wondered if he should at least hum along with the group, and he tried to anticipate which way, up or down on the scale, the heavy voice next to him would go. But none of them seemed to be singing the words all that much, mostly mouthing the end of a verse, a line, for the responses were entirely carried by a half-dozen very old women in a pew across the aisle. This choir was directed by a younger woman, and the voices were like those of young girls.

He could never remember his father being a religious man— all those Sundays spent in the library reading the Encyclopedia Britannica while the rest of them went to church—so this ritual before him seemed a little overdone, if not outlandish; one more reference to a part of his life none of them knew about, something lived before any of them had known him. "We didn't know he had arranged for this service," the secretary had told him this morning. "It's a traditional ceremony performed forty days after the death. I think you'll be interested." Which made her sound like his father and, come to think of it, wasn't that even the same phrase? Maybe she had typed that last letter. Right now, she had turned to look at him over her shoulder, as if to further entreat his interest, and the ambiance given off by the small candle in her hand gave the woman a flirtatious expression. But with a shift of light, she was all business and merely checking his attendance before facing front.

Next to her stood another of his father's employees, who could have been a brother to the man next to him as well as to the basso profondo who had lit Lazor's candle. All had the same broad, fierce brow that projected over deep-set eyes like a lintel balanced on the knifeblade of a nose. His father's expression could be similarly stern and not unlike the icons and the painted saints around the church. Their fixed frowns commanded vengeance for all wrongs done to a soul or to an individual or to a people. But sometimes this darkness in his father's eyes would glint like obsidian, like black flame, when a remark or thought had sparked a covert amusement, or by the ordinary pleasure of grilling thick pork chops for them in his backyard. The aroma of hot wax filled Lazor's head, and his stomach growled. He had had only coffee and a roll at the hotel this morning.

The priest had turned around and come to the portal of the screen, paused and raised his arms. The man's glasses and the jewel-like pieces of colored glass sewn into his ornate gown reflected the candle flames, a splintering of light beyond any theory. The priest had a short grayish beard and looked like the poet Allen Ginsberg. His voice rose into a falsetto and then fell back into a nasal flatness and then rose again. The leisurely pace of the ceremony had quickened, and the congregation was having trouble keeping up. They leaned forward in the pews urgently. The ritual became focused differently, and Lazor recognized the sibilant buzz of his father's old name—Josef Lazorcak. The others responded. Again, Josef Lazorcak and then again, Josef Lazorcak. Each time the congregation had responded with something, so it was like a dialogue between the priest and the others, as if to weave a spell around the name—Josef Lazorcak—or maybe it was a kind of rinsing of the name, Lazor would think later, to remove all the earthly matter that might have collected on it.

By now the priest had stepped down to a small table with a cross, which had been placed at the head of the aisle, and, by now, Lazor's candle had burned nearly down to the cardboard guard. The other candles had not burned so quickly, some only halfway down, and he wondered if this meant anything. Had he held it at an incorrect angle? Perhaps, a particular draft had singled out his candle, had swooped down from the enormous dome to blow across only his flame. Should he allow the candle to sputter and drown in its own melted wax or should he mercifully give it one quick puff? What was the protocol?

He looked around at the others but they were attending to the priest, who had begun to talk almost informally, smiling and relaxed. His father's name was mentioned and the priest nodded toward him, said something, which the others acknowledged pleasantly. The man next to him nudged him in the side and smiled. Meanwhile, an acolyte in green satin appeared with a silver tray that bore little white cakes. He presented them to the priest, then placed the salver on the table, where it received another blessing. Then the assistant, whose pale brown shoes poked out from beneath his jeweled robe, picked up the tray and faced the congregation. This gesture, Lazor was relieved to see, was also a signal that the candles were to be blown out, and the others began to move slowly toward the center aisle. The ladies of the choir had taken up a different hymn, something with a more lively rhythm, and the man next to him urged him forward.

One by one, each member of the ceremony stepped forward, took one of the small cakes and placed the entire pastry within the mouth. Without chewing, or even swallowing as far as Lazor could see, each circled the small table with the cross and then returned to the pews. The priest stood by, nodding, chanting, or saying something in Serbian, and he looked rather pleased and proud, like a chef presenting a newly created dish. When it came his turn, Lazor was held back with a gentle firmness by the priest, singled out; he hoped he looked at ease as the priest went through some special ritual that obviously had to do with him—the son. Then, he was given a tiny pastry and he did the same as the others, letting the cake dissolve in his mouth. It was made of whole wheat grains bonded together by honey and bits of nuts and coated with powdered sugar. The flavor was intense and burned his throat.

The dry sweetness of the powdered sugar still cloyed his mouth even as he sat in the office of the scrap yard that afternoon, and his throat remained dry despite a couple of trips to the jug water cooler in the corner. A large window looked out on the working place. It was a curious stockade, fenced off from the rest of the city by high walls of sheet metal. Slabs of steel of irregular sizes and shapes were arranged in bins around the yard's perimeter like the odd pieces of cardboard left over from some gigantic child's project. Lazor spotted some of the men who had attended the ceremony, but they now moved about the area in coveralls and wore heavy gloves to operate power booms and forklifts. At the far end, as in a lament to the crenellated skyline of the city, an enormous crane raised its tubular steel neck like the skeleton of a giraffe or, it came to him, of a creature that might have been born in one of those vacant steel mills along the Ohio.

Mrs. Pozar's expert fingers played upon the keys of a word processor. She still wore the tailored suit she had worn in church, and Lazor guessed it was a little more formal than her usual workday apparel. The office reflected a casual efficiency. No division, nothing marked off the area between employer and employee. His father's heavy mahogany desk was simply placed in one corner of the room, opposite Mrs. Pozar's area, and with a good view out the large window. Under the glass top of the desk had been placed pictures of them all, at all ages to make a pictorial history of camps and marching bands, graduations and weddings. Grandchildren were also represented and, in the case of Lili's children, Lazor guessed his mother must have sent them. He took this guesswork with him to the water cooler one more time.

"What will you do with his house?" Mrs. Pozar asked. It

was a direct inquiry, interested but not prying; a kind of straight-forward address he had discovered in the people of this city.

"I'm not sure yet," Lazor replied after a little. "I suppose I could sell it."

"Real estate is down right now," the secretary said, punching a key and activating a printer beside the processor. "If you want, until you decide, I could rent it for you. One of our men wants to move with his family. Closer to work. He'd be a good tenant."

"I'm sure of that," Lazor said. Several workmen with heavy gloves guided an immense sheet of steel grappled by a motorized boom operated by a fourth. The piece must have been about twenty feet square, and its surface was like a mirror in the sun, like a frame of molten ore, but for a dull spot at one edge where a circle, a man's height in diameter, had been cut out. Slowly, the apparatus with its several tons of scrap advanced to a bin and there, maneuvering almost negligently, the workmen deposited the heavy sheet with others. It settled silently into place.

"I'll think it over and let you know," Lazor finally said.

"Now, here." Mrs. Pozar arranged some papers on her desk top. "Here are these waivers. Your father had set up this corporation with the employees several years back, so the business would just carry on. They've chosen their own management. You get the house and the scrap yard stays with the employees."

Lazor had been looking over the documents as he slowly uncapped his pen. "If you wish to have your lawyer look these over . . ."

"That's not necessary," he told her, and started to sign. Her sigh made him look up. She was smiling broadly. "What?"

"Your father," she said. "Your father said you would say that."

Lazor blushed, caught off guard, as if some trait better left unknown had been revealed. He bent over the desk and carefully signed the several copies of a document that disclaimed any liens he or his sister or his mother, or their heirs, might have on the scrap yard. With his signature and power of attorney, he disowned them once and for all.

"Junk, Marcus," the lecture had continued several years

before, "is residue, something that has been used up and is useless." Once more, his father's arms had stretched out but this time to direct his attention to a flatbed trailer parked on the other side of the yard. Lazor had stepped away and then looked. A slab several inches thick was being lifted off the truck.

"But scrap, now that's different. Scrap is fresh, newly cast and ready to be made into something strong, something new. Only a part of its potential has been used up. It waits, always fresh, to be used well, to be made worthwhile." As they watched, the heavy piece of metal was neatly slipped into a storage stall. "Tell me it's all a dream, Marcus," Joe Lazor had said. "I dream of my village in Pannonia sometimes. The plains that rise in dust in summer. The little brick houses. Then the war and I'm in Belgrade. What a hothead I was. I would say 'Young Turk,' "—his laughter exploded—"but the allusion is not so complimentary. Then I come here and there is the time with your mother and you and Lili. Little Lili." The broad, dark face had looked down, like a weary runner's at the end of a race. "And then, I am here." Once again, the arms swept out, and a fist came back to thump the chest. "Is this a dream—this? Am I to wake in another place, then only to dream once more? Where had I been awake before and where was I in a dream?"

A loudspeaker mounted on a pole nearby had shattered the lull that had fallen between them. "Joe . . . Joe . . . THE CALL YOU WANT." Amplification had made the secretary's voice sound insolent, and Lazor would remember wondering if all talk in this valley had been made harsh because of the din of heavy manufacturing, the roar of the steel mills, which now rusted at river's edge while the level of speech remained loud and strong as if in tribute to what now lay silent, what—at one time—had to be spoken over. So very different, he had mused, watching his father stride across the yard, from the understated decorum of the boardrooms and family dens he frequented. Joe Lazor had taken the several steps up to the office, strangely built of wood like a Cape Cod cottage in this enclave of metal, pulled open the aluminum combination door, stepped inside and disappeared.

* * *

62

Once Marc Lazor found the key for the lock, the heavy wooden door of the old house swung open easily on its ancient hinges. He had stood on the low stoop as if to display his confusion to the neighborhood's children rowdily making their way home from school. They were both black and white children, and their noisy retreat from spelling and sums sounded vaguely threatening, a vernacular strange to him, so he had fumbled with the unfamiliar key ring, dropped it once and then stooped down to retrieve it. Inside, the house was larger than he remembered. The interior was dark and cool and offered a comfortable reception, and he could imagine how his father might have returned every evening to stretch out on one of the divans for a nap or maybe select a book from a stack on the floor. In fact, books seemed to be stashed in all parts and corners of the house, on chairs and tables and the treads of the stairs leading to the second floor. They were like provisions kept at various points of the house by an explorer, food and fuel stored at different altitudes of the Himalayas by a provident climber.

Someone had collected mail and placed it on a small hall table, circulars and letters, some addressed to J. Lazorcak and others to Joe Lazor. In a small foyer hung photographs of John and Robert Kennedy along with foreign-looking pictures Lazor knew to be of Serbian patriots. The dining room had been made part of a large kitchen that featured a restaurant-sized gas stove beneath many copper pots and pans that hung from a steel rack fixed into the ceiling. The functional, strong construction surely had been welded together a couple of blocks away at the scrap yard.

Marc Lazor located a mug and a jar of instant coffee and set a tea kettle of water to boil on the stove. If he looked, he was sure to find ingredients for a whole meal within easy reach either in the pantry or within the gleaming refrigerator. It might contain some pork or lamb chops or more likely some thick, black sausage. Perhaps in the basket on top of the refrigerator would be a dried-out hunk of bread. But Lazor sat down in one of the wrought-iron chairs and only contemplated his apparition in the polished door. He remembered a bedroom and a small bath upstairs, sponges nesting in a painted wire basket. There was also a room that was the actual library, books from floor to ceiling on all four walls, with a door leading to a small open deck just above where he sat in the kitchen. He had decided not to go upstairs. Clothes might still hang in closets and maybe the bed yet unmade, the covers thrown back and the pillows cast in the mold of the head they had supported. But this sentimental image was dismissed by the remembrance of his father's almost military habits. The bed upstairs would be taut and smooth and the pillows plumped into a bolster.

Later, he might look around for something to read, for he had just understood he would be staying overnight. Not here, not in his father's house, but he might find a book to take back to the hotel, a volume well-thumbed and supplied that he could look at—if not read, for he might not understand the writing. Just then, the phone rang.

That the service was still hooked up surprised him. Perhaps a computer oversight. He let it ring and ring, thinking the machinery might eventually correct itself, come to an electronic comprehension that no one lived at this number any longer. Even the phone upstairs in the library was ringing; he could hear it. The fierce alarms continued to pierce the tranquil proportions of the city house. What if he answered? Lazor asked himself. Who would be at the other end of the line? Someone who had not heard the news and who would ask for Joe. Ask not for Josef but for Joe. His father's circle had been small, and the obituary would have been posted at the Serb social club a few blocks over. Maybe, if he picked up the phone, a familiar voice would start discussing Balkan politics, the early history of Pittsburgh or the difference between junk and scrap. No, not a discussion but a lecture—one last performance.

But it was a child's voice asking for another child. How patient she had been, sure that someone would eventually answer. No, he finally convinced her, no Cynthia lived at this number. Then he picked up the phone again and called his wife to say that he was staying over another day. Nothing wrong; just a few small details he wanted to clean up before he left.

He took the mug of coffee out the kitchen door and onto a wooden porch built onto the back of the house. Firewood was stacked neatly at one end. He sat down on the steps, sipped the coffee and looked over the small garden beneath the ailanthus tree. Miniature shrubs and a profusion of weeds and plants that looked like weeds grew in brick-bordered beds placed around the sides of the yard. But there were no flowers except for the tubular bluish blossoms of foxglove that stood on spindly stems against the back fence. Lazor enjoyed the serenity of this surprisingly quiet neighborhood. Pittsburgh's center was only a short distance away, just beyond the Allegheny River.

"Of course this tree limits my garden to those flowers that can grow in dense shade. Like this digitalis, called foxglove by some." His father had turned from the pork chops to point to the plants. He rearranged skewers of sausage and onions, pepper and tomato. "So most of the plants here are poisonous and prosper in this shade along with the slugs and lizards." His laughter had been full and deep. "But I like to sit in the shade of this tree, a little like Bashō. He sat under a banana tree, that's what *bashō* means, banana, but the climate in Japan kept it from bearing fruit; only leaves and shade and, of course, his wonderful haiku."

The cooling coffee seemed to call up the memory of the meal they had shared, to refresh the flavors of the meat and vegetables and the crusty bread that had lingered within him, as water will sometimes bring up the faded outline of a stain on a piece of material. The old tastes mixed with the honeyed taste of the small cake that had melted in his mouth this morning. Down the block, a dog barked a few times and a woman called for a child to come home. The siren of a fire truck or an ambulance came near and then slipped beneath the coverlet of the city's hush.

Lazor wondered if he should weed the bed of parsley and basil and rosemary that grew around the roots of the ailanthus. The job would have to be done carefully, for their fragile stems could be pulled up by the more sturdy roots of the wild growth that overwhelmed them. But the light was failing, and he would not be able to finish before it got dark. And what of the rest? He knew nothing about gardening, though he guessed he could find a book somewhere in the house that would show him which were weeds and which were flowers. But it would take at least a day, maybe more, and then what? Wouldn't it all grow back again, a continual advance of unwanted vegetation? It was pointless, he figured, and sipped the cold coffee, a dry sweetness lingering in his mouth.

A Mechanic's Life

I

"How's your martini?" she asked.

He nodded and brought the glass to his lips. The pale, nearly colorless liquid mirrored the hill across from the terrace. He drank the view. He could almost taste the spruce trees, the pond, the road down to the village, as the whole prospect passed across his palate like a savory.

His wife had shrugged and sipped some wine and leaned forward to hug herself, as if to give him more time for his reverie, but then, with a shift of feet, she returned to their conversation. "You have so much machinery already." Her voice was nearly casual. "How did you know he wanted to sell it?"

"Little Bink called me. His father had asked him to call me. To give me the first chance at it," he told her. "It's in first-class condition, you can be sure of that. After all, it was Bink Card's very own brush cutter, and he only used it just to keep his fence lines neat. Of course, he serviced it himself. I really need it to keep down the brush from around those spruce trees over there." He had gestured toward the hillside. "The angle of the hill is too steep for the tractor. Wouldn't be safe."

"How much was it?" She lit a cigarette, one of the unfiltered kind that she continued to smoke though he had stopped all tobacco use years before.

"Only five hundred dollars," he replied, thinking how easy her questions were to answer. That hillside, for the first time since they had moved to Hammertown, would really look right. He would be able to control the undergrowth. "That same piece of equipment with attachments costs three or four times that brand-new," he continued, and took a handful of peanuts. "Also, now that he's in the hospital, old Bink needs the money. There are a lot of things I'll be able to do with it. I really do need it."

His wife had turned her gaze on the hillside. Her expression was like a search, an old bemused search of familiar ground, as if she might come across something she had never seen there but, at the same time, did not expect to find. Since they moved to this old farm ten years before, she had returned to the city almost once a week. He used to think she was having an affair, even half-enjoyed the idea, for it made her more glamorous to him, more interesting; so he was disappointed when she confessed to no more transgressions than hairdresser appointments and museum visits—which actually *were* alibis, but laid down to cover long, pointless walks through the city's streets.

"Well, that's fine," she said, letting the cigarette smoke drift from her lips. "Of course, you do need it."

He remembered her saying this when he bought the cultivator, his first piece of genuine equipment. He did not count the lawnmower, though it had been his first machinery purchase, because the lawnmower was the sort of cosmetic appliance that could be found on any suburban lawn and not at all in the same category with the cultivator or the powered snow-thrower, and certainly not with the high-wheeled tractor that occupied most of the space in the small barn. But the cultivator was still his favorite; it could turn and modify the soil. The machine's saracen blades had sliced through the earth's helm to transform the old feed lot into a sultan's paradise. He had always planted gardens that were too abundant.

When he would appear at the back door with baskets of green beans and squash, eggplant and brussels sprouts or onions, his wife would say, "What am I supposed to do with all these? What am I supposed to do?" The tomatoes seemed to depress her the most. She would let them grow soft in their casual pyramids on the backroom bench until they became compressed and juiced by their own weight. At first, she had tried to can some, to freeze the other vegetables, but she couldn't keep up, and he gave up trying to find recipes that would be easier for her to use. He reduced the variety and amount of vegetables he planted in spring, though the garden's area remained the same, the blades of the powerful cultivator churning and chopping the same plot of ground he had originally fenced off.

"I haven't seen Little Bink in a long time," she said with a final drag on her cigarette. She only smoked it halfway down, a habit originally meant to appease his criticism.

"I guess he'll be taking over the machine shop now. He's done most of the heavy work for his father, the last couple of years anyway." In fact, the younger Card had not called him about the brush cutter, as he had told her, but it had been the other way around. He had called Little Bink when he heard the old man was seriously ill and had been hospitalized. Just now, he had mentioned the young man's name to confuse her opposition to the purchase.

Little Bink had been an inventive kid in high school, using his father's tools, particularly the welding rig, to fashion weird and wonderful constructions from the scrap and parts of machinery that littered the Card place like the remains of a tank battle. The boy's concoctions could easily pass for modern sculpture. His wife had taken an interest in Little Bink, tried to get special attention for him at the local school, and even spoke to a friend of hers at the Art Students League in the city. But it had come to nothing when Little Bink dropped out of school his last year to disappear into the oily darkness of his father's machine shop. The old man had lost several fingers, walked with a stoop and bore numerous scars on his body, as if the machinery had become impatient with his repairs to it, had turned and nipped him, as he worked over it. Weeks after he had left school, Little Bink showed up at a church supper with his left hand completely bandaged, almost like a credential of his special apprenticeship.

The boy even looked different, something in his eyes when they met him in the village, like a mote from suppressed laughter, as if he had played some outrageous joke upon them and they would never know its nature. About then, she began her trips into the city.

"It's so wonderfully peaceful here," he said to her, and stretched out his legs. He fished for an olive in the bottom of his cocktail glass. "You don't know what it means to me to get back here and just soak up this silence, savor this—this peace."

"Yes, it is peaceful," she said, and stood up. "Bring in the glasses, will you? I think supper's ready."

The next morning he backed the old pickup out of the barn. The vehicle was a moving testament to Bink Card's ingenuity, for he had welded its different rusts together and kept it rolling long after it should have been junked. As the man settled into the lumpy seat behind the wheel, he was overcome with an appreciation for Card's skill and craftsmanship. To give a signal to this feeling, as well as to acknowledge his wife if she happened to be at the window, he raised one hand in a cavalier salute and tapped the horn button as he passed down the driveway.

"Bink Card is the last of an American breed," he would tell weekend guests. Some excuse would be found, perhaps a broken axe handle, to take these visitors down to the country garage so they could observe this native genius close up and in action. Sometimes, on the long plane trips that were a part of his life, he would find himself talking about Bink Card to the stranger in the next seat, about this rural genius who could fix anything, put anything right, while at the same time delivering a salty commentary on the times, local personalities and women. "Bink Card said," became a familiar prologue for the pithy, sometimes funny remarks he would repeat to his wife after a visit to the machine shop, some of them, he'd claim, almost folklore.

"You know yourself," she would say, "that if you heard anyone else say the things Bink Card says you would think him a bigot, a sexist. At least, I hope so." She was still angry about

70

losing the contest for Little Bink. "He's not folksy; he's a mean-spirited dirty old man."

But even now, as he rounded the corner just before the Card place, he half-expected to see the man standing in the wide opening of the barn, wearing stained coveralls and the rectangular black metal mask tipped back on his head, and with a cigarette smoking in one hand, as if the acetylene torch he held in the other had needed help.

However, it was Little Bink who waited this time at the end of the road, which resembled the path taken by a beaten army. Parts of tractors and old trucks poked awkwardly above the weeds like counters flung there by the same hand that might have carelessly knocked over the wooden silo. Bink Card had stopped farming when the boy was quite small.

Little Bink was spraying paint on a farm wagon that must have been his father's last enterprise. It had been put together from the chassis of a three-ton truck and the tongue and front axle of a manure spreader, and the bed was made of two-inch planks of oak bolted directly to the frame. The metal part of the rig was painted a bright green, the wheel hubs a strong yellow, and the colors set up a vibration that hurt the eyes. The boy continued to operate the spray gun with an unhurried motion of his arm, back and forth, back and forth to put an even coating of paint over the wood and metal. The glistening pigment accumulated on rusted bolt heads, joints and the hardened seams of old manure, so that the utilitarian assembly resembled a bizarre confection.

Little Bink had not turned to greet him, nor did he pause when the truck stopped, nor did he acknowledge the older man as he got out of the ancient pickup. There seemed to be some point on the wagon frame where the different films of paint would overlap and join, and everything, everyone would have to wait until that point had been methodically reached. The man leaned against a fender of his truck to await his turn, even enjoying the idea that he had a turn in the younger man's schedule. He studied the manufacture of the wagon and could see that the fresh enamel had covered faults and corrosion that should have been restored before being painted over. He wondered if Bink Card had had only enough time to teach his son just a few of his skills: those with the paint sprayer and the acetylene torch.

Abruptly, Little Bink stopped the spray gun and walked to the barn, holding the coils of hose to one side. The compressor was shut off, and it became very quiet. A herd of black-and-white cows moved slowly across a distant field, like pieces of torn paper adrift on a dark pond. The young man reappeared in the wide doorway. He stood there, blinking like his father, as if he had just come up for air, or for light, and he even held a cigarette the same way, fingers together and hands chest-high in the elegant pose of a woodchuck by its hole.

"Nice-looking wagon," the man said. Little Bink sucked on his cigarette and smiled as if there had been no point telling him this. "How's your dad?"

"Coming along," he answered. His voice was higher than his father's, nor did he resemble him much. His hair and complexion were very light, so that his face looked bald, without eyebrow or hairline. "His kidneys aren't so good." It sounded as if he talked of a worn part, something that could be replaced at the John Deere over in Green River.

"Well, if there's anything we can do . . ." Little Bink had smiled again and the man stopped, made to feel awkward by that sidewise expression apparently reserved for them whenever they met. "So here she is!" The man turned and quickly crossed the yard to the brush cutter. "Here she is," he repeated and tentatively touched one of the hand grips.

The brush cutter looked like something Bink Card might have thrown together on a Sunday afternoon, using a week of spare parts, just to keep busy. But this was how the machine was supposed to look. This primitive assembly was how it looked in every catalog, in every showroom, and that was the beauty of it, the man reminded himself, because the original design had been so perfect that no changes had ever been made. No frivolous fenders were mounted over the two substantial wheels, no tinny cowling around its powerful engine; nothing had been put on the machine that was not directly geared to its function of heavy-duty work. The design of its mechanics was frankly exposed and the whole construction was the embodiment of raw power. He grasped the two shafts by which it was steered. It was so perfectly balanced on its two wheels that he could raise its seven hundred pounds with only the slightest pressure and see-saw the whole rig on the axle's fulcrum so the teeth of the horizontal cutting bar lifted like the jaws of a hammerhead shark against the soft, gray belly of morning.

"Boy, she's a real man-killer, isn't she?" the man said exultantly. He had heard others so describe the machine.

"She'll get the work done, no question," Little Bink said. "But you got to let the machine do it. Don't try to push it or wrestle with her. That paragon gear onto it drives her at its own speed; no more, no less. You can't rush her or turn her by force. She's in A-one shape too. Pap used it only to keep down the fence lines."

"Yes, you told me that," the man replied. "But I guess she'll cut through almost anything."

"Well, I've seen her go through a stand of inch-and-a-half maples like they was straws."

"Inch-and-a-half, think of that," the almost new owner said. He knelt and expertly pulled out the dipstick to check the oil level. He slipped it back.

"Now you take sumac," the boy continued. "Why, hell, she'll take on three inches without a whimper."

"Sumac, three inches," the man repeated. He inspected the different cables that went from battery to ground and to another part; looked like the starter. "And the beauty of it," he said, "is that it's all right out here in the open; easy to get at, easy to fix—if there's a need to fix it. Well, here." He stood up and took a folded check from his pocket and handed it to Little Bink. The amount was for a hundred dollars more than he had told his wife.

The boy carefully inspected the check, as if it might be the first sort of paper he had ever seen. "Is it all right?" the man asked, after a bit. Little Bink nodded and gave that sidewise smile, then tucked the check into the top pocket of his coveralls. They pulled a couple of heavy boards out of the weeds and placed them against the edge of the pickup's bed. Little Bink stretched out a toe, in the graceful attitude of a dancer, the man

73

thought, and touched the starter button fixed near the drive chain. The engine coughed and started instantly.

The boy adjusted the throttle on one of the steering shafts and let the machine idle while he returned to the barn to put away different tools. He replaced them on their proper racks on the wall inside. The noise of the engine, only partially muffled, carved out a wonderful space around the new owner that put him in a joyous isolation from all men on this day. He could not yet believe that he owned this machine. He tried to imagine the glistening parts working smoothly within the roar; tried to picture them, tried—within the limits of his expertise—to name them.

The two men made no effort to talk above the engine's noise, and Little Bink signaled and then demonstrated that the new owner should run the cutter up the planks and onto the truck bed. The man tried to align the wheels with the planks, leaning against the steering shafts, and received his first lesson in the machine's imponderable inertia. It was as if he had tried to adjust the Sphinx.

Impatiently, Little Bink reached across him and pulled a gear lever and the cutter responded immediately, by going into reverse to back the older man up and into the barn and almost over a large anvil; all the while he desperately waggled different levers right and left, forward and back, at last finding neutral. The cutter stopped. Now, carefully, he put the machine into forward and it began to roll. He steered it with only a slight pressure on the hand grips. The wheels bumped over the ends of the planks and, with no hesitation, the whole mass pulled itself up the ramped boards and onto the truck. He found neutral again, rather deftly he thought, and Little Bink laid a screwdriver across the spark plug and cylinder head to short the ignition. With several mournful gasps, as if it had been only warming up to its full power and was sorry to quit, the engine quit.

As he drove home, he looked at the brush cutter through the rearview mirror. There had been an imperial quality about its power; slow but relentless. His ambition for it had already multiplied itself, for to merely trim brush from around young conifers would be a puny utilization of its power. He could foresee empires of clover where barbaric growth now rioted.

He was sorry his wife was not home—her car was gone—but he backed the truck into a bank in order to take off the implement, since Little Bink had been reluctant to loan him the two heavy planks. He had hoped she would be there to hear the smooth power of its engine, which started with just a touch on the starter button. With the malicious raw teeth thrust out in front, the brush cutter slowly wheeled toward the barn as he walked behind it, his hands resting on the grips to steer it, like an invalid recovering from paralysis. At the barn, he maneuvered and parked it beside the tractor and between the cultivator and the lawnmower, just behind the roller and the snow-blower. The bare, utilitarian lines of its manufacture somehow shamed their frivolous designs, as if a simple, honest workingman had been set down in a drawing room of dilettantes. He took a screwdriver and shut down the engine as he had seen Little Bink do, sorry for its silence for he was eager to try it out, but he had to prepare for a business trip in the morning.

II

By the time he returned from his trip, Bink Card had died and been buried. His wife gave him details as they had drinks on the terrace his first night home; it had been a small funeral and Little Bink was to continue the machine shop.

"I'm glad I went to see him," he said. "The veterans' hospital is near the airport, so I went by for a few minutes before my plane left."

"That was good of you," she said, and lit a cigarette. She seemed more nervous than usual, and even drank a martini with him.

"They had him hooked up to a dialysis machine, but I guess there had been too much damage. He didn't say much."

In fact, Bink Card had not talked to him at all, had even turned his head away and left him with the companionship of the machine at bedside. It hardly made any noise, only a low hum, and that surprised him, as if the mechanic should be associated only with noisy machinery. Card's skin had become the color of old-fashioned laundry soap, and the man wondered if all the fumes inhaled in the machine shop, all the cigarette smoke, had been brought to the surface, perhaps sucked up and pumped to the surface by the tubes that connected Card to this humming box. Maybe that had explained his silence too; maybe the machine had also filtered Bink Card's talk, those folksy monologues rinsed of their meanness and nastiness, so there had been nothing left for him to say.

After about ten minutes, a nurse had come into the room, and he stood up. She regarded them curiously to establish their relationship, and he had almost started to explain it, he told his wife, but then only nodded and started to go. But he had felt he had to say something, a farewell of some kind, so he had leaned over the dying man and said, "Bink, I promise to take good care of your brush cutter." He didn't tell his wife this part, nor that Card's right hand had lifted from the counterpane and the three fingers left on it had turned in the air as one. It was an ambiguous gesture.

"Listen," his wife was saying. "I'm going to the city tomorrow."

"Tomorrow?" he replied. "But I just got home."

"That's right," she answered, as if that explained something.

She had let her legs sprawl and then closed them together to trap a fold of skirt around her hands. "Though I don't feel I belong there any more. All the taxis seem to be full, and I can't find the corner where the empty ones pass. But there's a Monet show at the Met and lots of other things."

He smiled and looked away from her, toward the hillside. The weather had been dry and the underbrush around the conifers would cut very cleanly, and he had hoped she would be there to witness his first day with the cutter—to hear it. He had an agenda. In the morning he'd trim around the evergreens, just to get the feel of the new equipment. Then, in the afternoon, he would turn the cutter loose in a lower lot where brambles and sumac had infiltrated. So, he would be alone, but as he ate breakfast the next morning, the idea of doing it alone appealed to him; there was a purity about it.

When he pulled open the barn door, he found the brush cutter just where he had left it, though it seemed ready to chase the other equipment and snap at the lawnmower's plump tires. He reviewed the checklist for starting the engine—he had owned an official manual for the machine for some time—and then pressed his toe against the starter button. The engine turned over, coughed once and almost caught. He toed the button again. The engine almost started. He readjusted the throttle, checked the choke's position and pressed the button. Blue smoke puffed from the exhaust. Nothing. He held his foot against the starter button, a procedure the manual strictly forbade, and the crankshaft turned and turned and turned but there was no ignition. Yes, there was gas; he unscrewed the cap and checked the tank.

Probably an ignition problem, he thought; probably, some part of the ignition like the coil or the condenser was a little off. Maybe it was the sparkplug. With a wrench, he quickly removed the plug and was gladdened to see the gap was fouled by a gooey deposit of dark oil. He wiped it off and, whistling while he worked, cleaned the metal with a piece of emery paper until it gleamed like new. Just to be thorough, he checked and adjusted the plug's gap—he had all the gauges for this handy—replaced it and hooked back the wire. He touched the starter button. It almost kicked over but he could tell the battery was now losing its charge.

It would probably be a good idea to let the battery rest a little while he checked out the coil and the condenser. Moreover, the engine might have flooded. Once more, the functional simplicity of the machine impressed him as he began to take it apart. Even if he had not owned a manual, even if he had not almost memorized that manual, he could have worked on the machine, attacked the problem, exactly as he was doing now. He removed each part and laid it on the floor of the barn in a workmanlike manner. Every nut and bolt was easily accessible. The coil and condenser were neatly tucked beneath the metal platform that held the battery. Four bolts held this shelf to the chassis. The pure logic, the simple beauty of the arrangement thrilled him. He tried to visualize the genius who had designed the cutter; his name must be in some book somewhere, for this invention could not have been the product of an anonymous corporate effort. Individuality was written all over it. When he withdrew the four bolts, he discovered them to be much longer than he had supposed; apparently they were seated far within the engine block. One by one, he set them down on the floor with the other parts. However, the battery platform did not come off, would not even budge from its location, but remained fixed over the coil and condenser. It remained as solidly a part of the chassis, as if it were a part of it, as if it had been welded to it.

In fact, it had been welded to it.

With a rag he wiped the metal clean and saw the neat scar left by Bink Card's expert application of the acetylene torch. No doubt the threads on those long bolts had become worn and some extra bonding had been needed at this point. But the beauty of a machine like this, he reminded himself, was that there was more than one way to get at a problem. He took the manual to the open doorway where the light was better and studied it. His stomach rebuked him for the quick breakfast, and he noted the sun was higher than he expected. Then he found the right page. The diagram illustrated another way of reaching the coil and condenser; by coming from behind and through the space where the starter motor and timing gear were located. These parts would be a cinch to remove.

In fact, he didn't even have to change socket wrenches because all the fittings had been standardized. As he twirled off these bolts, he reflected on the modification Bink Card had made on the machine, appreciating how the man's practical, homegrown wisdom had joined up with the original conception— almost a synthesis. The driving chain and the rotor slipped off. It was all going much faster than he thought it would.

Three bolts had held the starter motor, and a couple of screws fastened a small black box that contained something that looked like fuses. The barn floor was beginning to resemble one of those illustrations in the manual, all the pieces neatly laid out. Now, he could slip his hand through this space and, with a small screwdriver, reach the condenser fitting. But a piece of steel, in the shape of a keystone, had been welded partway over the opening so he could not insert the screwdriver in such a way as to get a good purchase on the screw head. He could plainly see the screw head. It gleamed at the other end of the narrow channel like a pearl in an inner sanctum. He deduced that Bink, or maybe it had been Little Bink, had welded this brace at the axle for extra strength.

On his knees, he was clearly at a point of decision. He could reassemble the cutter and, by then, the battery would have probably recharged itself and the carburetor cleared. One touch of the button, and it might start. But what if it didn't start? He would have to tear it down all over again to this point he had just reached, parts spread out around him, and that would be a waste of time. The morning was already gone. He heard a car motor down at the house. He got up and went to the corner of the barn, though he would have been surprised if it had been his wife. It was only the delivery van from the dry cleaner's, and the driver waved to him, and he waved back. He watched the truck turn and pass down the driveway and out of sight. A bird sang behind him. It sounded like a robin, or it could have been a sparrow.

The left side of the brush cutter was even simpler than the right; that is, there were fewer parts to remove. Only three cotter pins held the clutch assembly and its control rod together. He left the carburetor intact, having read enough in different manuals to know that carburetors were a specialty for only experts to fool around with. Instead, he chose to remove the left wheel. With the wheel off, he would have a clear shot at the coil and condenser from the other side.

As he levered the heavy machine onto a cement block, he was again impressed by its substance and mass, and by the great power that lay within it, a power he knew to be there but momentarily at rest. If he could only reach it, get at it, he knew he could fix it.

The heavy-duty tire spun free of the ground, turning easily, well-lubricated and perfectly balanced. The wheel's ball bearings kissed like tumblers of a combination lock falling into place. The plastic cap pulled off easily and then the large pin it protected from dirt. Several washers slipped into his hand and he could see the wedge-shaped key snugged in the channel of wheel and axle. He put both hands on the wheel, braced his feet against the chassis and pulled. Nothing. It didn't move. After several more tugs on it, his back muscles straining and cramped, he took to whacking it from behind with a crowbar. Nothing could move it. It was fixed on the axle, maybe permanently attached. Yet, when he spun it, the wheel turned as if set into perpetual motion. A curious phenomenon, he thought, that anything could move so effortlessly in one direction yet not budge a fraction of an inch in another.

He stood up to stretch and walked into the small yard before the barn, pulling and massaging his back muscles. Far above, a tiny jet plane was silently scoring the afternoon sky, as if to divide the day into halves that would break apart along the white scratch left behind. The breeze had a whiff of pine on it, which made him look toward the hillside. Actually, he determined there wasn't all that much brush to worry about yet.

As he put the cutter back together, he started to whistle again. Even though he had not been able to repair it, even though he had not been able to get inside the steel case and reach the problem, he was pleased that he was able to return every nut and bolt to its proper place. Everything went back just right. He now worked with the easy familiarity of a professional, someone who really knew the equipment, and every part disappeared from the floor and found its correct location on the machine as in one of those trick photography sequences. Finally, the brush cutter was put together and looked as if nothing had ever happened to it. No one would know, he thought, that he had practically torn it apart, almost reinvented it. Well, Little Bink could probably tell, and he would have to call the boy and ask him to come and see what was wrong with it. Just before he left the barn, he walked back and touched the starter button. The engine did not start, but it still coughed and turned over, same as before, so he had not made it worse, and there was some kind of victory in that.

His wife returned from the city very late, and he did not see her until morning. He found her in the backroom preparing to load the washing machine. She did not answer his good morning, but held up the pants he had worn yesterday, then dropped them into the tub. "Those were your good jeans," she said sorrowfully, but she was not angry. "You should wear old clothes when you work on your machines."

"Well, it was the brush cutter," he replied. "I hadn't intended to work on it, but it wouldn't start, and I tried to fix it and one bolt led to another and . . ." She nodded and smiled and looked away from him, down into the washing machine, which slowly filled with water. He was eased by her casual manner. "It's probably just a little thing wrong with it. It ran great before. You should have heard the way it ran before. But it's something I can't fix, so I called Little Bink to come up and take a look at it."

"That's good." She nodded again.

Just as she spoke, a flatbed truck drove up the driveway and continued on to the barn. There was a large generator mounted on the back, and several cylinders of compressed gas. It was a familiar rig on local roads, as Bink Card had used it on his rounds to repair broken-down farm equipment. Little Bink was at the wheel.

"How was the city?" he asked her. "Did you meet some friends for lunch? I couldn't wait up."

"The city is still there." She shrugged. "I had to do a lot of little things that took a lot of time." She closed the top of the washer and reached into her skirt pocket for a package of cigarettes. She faced him.

"What?" he asked.

"What?" She lit a cigarette.

"You were about to say something, I thought."

She waved smoke away from him and toward the ceiling. "You can help me with the house. I'm way behind and have to get caught up."

"Sure," he replied, though he wanted to be up at the barn. He wanted to be there when Little Bink got the cutter going. He could picture the young man smiling to himself as he studied the

81

machine, as he reviewed a list of possible problems and then coupled them with their solutions. But it would be wiser to stay with his wife and help her. She usually hated housework and let the different chores pile up until they pressed a bitterness from her general good nature. But this morning she turned to the different tasks with a joyous bustle. They dusted and vacuumed, washed the woodwork, did mirrors and the windows inside, beat the rugs, polished the bathrooms, waxed floors; husband and wife paired up. Sometimes, as they worked, they would hear the clang of metal on metal, the blows of a hammer and the clatter of tools being dropped on cement. The truck's generator had been started up, and its whine cut through the morning calm.

"Sounds like he's got the torch going," he said to his wife. "I guess it's not a simple problem after all."

She nodded and smiled and handed him a dustbin; she had the broom. They had come, at last, to the guest room. He wondered if weekend guests were arriving; perhaps someone she had run into in the city, had invited up, and she was waiting to tell him when they took a coffee break. They had even changed the linen on the bed in the guest room, though no one had used it in a while, and she had displayed the same sedulous attention to ordinary details, such as the precise folding of the top sheet at the corners, which always seemed to key her preparations for a guest's arrival.

She had just aligned several journals on the bedside table. "There," she said. "That's done." The bed was between them. It was a double bed but looked larger because of the design of its counterpane. She looked around; her cigarettes were in the kitchen.

"I'll buy the coffee," he said.

"Good." As they walked back through the neat and expectant rooms, he noted the sounds of the barn were fewer but more emphatic, more serious sounding. Hammer blows fell exactly and their number was obviously considered, their delivery timed. Clearly, Little Bink had got to the source of the problem. He heated up the coffee made earlier and brought cups to the kitchen table. She had already sat down, already held a smoking cigarette.

They sipped the coffee, and he was about to speak, and then saw she was also going to say something, and then a geyser of noise erupted in the barn, a roar that permeated the air, a sound that caught all the particles of light in its billowing racket.

"Listen." She had leaned across the table, almost shouted.

"Yes, I know—listen," he cried. He was laughing and clapped his hands together. "Listen to that. He's got it started." He reached over and squeezed her hand, grateful for her presence. She brushed at some crumbs, swept them off and onto the floor.

"No, you listen to me." She shook her head. "Listen to me." She spoke above the roar of the engine. "I've taken an apartment in the city. I guess I'm leaving you."

He had heard what she said, heard the way she said it, the slight hesitation in her voice, which had been poised to turn around if he had hailed her and to turn in almost any direction he might have cared to direct her. But he was listening to the powerful noise of the engine and all its nameless parts, working smoothly to rhyme his heavy pulse.

Grace Peck's Dog

How exactly it happened, no one can remember: Had Grace Peck taken off before her dog or had they both disappeared together? Who had opened the door of the kennel? People had as many ideas as the county has kinds of corn. Some thought it might have been Clay himself, but you could make up a long list of suspects from the people who had had dogs destroyed, or their lives disturbed by Grace's phone calls. Perhaps some kind of a vigilante posse had been put together and they had crept up to the Peck place at night and released the animal.

Neighbors, farm families that lived within a mile or two of each other, used to meet at the Agway or at Bomberg's in Green River, and they would say to each other by way of a greeting, "Well, we had a call from Grace last night." That's all it would take. Quickly a committee would form in the aisle between the work shirts. Everyone had a story, everyone who owned a male dog that is, and it was always the same story but always of interest, as if the sourness in Grace Peck put up their wonder and kept it fresh.

Usually, it went this way. About suppertime, the phone would ring. Grace Peck would begin speaking immediately. No

84

need for introductions, once you heard her voice you'd know it; a flat, plain bran of sound ground from the corner of her mouth. "You better come and get your dog. He's up here making a disturbance and doing his business in our yard." Some nights she'd make three or four calls. Sometimes, there'd be no calls but dogs would disappear, never return home, and the owners would know why.

Sometimes, a farmer's wife would admit she had made the mistake of trying to talk to Grace Peck. Why didn't she have the dog spayed? Why didn't she breed her? What good was the animal just locked up in her cage, on cinderblocks, in their backyard? Was it fair? Humane? The line would go silent, but not because the questions had stumped her. It was more the silence of a peculiar amusement, and the long pause would stretch across the telephone line, until the questions had lost their momentum and fell back on those who had asked them.

There were stories, too, of how owners would drive up to Peck's and how two or three male dogs would always be hanging around, their own mutt among them, as if standing guard by this cage set on cinderblocks in the center of the yard, open to the various air currents. They were like courtiers, someone said, waiting recognition or hoping for a favor from the tongue-whipped, stiff-legged Doberman locked inside. She was a lithe, handsome animal, built for speed and sport.

Grace was never around at those times, but more than one dog owner, driving home with his love-smitten hound in the backseat, would tell later of movement seen at the kitchen window; so she might have been watching the whole time as he had been trying to coax and finally drag his animal into the car. More than watching, some felt she had been directing the whole business.

Then Clay Peck was alone. People became aware he was by himself about the same time the phone calls had stopped. And then, the Doberman was loose. She was reported everywhere at once, an ebony dart that streaked across the countryside. She was seen in Irondale, on remote hilltop pastures, at the crossroads in Hammertown, and even on the outskirts of Green River. A movement would catch the eye, a speck flicked across a distant hillside, and it would be the sleek Doberman, racing like a greyhound and now accompanied by several male dogs who galloped after like bodyguards escorting a queen hell-bent on some state emergency. She was making the rounds.

It was as if the Doberman had kept track, made a mental list of all those sad animals who had made their pilgrimage to her cage to keep a vigil at her captivity, and now that she was free, she was making visitations, returning thanks, you might say, and these expressions of gratitude were as unexpected as they were joyously employed. Some wondered if the dogs had talked it over, among themselves of course, had planned the whole thing as they gathered around her cage in Clay Peck's yard. Whatever; once liberated, it seemed her first and only desire was to join a canine Witches' Sabbath.

The lower part of the county became one large rutting ground. Now phones rang again but for a different reason. "She's here!" the hysterical cry would screech across the wire. "She's here!" Panic, pity, wonder and scorn made for wordless response. The phone would ring in someone's kitchen, and there'd be no time for salutations. "She's headed your way!" the alarm came through. "Look out for your dog." The owner wouldn't even hang up the phone, just let it bang against the wall on its cord, to rush outside, but always too late. The last giddy convulsions had already begun behind the tool shed. How did she get there so fast? How did she get it done so quickly? *The Green River Sentinel* published a whole page of angry letters to the editor, two weeks in a row. The minister at the Irondale Presbyterian Church put out a sermon on it. The sheriff was pressured to hire extra deputies, local dog wardens had already used up their budgets, and mothers waited with their children until school buses arrived in the mornings, met the return trips in the afternoons.

One morning, George Winkler heard a ruckus behind his novelty store in Irondale. Two large mongrels were going at each other's throats while, to one side and in the shadow of a sycamore, a black Labrador solemnly humped Grace Peck's dog. Winkler reported the male's expression to become more and more sad and then, like a signal of some sort, the tip of its pink tongue popped out to one side of the black muzzle. But that seemed to be the only fight to take place; it was in the first days of her freedom and the word seemed to be passed around among the dogs that there'd be no need for such combat, that there was plenty to go around and she was bringing it around as quickly as her four slim legs could bring it around.

An afternoon later, Red Schuyler nearly wrecked his car on his mail route to avoid the Doberman as she trotted down a back road carrying what looked like Miller's German shepherd along with her. It was a ludicrous sight, as Red described it, with the male dog hung up and jigging along as fast as he could on his two hind legs, but the Doberman didn't seem to be concerned about him or his pleasure; a preoccupied look on her face, he said, as she pursued a commitment elsewhere. Most of the men laughed, but some of the farm women said something should be done. Others said they weren't sure.

In Boston Corners, the Taylors' Irish setter was found strangled on the very chain that had been supposed to preserve his chastity, but which apparently had tightened around his windpipe at the critical moment so he was found dead one morning in the barnyard, tongue hanging out the side of his mouth and, some said, an all-knowing look in his eyes. Something had to be done, people said. TV people from New York were beginning to show up with their cameras.

Other dogs just plain disappeared. Nothing could keep them home, not even plates of the most extraordinary food. Pork guts and beef testes were left to rot untouched in the empty sunlight. The tears of children, the calls of old masters—even letting the dogs sleep indoors at night—nothing worked. Tie ropes were broken and collars slipped, fences tumbled over and kennels mysteriously undone, some even chewed right through. The county was in turmoil, put into a heat like a pressure cooker. Families began to come apart. Attendance at PTA and Grange meetings fell off. Veterinarians stopped answering their phones. Children began to look at their parents in peculiar ways. The annual carnival run by the Green River VFW was so poorly attended that the post had to take out a second mortgage on the clubhouse just to pay for the party they had hoped would satisfy the first mortgage. A beer-and-bitch posse sponsored by the Irondale volunteer fire company was a lot more successful financially, except that one of Ike Vosberg's barns burned to the ground while the firemen were out chasing Grace Peck's dog. The slim, swift animal slipped through all the roundups and sweeps, all the stratagems and nets, like a sliver of tortoise shell through the coarse weave of an Afghan throw.

Somehow no one blamed Clay Peck. It wasn't his dog, after all, but hers. He continued his work and routine as if nothing unusual were happening. He'd be seen driving through all this confusion and uproar, his carpentry tools neatly put into their steel cases in the back of his truck, on his way to some job where he would carefully measure everything several times before he cut the wood to make a perfect fit.

Then the dog was gone. As when she got loose, no one could place the exact day of her departure, or even the nature of that departure; nothing dramatic, no bellow or yammer trailing off into the distance—nothing like that. She was just gone. People could remember what they might have been doing when they realized she was gone; hanging up wash in the yard, opening the new Sears catalog or stepping out of the milk parlor to take a breath—something like that—but to put a time or date to it couldn't be done.

In retrospect, the signs of her abandonment are clear enough. Dogs, sitting stiff-spined at the end of their tie ropes, suddenly went limp, turned and ambled back toward their water dishes to drink them dry, then turned around once, twice and finally lay down. Some of them slept for days. Birds seemed to sing louder and air currents carried other, smaller sounds, hushed until now by the straining uncertainty that had ravished the community.

A few years later, a TV news program featured a story about the Canadian Mounted Police trying to capture a large pack of wild dogs that raced back and forth across Canada and as far north as the Arctic Circle. No one talked about this straight out, just picked up their mail without comment, but a few glances were exchanged, a head nodded here and there at the Agway in Green River. Someone got a card from Grace Peck, posted from Atlantic City, and she was doing fine. Clay still goes about his business.

Touching Down

In this dream, Taylor pulls back on the stick for that last fraction of its radius, into the pit of his stomach, and feels the controls go mushy in the stall. He hovers just above the earth, waiting to touch down, waiting for that first kiss with the ground.

Then he woke, and turned over in bed to tell his wife about the dream before it dissipated, reached for her across the empty bedclothes to find her gone and this vacancy another dream but one from which he would never wake. The thick stick of his erection pushed into the melange of sheets that held him like something caught, suspended, and he groaned and pushed against the mattress with the remembrance of her. A joy stick! The term had tripped her laughter on one of those first nights—someplace like Buffalo and one of those dumb places where they had carelessly landed to scatter their clothes around the bed, and make a scene of sweet disaster. Later, before sleep, she always hung his service jacket on a chair and the silver wings on the breast of his tunic would catch the light of the neon sign outside the window. HO–TEL. HO–TEL. Going from blue to red to blue and back again.

But it's a French name. I bet it is, she had said with a roguish wry of neck. No, I mean it comes from the name of the Frenchman who invented the control stick. From the other war. The first war when planes were no more than big kites with motors and flying them had been a kind of mortal ecstasy; when all the flimsy parts had been named innocently, no puns intended, nor had the mode for destruction been so defined. That's why he never flew again, save in his dreams.

Because she sometimes had asked him why he never flew again. This morning, he almost answered her, with his face into the pillow, but her spirit had already departed. Outside the window, the Eastern sky was growing light, toward the front; he laughed at himself and swung out of bed. If it had been fun, he might have kept it up, but he wasn't the only one. Sometimes he heard from others who had been in the 55th, and few of them had got into a cockpit again after that last touchdown in Essex. Just think of it, he might have said to her, he hadn't been old enough to vote but he had been given this fabulous machine to operate, a machine that weighed over three tons and was powered by a 1500-horsepower engine and which mounted six guns triangulated to make a terrible new history at four hundred yards. It had been so methodical, so joyless—not even the "sport" the older English pilots had talked about in the early days of the war, the Battle of Britain. It had become serious business.

"I've been thinking about flying again," he told his daughter, and the abrupt statement challenged whatever her warrant had been to phone him. In her silence, he could hear the sounds of a brief being assembled; once again he had shrugged off her concern for him, had not let her finish, complete her idea; he had usurped her initiative.

"Don't do that," she said finally. Her voice was oddly thoughtful. "It's too dangerous."

"Naw, not dangerous."

"But what's the point?"

"Does it need a point?"

"Well, I mean, the firm has its own jet. You can go wherever you want. What can you do in those little planes? Take off and land someplace, have a Coke, then take off and come back; have some coffee."

"Yeah, something like that." He could visualize her eyebrows rise toward her hairline. He had freely admitted his intention had no purpose. And just to confess more evidence of his folly, he added, "It would be fun."

"Look." Her voice took on that commanding tone he remembered her using with playmates as a little girl. "Look, this is the sort of stuff that really worries me. You are not dealing with the realities. I called to see if you had cleaned out the closets yet. You must do that, Daddy. I bet Mom's clothes are still hanging there. Everything. I've asked you to send them to me. I can wear them—some of them."

That had been a lie, and he was grateful to her for it on this morning of the dream. Leaving the bed, he walked into the large dressing room and through the aromatic grove of dresses and gowns, slips and all the rest. He tried not to look at them, for he would helplessly pair up a garment with some mundane turn of the past, round a corner of his memory to find her standing at the front door, going through the mail.

"I'm not afraid to die," his mother had said last week. Her voice had been calm, serene. Low cumulus clouds hung like great mirrors over the rolling Pennsylvania countryside, and her eyes were caught up, lifted up by the alternating currents of their brilliance. "It will be like a wonderful, long sleep," she added after a moment. "But I think back on my life and wonder what I did to deserve this kind of finish."

Outside her room, a nurse's aide pushed a jiggling cart of food trays down the corridor. His mother had pulled at the wheels of her chair to bring herself closer to the large pane of glass. "There are my little birds again." Her voice was full of wonder.

"If I could figure a way of mounting it, I'd get you a feeder," he had told her. Her room was on the third floor of the clinic and the large window was sealed Thermopane.

"It doesn't matter," she said. "Somebody on the roof above

drops bread crumbs down and they fall onto that casement out there. See?'' She raised one crippled hand to point to a sparrow that had just darted into the area to light on part of the framework. Then the bird flew away. ''Not the kind of ending for both of us, I would have thought we'd have,'' she said, and looked down with a curious smile.

''We have to make the best of it,'' he replied. Where was the glossary for such moments, the handy list of snappy sayings? Surely, it was one of the cruelties of this life, he thought on the drive back to Pittsburgh, to be required to attend these occasions without being given the words for them. Nor did any amount of practice seem to help.

It was during this drive back to the city that he had acquired the material for his dream. About ten miles south of the small town where his mother was hospitalized, a small airstrip had been laid out parallel to a ridge of hills. The place was the site of a glider club, and road signs promoted rides. He had passed the spot many times, in all the different seasons and weathers through which he had driven to visit his mother, but this particular Sunday was so gloriously warm and sunny, such beautiful flying weather, that he had turned off the highway and onto a dirt road that jostled his car past a row of thin-winged gliders and several corrugated-steel hangars.

Taylor was not unmindful of the echoes the scene sounded in his memory, and the soaring vision of two gliders riding the thermals that rolled up the Allegheny foothills inclined him to dawdle, to loaf. His mother had slipped into a half-sleep, giving him leave to go earlier than usual, but he had no reason to hurry back to Pittsburgh.

As he braked the car, turned off the ignition, a Piper Cub gunned its engine and the plane's tail lifted with the pull of the towline connected to the slim glider behind it. Within seconds, both broke ground and lifted with a lazy innocence to pass through a balmy sound barrier so, all at once, the field was restored to the hush of the meadow it had once been. The warm breeze enveloped him. Above, the huge omnibuses of cumulus clouds appeared about to collide, but the spaces between them never varied—just right for a little hide-and-seek, he thought with an old giddiness that surprised him. Farther above, at about forty thousand feet, was a layer of cirrostratus, which would bring rain in a couple of days. But, here on the ground, all was sunny and warm, and he walked toward a nailed-together operations shack where a couple of soft-drink machines on the porch stood out like something from an Andy Warhol painting.

Gliders parked nearby presented the same fresh, efficient lines, and it was easy to see the pride their owners took in their clean beauty as they pulled them about, readied them for flight with a satisfaction that no amount of casual handling could disguise. "Want to take a ride, sir?"

The young man looked at Taylor with an eager friendliness, the look of a proselyte. Behind him, a young woman sprawled on the blue-green grass of May, taking the sun. She wore denim shorts and a sweatshirt, same as the young man. "No thanks. Just thought I'd have a Coke and watch for a bit," Taylor told him.

"You're more than welcome," the other said, and walked on to help a pilot haul his craft into line to wait for a tow aloft. The woman on the ground raised one hand and placed it across her face as if the sun had become too strong for her, or maybe, Taylor thought, in an instinctive purdah from his stranger's gaze. A low-winged plane, a kind he'd seen used for dusting crops, whispered down an invisible channel in the sparkling air, ready to take up the dray-horse chore it shared with the Piper Cub that had just taken off. At about two thousand feet now, this other plane had banked to the left and released its fragile ward to the whims of the rising currents. The air brushed Taylor's face with the sweetness of timothy.

At the far end of the field, another glider banked sharply, its long nail of a wing pointing straight down as if to punch a hole in the corn lot below, and then it leveled out and started the final glide path. Almost imperceptibly, the paper-thin silhouette began to settle lower and lower, and at this moment, his dream must have been framed, and within it the old urgency, how the suspense would catch the breath about now—switches off, wheels and flaps down; the procedures clicked through and the control column pulled back to his harness buckle. Nothing to do but wait, to hover and hope for the best, that the ground would be in the right place. "You've done well," his mother had said as he left, taking his hand in both of the horned crooks her hands had become. "You've done well," she repeated as if to address the ambiguity he always heard in this commendation. Without a sound, the glider had touched down on the grass and rolled to a stop.

"You mean you want to fly to the Coast?" His younger colleague colors and glances down at the documents between them on the conference table. Paul White has been counting on this trip, Taylor knew, to score points with the banks in California as well as to extend his affair with the wife of the firm's budget director, enjoy her on the other side of the continent, as it were. She was the most recent of the man's conquests.

"No, no, I mean actually fly. I've been thinking of taking it up again." He watches the younger man's face take on some calculation. This information was being filed away, perhaps to be used later on. White was brilliant, but he was of that new class of MBA graduates who seemed to have studied politics more than ethics, with a course in killer rhetoric thrown in that made for long, sanctimonious preambles at board meetings, so the draconian judgments that followed were almost to be welcomed. Sometimes White reminded Taylor of the lachrymal walrus in *Through the Looking Glass*.

"I used to do that, you know—in the war, I mean."

"Yes, I heard that," White replies, and collects his agendas and reports.

"Did you ever see that Disney cartoon about the Three Little Pigs?" Taylor's lungs hurt as he holds back his laughter. White's face has become whippet sharp, attuned. He's just heard a looney tune in the old man's head— something he could casually inform another partner of, an item, say, for an ad hoc committee on early retirement. "There was a song from that cartoon we used to sing, about the Big Bad Wolf, except we changed the lyrics." With a gleeful use of his authority, and knowing the very example of it could be used to undermine that authority, he begins to sing to the other man.

"Who's afraid
Of the big Focke-Wulf?
The big Focke-Wulf?
The bad Focke-Wulf?
I am . . . I am . . . I am."

The muffled commotion on Grant Street far below mills the silence in the conference room into a weave that neither seems able to tear through. Paul White looks incredulous and expectant—not believing the luck of this leverage just given to him. Taylor looks over the man's shoulder and at the Pittsburgh skyline behind. The bulbous silhouette of a 747 has just passed behind the mirrored fantasy of the PP&G towers, coming in for a landing at the airport south of the city. They seem to be the only people in the huge building.

"Well." White finally speaks. "All I need then is the report on the Irvine merger."

"I'm having it touched up for you," Taylor tells him. "I want you to go in there Friday with the latest rundown we can put together. I'll drop it off at your house tomorrow. The Lear is all cranked up to go at four. Maybe I could give you a lift to the airport?"

"No, that's okay. Margaret is taking me out." White looks pained as he stands up. Clearly, this is not the way he would run the firm when he takes over; say, next week. He was such a correct fellow except when it came to other men's wives, and on this matter, he never spared Taylor any of the details. But dropping reports by each other's houses was not the way he would do business. "Very well, then," he says, and bows with a ludicrous exaggeration of deference to leave his superior sitting at the end of the long table.

Taylor takes a deep breath and then goes to the large window that takes up almost all of the room's outside wall. The processed air of the building's central system is lacking in sustenance; needs some grit put back into its manufactured purity, he thinks, and not for the first time. He looks out on the airless and near-noiseless panorama of the city's skyline. Sometimes, he would stand at this window and look out sideways from one corner of it as if to find another cross street had been included in the familiar display, as if the whole building might have been slightly rotated on its foundation during the night. But the glass was fixed permanently on its designated prospect, sealed tight and without even a small portion hinged to open for fresh air. He takes several breaths to make up for one.

Their CO had flown the old open-cockpit planes before the war, and he had described fondly the feel of the slipstream in his face, how a sense of the plane's performance was given by the sting and bite of the wind on his cheeks. Of course, none of that had been possible six or seven miles up, enclosed by super-tough Plexiglas and with an oxygen mask clamped on, but coming back over Wormingford, settling into the final approach over the tops of English oaks, most of them would slide back their canopies and let the ground air blast into their mouths and up into their nostrils, like a cleansing of some kind.

Not as many came back the day of the Nuremberg raid as had taken off before the sky grew light. In the ready room, someone had mentioned his grandmother heated her farmhouse with a Nuremberg stove, and another had joked about the heat turned out by the Panzer stoves made there. Truly, several hours later, the sky over Nuremberg was plumed by coils of thick black smoke, like smoke from stoves, though the process was reversed, a film going backwards, as the oily spumes descended rather than rose, seeking out the stoves that were to exhaust them. No time, no mind for such subtleties then—no mind at all, just reaction; spontaneous spasms of muscles.

When the German fighter drifted across his gunsight, a casual sideslip as if the pilot wasn't all that interested in the B-17 below, Taylor's gloved fingers hardly pressed the control head, an indifferent grip such as he might give someone like Paul White. His guns fired no more than two seconds, if two seconds could be counted, and the fighter had burst apart like a mario-nette losing its strings. As he veered off, hoping none of the debris caught his stabilizer, he could see the pilot in midair, with his knees up in a sitting position as if someone had pulled a chair out from under him. A joke, almost funny, but the man had lost his head as well.

Back safe over British soil, wheels down and the P-51 eased into that unmarked groove, Taylor had pushed back the canopy and let his head lean over the side to take great gulps of the sweet air rising from the green countryside, spiced with the fumes of high octane and overheated glycol. The queasiness of the final stall continued to turn in his stomach even after his wheels had tapped the tarmac, as he rolled toward the line-up. Only then, he felt his ass was wet and cold and he realized he had voided his bowels somewhere back there, over Germany, which was not an uncommon salute in these sorties. The field's laundry gave twenty-four-hour service. The fighter was to be his only kill, not counting a probable he shared with a wingmate, but he had done well, as his mother might say.

Most of them were waiting for him on the line; his crew, the rest of the 55th. The CO was waving a bottle of wine. Taylor had let the huge Merlin whine down, wondering how he could handle this occasion, whatever it was about, with his pants full of shit. The confirmation had been radioed back, had overtaken the Mustang and beat him back to the field. He had got Grossman, the Hans Grossman with 162 kills that went all the way back to the Spanish Civil War. As the CO poured wine over him, he had been thinking it was somehow not fair; this unearned success, this lucky hit on a pilot of such consummate skill, a man who had been at the business for almost ten years—half the lifetime of this kid who couldn't keep his pants dry, who had brought him down.

Taylor rarely thought of the event, certainly never considered it a high point in his life; nor, standing before the cityscape of Pittsburgh, does he indulge in any sentimental speculation as to what and where Hans Grossman might be today had he not drifted into the range of his six Brownings on that March morning in 1945. The man had grown careless or maybe just tired. He could see the end of the war as well as they could. But that American bomber looked a bit too wobbly to leave alone; so perhaps, just one more trophy. No, it was another life, nor had it been any fun. That was the answer to the question drawn from him by the naïveté of those powerless gliders, those near-silent flights that had caused him to dream and wonder. He presses against the window, longing for a lungful of real air. The sky above Pittsburgh is immense and empty.

But the next afternoon, a pewter lid of stratus clouds fits tightly around the horizon. He had seen the prediction of this weather a few days before at the glider field. Moist air flows through the open car window as he steers his car around the gratuitous but graceful curves of the expensive suburb where his younger colleague lives with his family. The intricate maze of winding lanes governs the speed of the car, a very slow circuit during which, no doubt, a person was meant to appreciate the expansive lawns that stretched out on either side like the playing fields of an exceptional game; the snug, modest mansions set at their far end were the goals.

He sees Paul White standing on his lawn as he pulls round the final bend of the road. The man's face is turned up against the low overcast and his eyes are even more mournful in the gloomy light, as if he was so sad to consume the best oyster. How did some of that go?

> "I weep for you," the Walrus said:
> "I deeply sympathize."
> With sobs and tears he sorted out
> Those of the largest size . . .

"Perfect timing," Taylor says to White as he swings out of the car, bending back to pick up the portfolio on the seat.

"I just sent Margaret off to get some gas," White advises him, deflecting the pleasantry. "Naturally, she forgot to get any yesterday and it was on Empty." Then, as if he remembers their relationship, that Taylor is still the chief, he adds with a laugh, "Nice weather you send me off in."

"Oh, this is nothing. The Lear will punch through this cover and you'll have sunshine the whole way." But White has ceased to attend to his response, in fact has reached for the folder, and Taylor feels that his words are extraneous. "You'll find an interesting update on Tokyo. It's a good job."

White has nodded, opened and shut the folder, a matter of form only and then he looks over Taylor's shoulder. His face becomes abruptly disinterested, focused on something happening on the street. A car has just gone by. "Look at that!" White says almost gleefully. "I can't believe it."

"Believe what?"

"Listen, do me a favor. Give me a ride, follow that car that just went by." Taylor glimpses a station wagon just rounding the curve. "It's not far," White answers his frown. "I know where she's going—it's just around the bend. Quick."

Strangely amused by his willingness to be of service, Taylor puts the car in gear and they pull away from the curb. White holds the report in his lap, folds and unfolds it with a curious anticipation. "It's our own plane, of course," Taylor reminds him after clearing his throat, "but the pilot has already filed his flight plan and ETD. The sky gets very full these days."

"This won't take long." White laughs. "She's one of the original Hoovers."

The car has come to the bottom of the hill, where an abrupt turn to the left ends in a cul-de-sac. A very large garden nursery has been established here, almost as an embarrassment of shrubbery and flowers to the prim plantings of the minor estates around it. The station wagon has already been pulled into the parking area, the only car there, Taylor notes, and its driver has walked partway into the front area, a space crowded with pots of blooming begonias and impatiens. No one seems to be around.

"Thanks," White says quickly, and jumps from the car. "I'll call you from L.A." He trots through the gate and says something to make the woman turn around.

Taylor recognizes her. He recognizes the agreeable mystification at Paul White's sudden appearance as the same expression she had shown him about a month ago, at her own table in fact—and his memory quickly sets that table with the silver candelabra, the antique French china and, among the other guests at that table, Paul and Margaret White. She had asked

Taylor about investments in Mexico; they were thinking of buying a house in Cuernavaca. It had been the polite small talk of an agreeable hostess trying to amuse the single male guest: Her husband, just retired from the Mellon Bank, probably knew everything there was to know about Mexican properties. On this gray afternoon, he calls up her broad, handsome face in the candlelight; a few interesting lines just appearing around the eyes, the mouth humorous and full.

White has engaged her in earnest conversation, his head thrust forward as it did when he made a point in a board meeting to pin an opponent down with unrelenting logic. Taylor wants to pull away but he is caught up in the scene, mindful that White has caught him up in it. He has been coopted, as his daughter might say. The woman is smiling again, a rather wary, interested expression, and he can see her head almost turn his way, toward the entrance, but something stops her, as if she doesn't want to see—as if not seeing she might not be seen.

But this is all in his imagination, he thinks, and none of it matters anyway, for she looks entrapped by whatever White is saying to her. He has just waved the portfolio in the air like a proof of something, and then places one hand at her elbow to guide her farther into the potted sylvania of the nursery. Their figures pass between aisles of bagged fruit trees and then, at the far end, disappear behind a silvery-blue screen of tall Norwegian spruce.

All of it has happened so fast, Taylor thinks he must have missed something, some prologue that might have introduced the subject, stated the theme of this little drama. He is angry to have been made a part of the man's sordid foray, an ally to this quick pickup. Even worse, White could be playing him, feeding his imagination this greasy morsel while—at this very moment—he might be having an innocuous conversation with the woman on the qualities of different conifers. A voyeur in spite of himself, Taylor does not want to believe what he has witnessed without proof. Why couldn't he accept the realities, as his daughter said yesterday: the truth of men and women, the

100

death of his wife, the unearned victory over a Hans Grossman. He required confirmations.

He had looked for proof in a similar setting. The pine trees were real and not part of a suburban nursery, but a forest that came down to the shore of the New England lake his prep school overlooked. The football field nearby had been a testing ground, where some of them had proved themselves and others had merely witnessed. That spring almost the whole graduating class had enlisted in the Army Air Corps. The heat of war had given them a fever, and they believed the soupy, sentimental ballads of that time. Most would be transferred into the infantry: a kind of first lesson, that, in institutional treachery. But he had been one of the lucky ones. He had been taught to fly above it all.

Nor had any of them believed Zack Berry. Star halfback and fast talker; how many times had Taylor led him through the line to hear later how wonderfully the guy had done it on his own? But this last boast was too much. She was a townie, a frail, pretty girl whose father owned the village drugstore where they hung out. She'd sometimes work the soda fountain, making frappés for all of them. On warm evenings, Taylor often passed by her house, and he would linger in the dark obscurity of a full-leafed maple to listen to her practice the piano. He would stand on the sidewalk and follow the shape of her blondness as she swayed over the intricacies of the same piece. Later, he would know the music had been ''Clair de Lune.''

But she had been like a catamount, to hear Berry tell it. Wild and hungry and so excited by his halfback moves that he had to dig his shoes into the earth just to keep her on the ground. Down near the lake, he told them. She had given him something to remember her by; Berry had laughed at his own wit, his banal interpretation of the song title. They couldn't believe him, his luck. Taylor had not wanted to believe him; yet, the morning of their commencement, he had wandered away from the parents' reception on the football field. The woods were deep and heavy with the moist pungency of conifers and loam. It was almost as if he had to learn to breathe again, and his heart pounded in his ears as he stepped soundlessly over the carpet of pine needles. He held a half-empty cup of hot chocolate and his other hand pushed aside the low branches of scrub birch.

Unexpectedly, like coming on a patch of smooth air in a turbulent front, he came upon a small clearing. It could have been a place where deer had slept the night before, or that natural bedding of moss and small grasses often found neatly tucked into a forest floor, and his heart had almost torn from his chest. Could this have been the place? Strangely, because of the spot's nearness to the open field he could clearly hear the exclamations of parents; somehow this risk of discovery, the risk to her reputation—that would have been like Berry—lent it credence. The pine needles, some of the surrounding area looked roughed up. He sat down on the trunk of a fallen tree and sipped the last of the chocolate. He had almost reached out as if to repair the scarred soil. He had wanted to smooth it over, then touch the ground.

Success

for Mischa

My half-brother is buried in one of those towns along the Muskingum River, south of Zanesville, Ohio, where people speak with a gentle slowness that is a reflection of that water, flowing by places with names like Malta and Blue Rock. This is a family cemetery but one I have visited only once—actually, the last time I was to see Will—when we attended our father's funeral.

They lie several graves apart. Both reached the same, venerable age, though Dad has been dead many years and I have only just come to the age of my brother when I last saw him, tending his grief over our father's simple country bier. We had different mothers, and mine was a generation younger than Dad.

"Not even a full commander," Dad had written me in a last letter, and I thought of that as I looked at Will standing over the pine board coffin, his face in his hands so the one narrow and two broad gold stripes on his uniform's cuffs gleamed dully in that rural parlor. The war in Korea had called him back in service. "But as a clerk. He gets medals for counting socks. Ha!"

My father had been feeling very full of himself that evening, very satisfied with the small honor conferred on me earlier that afternoon. He looked around the dining room where we took coffee and cognac, as if the gleam of the room's paneled walls put an extra polish on his delight. "He's not like you at all."

"We could drive down to San Diego tomorrow, if you want." Sally has just reached across to switch on the wipers, and two fans of colored lights erase the mist that has collected on the windshield. I have put our car first in line for the small ferry that goes across the inlet of Newport Bay. "It's just a big navy place, but if you want."

"There's no point in that. There was nothing unusual about my brother's service record. I'd rather you show me California."

"Where is that damn boat?" she wails. It is very dark beyond the ferry slip, and the shapes of dreadnoughts plow back and forth across the watery lane we are about to traverse. "I'm starved."

"You are beautiful in your hunger," I say, but she doesn't laugh.

"What's that from?" Her eyes spread wide, an expression that has begun to disturb me lately by its frequency.

"An old John Wayne movie." I tell her about the film. Wayne plays Genghis Khan and captures Susan Hayward, a princess of some sort. " 'You are bew-ti-ful in your wrath,' he tells her."

"They've named the airport here for John Wayne. I showed you his statue." Her fingers go to one ear, to adjust an earring, and several heavy bracelets slide down her bare arm. "But I don't remember any of the Khans. Genghis, son of Kubla, I suppose."

"Something like that." The shop windows along the street show resort merchandise. One shop specializes in swimwear, scraps of colored bikinis suspended in midair, a wild parody of leaves swirling in an autumn afternoon. This afternoon, Sally wore the same sort of costume.

"I should have taken you by the back road around the bay. We'd be there by now. My tummy is in shock."

"And a very pretty tummy it is, too."

"Thank you," Sally says with that easy acceptance that

amuses me. It is her way to receive praise for something unearned—her extraordinary good looks in this case—as if they were something she had worked hard to achieve.

I turn the wipers on again. The red lights on the dock have not changed. Two young men with knapsacks on their backs are talking to the deckhand. No lights approach from the other side.

"You don't remember the ferry that used to be here," Will said to me. We had just come from the cemetery, and he had turned the car down a small road that dead-ended on the river's bank. The area seemed parklike, and I wondered who mowed the grass. A trailer set within a neat arrangement of picket fence and trellised roses was about a hundred yards downriver. "Dad put up the money for it, and, I guess, kept it going because of a barbecue run by some colored boys across there that he liked especially."

He had started to laugh, but the sound got caught halfway up his throat. "C'mon," he said, almost gruffly, and got out of the car, turning back to toss his navy cap on the car seat. His hair was thick—even with the crewcut it looked dense—and there was only a slight tinge of gray above the ears, which in summer would probably look blond.

"The hairs on your chest are silver and gold," Sally said this afternoon. She was studying my chest, part of a close inspection she often makes—not so much to find defects as, perhaps, to satisfy a curiosity about the body that has washed up on this part of her beach.

Will and I had come down to the river's edge. Across the Muskingum, on the opposite bank, was what looked to be a small hamlet entirely composed of trailers. They resembled fresh decks of cards all lined up and ready for play, to be dealt out. One of them had a sharp spike of stainless steel, the horn of a unicorn, rising as far toward heaven as necessary, as far as the purse of the congregation could afford.

"Gosh, Sonny." He used my family nickname. "That was a long time ago."

"You went with Dad—across there?"

"When he'd let me." Will looked very smart in his uniform, and the short line of ribbons on the left breast might not have been for valor, for bravery under fire, but they stood for doing something right, a job well done, and not always a duty, I guess, that had been pleasurable.

"Why, he's a runt," Dad had said. "He always was a runt, mentally and physically and morally. His mother spoiled him." We were having drinks at my hotel in New York before going to the theater. "Can you imagine running a furniture store? In Columbus?"

"Is that it?" Sally says, and leans forward to look through the windshield. We watch lights approach the ferry slip, then veer off. A large ketch passes in review.

"You want to cross over?" Will asked. "I think the place is still there, and I could use a little grub."

"But there's no—" I had started, then turned around to follow his gesture. A man had come out of the trailer and was walking toward us quickly, tugging on a windbreaker.

"Will, you're sure a sight for sore eyes." He started to talk from yards away. A hand went out and Will met it with his own. "Awfully sorry about Mr. Meghes," he added in a hushed tone. For a moment it felt as if the open bank by the river had been enclosed by four walls and a low ceiling.

"Elwood, you may not remember my half-brother," Will started the introductions.

"Gosh, it has not been my opportunity," the man said, taking my hand with a rush. "But I certainly do know who he is. I am only sorry, sir, that my honor at your acquaintance accompanies your sadness."

"We'd like to cross over," Will said. "Can you give us a ride?"

"Sure can. Surely can," the man said, and headed for the riverbank and a small landing where a motorboat was tied up. The back of his jacket said GAYSPORT ROCKETS. "I'm a little timid about asking a navy man like yourself to get into this rowboat of mine."

"Elwood, this is the largest boat I've ever been on," Will said, and then gave that laugh that used to make Dad grind his teeth. A jackass braying, he called it. A salesman's laugh—it does everything but clap you on the back and slip you the signed contract.

"Are you going to turn mean like that?" Sally has leaned close. Her perfume whets a second appetite. "Your father was an exceptional louse."

"Are you sure this restaurant is open?" Lights come out of the dark and approach the ferry landing. The car behind us starts its engine.

"Of course it is open. This is California, not Ohio, or any of those poky places you talk about in your sleep. At last," she says as the ferry nudges into the slip. She has taken a prim, expectant position on the seat, feet together and hands clasped in her lap. Not too different, I suppose, from the attendance she put upon a lecture at UCLA only a few years back. "Here we go."

Will had stepped carefully onto the center seat of the boat. I took the bow. Our boatman stroked the outboard motor, one-two pulls on the starter cable, and the engine started strong and smooth. We drifted away from the small dock, and then the skiff pointed toward the opposite bank as the engine took over. The river's water, like thick brown cream, curled up and away from the bow.

"There's more current out here than you might think," Elwood shouted over the engine's noise, and—as if to illustrate his pronouncement—the outboard engine groaned and labored. I can remember thinking it was a line often rehearsed for this point in the river made known by the engine's effort. Meanwhile, my brother had said something that I couldn't hear. Elwood laughed and nodded and steered us toward the opposite shore.

*   *   *

107

"Your brother stayed in the navy?" Sally asks. We have just bumped up the loading ramp, and I follow the crewman's hand gestures to brake the car inches from the edge of the ferry's foredeck.

"No, he was only called back to be some admiral's aide in charge of materiel supply. Actually, he wasn't called back but invited. They needed his experience, I suppose."

"Then back to selling furniture."

"Well, that wasn't quite right, either. Will owned a chain of stores all through Ohio and West Virginia." The ferry's engine vibrates beneath us, and the boat pulls out of the slip and into the bay. It is strange to sit still in one conveyance and be moved someplace by another. Quickly, we are away from the land and into darkness; nothing but water ahead through the windshield. "Scary."

"I love it," Sally says. She sits forward, on the edge of the seat, as if to get a better view of our isolation. "It's like being lost. I love to get lost. You always want to know where you are all the time. With a map."

"Look out there," I say. The shoreline has completely disappeared. "We could be anywhere. Going anywhere."

"I know." She almost bounces on the seat and leans forward. Then, she turns to sit close, as if to rejoin me and leave her own excitement. She smooths the lapels of my jacket, even looks at the stitching. I sometimes wonder why she pays so much attention to the small articles of my life. She gives them a value—say, the leather case of my reading glasses—as if their worn and frayed edges can be read as a history without her, a time in my life before I had met her and had even managed to do without her.

"Some reason people talk more Southern on this side of the river," Will said. We watched Elwood reach mid-channel on his way back. The small engine groaned against the current. "And that's funny since it is the west bank and not the south. Dad liked it for the atmosphere. More relaxed, I guess."

What was left of the town was more than relaxed—it was defunct. A bank of yellow brick stood on one corner, boarded up.

The gas station opposite was also abandoned. Several houses looked vacant; one was a burned-out shell. Two streets up, the neat rows of trailers began, and just across from the development, a small concrete block building sat in the middle of a very large parking lot. CRAIG BROS. WORLD FAMOUS BAR–B–CUE.

"They used to do a helluva business on the weekends," Will said. "This parking lot was bumper to bumper." He pushed through the screen door to lead me into the humid and spicy interior. Several black men in stained aprons and wearing Cincinnati Reds baseball caps greeted us. A booth table was cleaned up with a flourish. "The ribs are plenty okay, too," Will advised me.

"What are you going to have to eat?" I ask Sally.

"This is definitely a night for bouillabaisse." The ferry has encountered a little chop, for we are about midway across. The boat rolls slightly and I tug the parking brake. "How do you feel?" She takes my hand. "Still adrift?"

"It's weird." Our car noses across the open water almost silently. I turn the wheel left, then right, but we continue the simple, straight course across the bay. A small deckhouse is set halfway back, and I wonder if there is anyone at the wheel, or is the whole affair strung on cables underneath the water? "Humbling. Makes for honest appraisal."

"Oh just a chip in the big ocean." She pulls my hair. "Mister Wonder plays the common man. Are we going through that routine again?"

"What are you doing?"

"I'm starting the car to drive it over. I want to see if you can float like that awful soap you carry with you." There's a sudden rapping on the rear window and I quickly turn off the engine. "This purity-and-humble trip is beginning to get suspicious."

"If these ribs aren't world famous, they ought to be." My opinion had pleased Will; even his eyes seemed to smile. Nor was I being only courteous. The sauce was rich and peppery and left a sweetness in the mouth. Thick slabs of Idaho potatoes, cut lengthwise, fried crusty on the outside, accompanied the bowl of ribs. Will had ordered chicken.

"One of the last times I was here with Dad, we sat right in this very booth. He spent the whole afternoon talking about you. Jesus, Sonny, I used to hate you. Every time there'd be some piece about you in a magazine or like that, he'd call me—call me in Columbus to make sure I picked up a copy."

Will handled the chicken bones with a particular delicacy, picking up each one to suck out the last of the sauce and marrow. The way he went through the barbecue didn't go with his uniform—or rather emphasized the borrowed nature of the formal clothing, put on temporarily and for a special occasion, but not changing the basic nature of the body underneath. I had a sudden picture of him dealing with the admiral he had served and how this same straightforward manner must have made him so very valuable. Perhaps it was the reason the navy had asked him back.

"But then I figured"—he wiped his fingers on some of the paper towel provided us for napkins—"he was only using me as a way of getting even for something he felt my mother's family did to him. And, lordy, that happened before either one of us came aboard."

Now, that was a trait that Dad would laugh at, the way Will had just used this nautical term, a figure of speech so different from his own language that its affectation was almost comical. "The whole family was like that," Dad would say. One time he wrote me a long letter about their history—or his history of their history—that would have done justice to Trollope in its examination of what he called their "riverboat how-de-dos." "Not one of them ever got above cabin class," he wrote, "but you'd think they owned the river from the way they put on."

Will had been laughing behind the paper towel he held to his mouth. His eyes were very much like mine, set close to the nose, but large, so they gave the appearance of space between them. My hair has just turned the same amount of gray as his had then. "Once I caught on to all this," he said, "I used to fool the old guy." His laughter got smothered and the paper towel went to his eyes. I picked through the bones on my plate.

110

The three men behind the counter hunched over a small radio like a trio getting ready to sing. A ball game was in progress. Above them, a large electric clock advertising Dr. Pepper went through a full minute. "Well, hell." Will finally shrugged and laughed. "What I was going to say is that I would purposely tell Dad about some little trick I had pulled off, a big sale of some kind, just to see how long it would take for him to bring up something you had just done.

"But I'd always trick myself. He had that way, you know, of getting you to outsmart yourself. He'd just sit there, not saying anything, watching and waiting for you to go on . . . to go too far. One time, I called him to tell him I had just got this contract to furnish all the Holiday Inns going up on the interstate. I mean every room in every one of those places along the highway—that's all my furnishings inside. Drapes, lamps—the whole caboodle. Do you understand? Well, I remember he listened and then he paused, like he was reaching across his bed for something that might have slipped down the counterpane, and then he told me about that prize, whatever it was was, you had just won."

A cheer went up behind the counter. Cincinnati had won. The three men broke apart to resume a meticulous cleaning and polishing of equipment, grills and large pots. One cook stirred a huge vat of the world-famous sauce, getting ready for the weekend probably.

"You gentlemens for dessert?" The table was quickly cleared and sprayed with some sort of cleaner and then wiped dry. The man's white hair stuck out from beneath the baseball cap.

"I recommend the lemon ice," Will told me. "It's their own concoction and is much like that other stuff. What do you call it—sherbet?"

"C'mon, Will," I said. He knew what it was called, just as he had known the name of the whatever-it-was-prize.

His head, rounded by the short haircut, tipped back on his shoulders and he looked at me out of the corners of those large gray eyes—the same eyes I see every morning when I shave. They crinkled as he smiled, and one of them winked over the

111

can of Dr. Pepper he lifted between us. "Hello there, brother," he said and sipped the drink. Then his expression changed, looked uncomfortable with what he was about to say. "Where does it come from, Sonny?"

"What?"

"Where do you pull it from—all that stuff you do? By golly, it just amazes me." He shook his head and got up to pay the bill. He moved toward the counter with the cocky assurance of an old patron, someone more than familiar with the place.

Sally's eyes glance at me off the car's rearview mirror, which she has twisted toward her face. She has uncapped a lipstick. "Sorry about this. You can fix it back straight before we dock."

She changes the set of my life with a casualness that often seems like impertinence. The moment I arrive, she starts pulling the clothes out from my luggage, supposedly to hang them up, but actually to audition the collection and find something she can put on.

"That's the shirt I was going to wear to dinner," I often say. The shirt drapes over her shoulders and goes to her knees. Or my bathrobe is a favorite. Or a sweater.

"I would like to slip under your skin," she said this afternoon. We've just come from the beach and showered off together.

"Lordy, why?" I am truly amazed. Her body, the luster of its complexion, works its usual paradox of wonder and sadness on me.

"To put you on. To become you." The ferry's engine has throttled down, and we seem to coast, headlong, toward a berth that looks much too narrow. My foot has gone to the car's brake pedal.

Will had called from the restaurant, so by the time we strolled through the empty streets and down to the riverbank, the small boat was more than halfway across the channel. The sky had become overcast, a luminous pearl screen that cast no shadows.

"He did the best he knew how for the both of us," Will said.

"I have no regrets and no anger left. Each of us serve as we are made to serve." He sounded like the churchwarden he was— something else that raised Dad's scorn. *Why can't those people order a cup of coffee,* I remember him saying, *without quoting the goddamn Scripture?*

"There was never anything bad between you and me," Will had continued. "Never was. Time was our distance; only that and nothing more." Just off shore, Elwood raised one arm in greeting. "We have served each other as best we could." My brother reached down to receive the small line that our ferryman tossed him, and pulled the idling motorboat into the bank.

"Kindly take my brother back across and, if you don't mind, drive him back to the house, so he can get his car. . . . I'm going to stay over here for a little bit," Will explained to me. Something in his tone indicated he had planned this from the beginning. "Well, there's a couple of Dad's old cronies over here that I want to call on. They're nothing much and you have a plane to catch."

We shook hands with an awkward heartiness. I remember saying something about him coming East, and he nodded as he handed me down into the skiff. Halfway across, just as the engine began to buzz against the river's grain, I turned to wave at him. He stood on the riverbank, very much at ease, hands in the pockets of his dark blue uniform. I expected him to wave, but when he did not, I kept my own hand down.

The cemetery in Ohio is set back off a road that is fronted by a convenience store, an ice cream stand, and a business that had once kept plumbing supplies, but which I remember as being closed. A welded iron arch bends over the entrance. OAKCREST CEMETERY. But there are no oaks, not a tree of any kind, and the gravestones stick up from a terrain as flat as slack water.

"And that's a funny thing," Will wrote in his last letter. "I've been going through the records in my position as the chairman of the cemetery board, and I came across this whole bit of correspondence Dad had had with the iron foundry that made the arch and gate. It seems they got the orders mixed up and they sent us the arch for a place in Iowa and they got ours. But it must

113

have tickled Dad to leave this wrong one up, or maybe it was too much trouble to switch them around. There was a war on. But can you imagine some cemetery out there on a hill in Iowa, with lots of trees, called Golden Shore? I guess, in the last, it's all interchangeable.''

Some time later, a Polaroid photograph arrived in the mail, sent by one of the cemetery's board members at Will's written request. His stone is a square chunk of red marble. It bears his name and dates. It records that he was a Lt. Cmdr., USNR. Then beneath all that: "THE OTHER SON."

"You should have waved anyhow," Sally says. Miraculously, the ferry has neatly made port without my help, but with only an inch to spare. I start the car, and we bump off the boat and onto the road. Today the light was particularly luminous and with the same purity that strikes the Mediterranean coastline with such energy that even the blackness in shadows becomes a color. Some of this light seems to lie upon the leaves of the palm trees that tower above the street; though there must be a trick to this, one of those California illusions that beguile the Easterner, because it has been dark for some time.

She directs me toward a final turn. "Feeling better now to be on dry land?" This side of the bay is more residential, fewer shops and more cottages. The restaurant is small and cozy. The air is fragrant and the candlelight is full of prophecy.

"Thanks for the shortcut."

She looks wide-eyed and shrugs. "It wasn't so short, as it turned out. You could have found the way here on your own." She takes up the menu. "Let's eat."

The solid ground beneath us, even this table I lean across to kiss her for her confidence, undulates with the memory of the passage. Maybe this small peninsula has separated from the mainland and floats the two of us out into the Pacific as we dine by candlelight, drifting farther and farther so that we will be at sea by dessert. Not drifting but launched, and not cast off but wound up and set going by a hand too shy to wave and too distant to be seen.

On Silver Skates

The green balloon rose through the tree. Hendrick remembered thinking some kid his age must have let the string slip through his fingers, distracted by the puppet show or the clog dancers or some other event at the park fair so the balloon quickly escaped. Hendrick remembers how the balloon had made its way upward through the tree, climbing dextrously from limb to limb like a gymnast or a monkey in a zoo. Each bump against a branch, any contact with a leaf twig could have punctured the thin skin, but the balloon remained a perfect oval, a green idea rising higher and higher as if guided by some intelligence on the ground, perhaps by the boy or girl who had let it slip away.

Or maybe he had done the trick, willing the balloon its safe journey, maybe making a bet with the powers that govern such things: that if the balloon did not burst, then this day would come out all right. He would not do anything dumb or silly to embarrass his father during the park fair and the day would come out all right. He had held his breath as the balloon bounced against the maple's canopy once, twice and then again, blindly feeling for an opening and then, suddenly, it slipped through the leaves and into the uncluttered air. Free.

"Where have you been, Skippy? I've been looking for you."
His father had appeared, and the question was snapped toward
him as the older man made his rounds, as a shortstop might whip
the ball over to Stan Musial at first base. Hendrick had fallen in
beside his father, almost running, taking three steps to the man's
one stride. "You're my right hand. Did you deliver that message
to the Dixie Doodles?"

"Yessir."

"Good man. Now here's the mayor. Over by the puppet
stage. Now, look sharp," and they set off in that direction, the
right hand with the small ruby ring on its little finger already
extended as they neared the official party. "Mr. Mayor, welcome. I'm Butch Hendrick."

"He runs special events for the parks," an aide quickly told
the mayor.

"Why of course, Butch. This is an outstanding occasion.
Outstanding." The politician's huge black hands not only en-
veloped his father's hand, but then they moved to grip his shoul-
ders, his upper arms, as if to estimate his volume for a package.
Then the genial face lowered over him. "And this must be young
Mr. Handrack."

"Hendrick," his father said. "He's my right hand."

"I can see that. Indeed, I can see that. Now, what I want
to know is when is that barbecue going to get ready?" The
politician rolled his eyes and everyone laughed. Some looked at
each other and then laughed. "If you think I'm a good mayor—I
am a chief justice supreme of the barbecue."

"That's going to be in about an hour. After the golden-age
horseshoe contest." His father had to say it fast, because the
mayor and his party were already moving toward the next exhibit, greeting people, posing for a photograph. "A great man,"
his father told him. "He's going to be governor someday. The
first black governor. Did you see how he kept holding on to me?"

"Yessir."

"That was the old fraternity one-two, secret whammy. I tell
you, Skip, he's going places, and yours truly is going to be on the
train. Now we got to check the concessions. C'mon son. No time

for skylarking.'' The green balloon had disappeared into the blue sky.

"*A Sky Full of Balloons* is just a classic,'' the woman is saying.

"Well, thank you,'' Hendrick says as he signs the book.

"I must have worn out a half-dozen copies with my own children and this one is for my first grandchild. Of course, we love your other books, too.''

"That's very good of you,'' he says, and returns the book to her. It has been a slow morning in this bookstore but just as Hendrick is getting a little hungry, a little thirsty, business picks up. He has noticed several middle-aged women—grandmothers seemed to buy a lot of his books—working their way through the humor and travel sections of the store toward where he sits at a table piled high with his own books.

"Do you do many of these?'' The customer points to the placard beside him. Over his photograph is a banner of type: MEET STANLEY HENDRICK. "It must be difficult to leave your own family.''

"Actually, I'm alone these days and my son—our son—is off on his own on the West Coast.''

"Oh, I'm sorry,'' the woman says. "Well, you do beautiful children's books, anyhow,'' she says.

"Thank you.'' It is almost noon in this small city where his publisher has put him down briefly to sign books, appear on a local television show and speak to the students of an art institute. In Los Angeles it would be not quite nine o'clock. Tomorrow he will be in St. Louis, where Stan Musial became a legend, and where the difference in time from Los Angeles will be one hour less.

"Stan the man,'' his father would say, taking his small shoulders in a grip that somehow conferred honor by way of the pain, perhaps because of the pain.

"This is your little boy?'' the woman asked.

"This is my man, Stan,'' his father said, and Hendrick remembers turning away to better handle the glory. The woman

117

was one of the Dixie Doodles, an all-female barbershop quartet that was to appear later on the wooden stage set up in the middle of the park. The members of the singing group represented the four possible variations of height and weight as their voices registered the different ranges between alto and soprano.

"What's the matter?" his father asked.

"It's this darn tie," she replied. She was already in costume. "It scratches my neck." The Dixie Doodles wore a version of a man's tuxedo but the bow tie was of red plastic and fastened around the bare neck, and this tie seemed to bother the plump bare neck of the second alto.

"Let's see," his father said. The smoke of the barbecues hung above the park. By the lake, boys and girls waited for pony rides. "I see the problem," his father said. The singer had bent her head forward to allow a close inspection of the bow tie's clasp. "I think I can fix it. Stan, shoot over to the bingo hall and tell them the prizes won't be here until four o'clock. Then meet me at the Texas Red Hots stand. We'll have one of their Numero Unos. On the house. Wait for me there. Don't leave. I'll get there. Now step on it. The bingo people are waiting to hear about the prizes."

How fast he ran; no one ever knew how fast he could run. Some springy substance was set into the soles of his tennis shoes that day which is unavailable in Korea or Taiwan, where sneakers are manufactured now. The Spring Element or the Jump Factor. Hendrick takes out a notebook he always carries to jot down such ideas. Could be a book in this. As he writes in the spiral journal, an image develops, and he quickly sketches an old-fashioned, high-topped tennis shoe with the wing emblem on the ankle. A second sketch and the wings have come full-feathered, like Mercury's sandals, and the shoe seems ready to fly off the page. Messenger to the gods, Mercury.

Or Hans Brinker and his silver skates. Wasn't that to do with delivering a message? He couldn't recall the plot. Young Hans was on a mission of some sort, wasn't he? The canals had frozen over and the children had slipped off their wooden sabots and donned skates. He remembered his mother reading the story

118

to him, resolutely pulling the narrative from the page, word by word, as his father called from the side yard, slapping a baseball into the mitt. Thwack. Thwack.

Why silver skates? Because they were better, elite, faster. A prize. The dike had sprung a leak. Step on it, Hans. Skate over to the bingo hall and tell them there's a dike here that's sprung a leak. The message always got through. The speed of sound meant something then. With all the technology since—there's a whole section in this bookstore on computer literature—sound still traveled at the same speed. Even slower, maybe, slowed down by the technology. Or maybe everything else had started going faster. Phone calls to California, for example, had a way of overlapping themselves as if the sounds walked around the corners of the conversation and he heard his own voice coming back, was made to listen to his own banal language.

"How are things . . . are things?"

A journey through the universe; then, "Fine."

"Well, what are you . . . what-are-you . . . doing . . . doing?"

Another trip around the cosmos. "I've had some offers but nothing . . . nothing firm . . . firm. I have to go . . . to go.."

"Good-bye . . . bye . . ."

" . . . Bye . . . bye . . . "

A woman has been looking at him from the cookbook section and Hendrick almost motions to her. He might ask her, would she mind, on her way over, seeing if there is a copy of *Hans Brinker, or The Silver Skates* somewhere in the large children's-book section around him and bringing him a copy. He can't leave his post and he's not sure about the story. Maybe Hans was given no such mission. Wasn't there a sister who also was a skater? He ought to check it, but he's just been handed another of his own books for a signature, and it is the new one. Two more customers wait their turn, arms holding books with familiar jackets. His colors, his palette as the professor called it when introducing him yesterday, really are unique and all the more apparent when seen against this sort of background.

Clearly, the woman in the cookbook section is waiting to speak to him, though she clasps only Betty Crocker to her bosom. An old hand at such encounters, Hendrick identifies her

119

as a curiosa rather than a book buyer; perhaps, someone who has tried to write children's books herself and has come just to verify her suspicions about him—that he is no different from her, no more talented, and that it is living in New York City and having all those contacts that makes the difference. She looks about his age, maybe older.

"Do you read to your children?" The customer who asks the question blocks his view. Her expression is already delighted by the answer she expects to hear.

"I used to read to my son, but he's too big for that now." A funny picture of his son trying to crawl up on his lap like some large hound that still thinks he's a puppy? Hendrick wants to laugh but, fortunately, the woman persists.

"What does he do?"

"He's in college."

The new book would be the reverse of the old idea that the simple, ordinary article—say a pumpkin or a pair of tennis shoes—was intrinsically better because of its ordinariness, that there was something magical in the worn and odorous seams of the old tennis shoes that made the wearer run faster than the new rich kid on the block in his crisp Keds. That sort of crap had pacified the have-nots for centuries, Hendrick thinks, and he had contributed to the propaganda himself. Even if any of it had been true, all of it—along with the speed of sound and other such verities—had been clicked into the wastebasket. Brinker's skates went faster because they were silver, they were better. No mystery to it. That's why he got the job, that's all there was to it.

For hadn't he run faster than the speed of sound, only for the people at the bingo hall to look at him funny? They didn't seem to much care when the prizes for the games arrived. He was out of breath, the words urgently formed on his lips, and they had only looked at him and turned back to their preparations, setting up tables, fixing the wire baskets that would mill the numbers for the afternoon's games. They wore satin shirts in different pastels that were intensified by the colored gelatins placed over spotlights mounted at different locations. Hendrick remembers those colors to this day; in fact, he could reproduce them in his studio, weak tints made mean by the peculiar light thrown on them.

He had hung around the bingo hall for a little bit, then started across the park toward the food concessions and the Texas Red Hot stand. He knew he should take his time, that he had gone too fast before and that he should slow down. No one, not even his father, had realized how fast he could run. He had to kill some time, not get to the food booth too early, so as not to hang around there by himself, answering silly questions, alone. He took the long way around through the antique displays and the canned preserves and then coming to the grade-school science projects, which fascinated him though he hoped no one would discover him looking at them. How things worked had always interested him, and these crude models of cardboard and balsa wood seemed to give answers to questions he hadn't even formulated yet, answers that teased him but never satisfied his curiosity.

"What makes balloons go up?" a voice in his lap was to ask him years later.

"Okay, balloons are filled with a gas that is lighter than air—like helium. Hydrogen used to be used but that was too dangerous, it would explode. But helium, it's named from the sun, is safe. So, enclosing a batch of helium inside a balloon sets it apart from the ordinary, heavier air—separates it within the balloon's skin—so it is different from the regular air and it rises, pushing the balloon up."

"Get back to the story," the voice would say.

Hendrick wonders if he should sign the *Betty Crocker Cookbook*. The lady who has just come before him looks as if she is about to hand it over. *Best wishes from Betty Crocker via George*. He has a sudden reference to the old story about H. L. Mencken taking the Gideon Bible in whatever hotel room the Baltimore Sage found himself and autographing the flyleaf, "Good luck from the author." Instead, he looks up at her with what he feels to be a pleasant expression. She continues to study him as if he were something strange imported to her part of Pennsylvania, like a traveling display of moon rocks.

"You don't remember me, I guess," she finally says.

121

"No, I'm sorry." Quickly Hendrick runs a check of her eyes, her nose and mouth, and tries to imagine how they might have appeared some years back. Pretty far back, apparently, because nothing about her looks familiar.

"I was Joanne Schneider's roommate the year you dated her," she says.

"Oh, yes," Hendrick replies, trying to remember that year, and then the image of Joanne Schneider takes form. All one spring he had tried to seduce this economics major from Hartford—he thought it was Hartford—but with no success. Then, one afternoon at a deserted beach, as he had trudged back to the car to get them more beer, he heard her cry his name from a distance. He turned. She had removed the top of her swimsuit to bare her breasts to him and the sun and the seagulls. Obviously, she had no preference. Then, after letting him see her, after allowing him his portion of this vision, she had pulled on a long-sleeved sweatshirt. That was to be the extent of his adventure with Joanne Schneider. "Of course," he is saying. "I remember you very well."

"I was Alice Emerson then."

"Yes . . . Emerson."

"But my married name is Roberts, though that's my ex-husband, who is something of a zero."

"I'm sorry."

"Well, that's the way it goes. You married, did you?" She looks at him closely, perhaps just remembering something Joanne Schneider may have told her.

"Yes, but I'm divorced also." This bit of biography does not surprise her and she nods, so he finds himself adding, "But my former wife and I seem to have a very good relationship. We have stayed friends."

"Children?"

"We have a son. He's in California, in school." While Hendrick's attention had been pulled elsewhere, toward making these books piled high around him, putting together these inventions of paper and color that give no answers as they contribute to falsehoods, the boy in his lap had become large and bored; impatient with the wordy explanations of phenomena, probably

122

even doubting their truth. He had slipped off his lap and gone to California.

"He must be very proud of you," she is saying. "To have a famous dad like you. All my daughter has to look at is a father who deserted his family to take up with a younger woman."

Then her face seems to come apart like newsprint in the rain and she weeps uncontrollably, hugging the cookbook to her bosom. A customer behind her makes a quick assessment and moves away. Hendrick wonders if the other woman still might buy the book on her way out, even unsigned.

"My daughter is dying of leukemia," the woman in front of him is saying, "and I don't know where she is." She holds onto the edge of the table, his books between them. Hendrick leans forward and caps the pen he has been holding in his right hand. "My ex-husband and his wife gave her a new car and a bunch of traveler's checks, so she's out there somewhere, just driving around the country. I don't know where she is."

"I guess she has lots to think about," Hendrick says.

"But I don't know where she is. Oh, well"—she shrugs and corrects herself—"I heard from her last week. She was in Arizona. She called me to say her white cells had gone up only thirty and I got so . . . so . . . " Again her face becomes gray. She hugs the cookbook and continues. "I got so excited, thinking it had stabilized and then I called her doctor and he said she had meant thirty thousand cells, not thirty. So, she's out there. Camping out. Can you imagine?"

"I'm sure you'll hear from her," Hendrick says. "She must have a lot of things to think out, put into order. She has to come to terms with what's happening. She probably needs a little solitude."

"Who needs to be alone?" A quick anger restores her control. She uses a delicate handkerchief with lavender embroidery to wipe around her eyes, her chin. "Of course, we were never close, but I thought that now . . . now that this . . . well, now."

"Maybe you could leave messages for her?"

"Where can I leave messages for her?" Hendrick did not exactly hear her reply because his own question had started a race through his imagination and he automatically reached for his notebook and then pulled back. He would have to remember the idea. Hans Brinker as a Western Union boy. They wore brownish-green uniforms and pedaled about on bicycles with yellow envelopes that people were always afraid to open. Mother died this morning. Dad passed away last night. Your services have been terminated. But this time, this story, it would be good news. The bicycle chain had broken and Hans had to run the rest of the way on his silver sneakers. *Hans, take this message to Fort Bingo, and if your bicycle breaks down, run the rest of the way.*

And he did run eventually, until he found himself in the back part of the fair on the edge of the park where the tents and trailers that belonged to the performers had been put up. Here, the aromas of barbecue and cotton candy and soda pop gave way to smells he could not identify save for their greasy quality. An odor of old tires, all the miles they had turned over. Something like the cold cream on his mother's bureau top. Old laundry. And music from radios, from records on portable players.

The Dixie Doodle trailer was aluminum and had vanilla-colored venetian blinds that made the windows look like the lined tablets he used in school. He could have practiced his penmanship on the parallel lines of those windows, making the exact copies of the Spencerian alphabet that the writing teacher would hold up to the class as an example of how it was to be done; but this time the letters would be poorly made. The paper would not hold still. It kept quivering slightly as the trailer trembled. His tennis shoes pawed at the earth; the mission waited and the messenger, ever mindful of his command, raced on toward the Texas Red Hots stand, hoping to arrive late.

"Actually, I've thought of leaving messages with the police," the former Alice Emerson is saying. "This car they've given her is a red Thunderbird with a Wisconsin license plate. There can't be many of those in Arizona. I thought I'd call the state police and have them track her down."

"I wouldn't do that." Hendrick is looking over her shoulder. A very pretty young woman is standing toward the rear, obviously waiting for him. He recognizes her as one of the students he talked to yesterday, and she has come to take him to lunch and then on to another bookstore. "She'll find her way back. You must let her find her way back."

"I suppose I might as well buy one of your books," the woman says. "I have a grandniece who might like them. Which one do you recommend?" None of them will do, her tone suggests. "What's this one about balloons? That's supposed to be your best, isn't it?"

"It's done okay," he replies, uncapping his pen. Good wishes. Good luck. None of the standard salutations seem appropriate. Had they ever been suitable? He always appreciated the endpapers of this book. The round shapes glowed with the colors, pungent like ripe fruit, and he is suddenly very hungry. He signs only his name and the date and—after a little thought—the city where he is. St. Louis, tomorrow.

"I sometimes hear from Joanne. I'll tell her I saw you." She has gathered his book up with Betty Crocker's, and leaves. Hendrick is ready to go also and he stands and smiles at the student, who quickly approaches. He appreciates her perception of his predicament, her savvy, as she moves smartly in dark blue boots down the aisle toward him, her youthful stride putting her quickly between him and the next bright-eyed matron.

"Busy morning?" she asks. Her smile suggests a conspiracy between them—artists versus the public. Hendrick estimates the hope and courage in this young face. "What would you like to eat? Sandwich? Pasta? I've been given a blank check to use with you."

"As a matter of fact, I've been thinking about some chili."

"Chili!" The young woman looks disappointed. Perhaps this has been her once chance not to eat chili. "This town isn't very big on Mexican food." Her face scrouches up, then smooths out. "Okay. I know a place."

"It needn't be anything fancy," he says, following her out of the store. "Just some Texas Red Hots would be fine."

"All right, I'm supposed to ask what they are. Okay, what are Texas Red Hots?"

"Hot dogs with chili and chopped onion. Sometimes little red peppers. The peppers turn an ordinary Texas Red Hot into a Numero Uno."

"Numero Uno," she repeats with a little laugh, surprised, maybe even pleased by this new thing he has shown her. She drives with a skillful daring that has Hendrick casually feel for his seat belt and then decide against it. She wears none. "Am I going too fast?" she asks.

Yes, too fast, he says to himself, because if they get there too early no one will answer the phone in California. It will either be too early or too late, a null point where the circle that defines the right time comes full round on itself; separating all the moments, all the conversations from their earthbound moorings, and they become lost.

He had run too fast, so he had wound up at the Texas Red Hot stand before his father. The boy behind the counter didn't seem much older than he; only the long red-and-green apron and the white chef's hat made him seem older. Also, the long-handled spatula with which he scraped down the griddle set him apart from every boy, everywhere in the world. Hendrick's father had said he could have a job like this at next year's fair, because he had been disappointed that he was still running errands, tagging along to be introduced as a right hand.

Business was slack, and the kid in the apron spent a lot of time scraping the griddle, neatly lining up beads of grease into perfect straight furrows and then pushing everything cleanly off into a small trough alongside the iron plate. Hendrick admired the technique, tried to follow the procedure while ostensibly watching the ring-toss booth by the pavilion.

More grease must have oozed up through the surface of the iron griddle, because the whole scraping and cosseting of the hot metal had begun again. Sometimes, the boy would strike the edge of the spatula against the stove's top, smart whacks of metal on metal that made Hendrick envious of their commanding ring. Next year, he could do something like that, stand there all day and clean off the griddle. He wouldn't care if he had customers or not. His father would be making the rounds of the festival, maybe with the mayor who had just been elected the first black governor, and they would come by the stand for a couple of Numero Unos and his father would introduce them.

126

"Why, of course," the first black governor would say. "I remember Stan. He makes the best Texas Red Hots in the land."

Then his father did appear, but by himself and trotting around the corner of Pavilion A, taking those small, dapper steps as if he were coming in from the infield after making the inning's final out, a snappy double play that had the crowd on its feet; but he would ignore the standing ovation, not out of modesty, but because it was his job to deliver such perfection.

"Been here long?" he asked, a little winded. His face looked pink, as if he had shaved since they had last seen each other. "Okay, we'll have two of your best Red Hots," he told the kid at the counter. "And make them Numero Unos."

"What's that?" the boy asked. "We got nothing like that."

"Numero Unos? Sure you do." His father looked incredulous, and stepped closer as if to peer behind the counter. The cook scraped the surface of the griddle, smacked it with the spatula.

"We got Red Hots and we got hamburgers and we got Polish sausage. We got no Numero Unos."

"Hey, buddy, you know who you're talking to?" His father gave half a laugh and stuck out his jaw. "I put this whole thing together. I'm the chief here. I run this place. I'm Butch Hendrick. Don't tell me you have no Numero Unos. Where's your boss?"

"I *am* the boss," the boy replied. Hendrick remembers the kid's feet, how they went apart and took up a stance behind the ankle-length apron. He held the spatula blade down against the hot metal. Across the way on the stage, a magician in clown makeup had begun to do tricks.

"Hey, Skip, don't wander off. We got to get this straightened out. Okay." His father turned back to the other boy. "Okay, then, give us a couple of Red Hots."

"That'll be two bucks," the kid said, not making a move. Then it was like the pantomime act earlier that morning, both of them stuck in a pose. If he hadn't shown up early, none of this would have happened. His father could have worked it out if he hadn't been there, before he got there, and none of this would have happened.

"Okay, here," his father finally said.

They had walked toward the magician on the raised stage as they ate the wonderful hot dogs with chili, Hendrick leading the way and his father talking. "There's a lesson in this, Stan. It's my fault because I wasn't paying attention and let the ball slip through. Took my eye off the ball. Can you imagine no Numero Unos? Whoever heard of such a thing? But it's my fault and it won't happen again. I can promise you that in capital letters, buddy. Because I'm going to get somewhere. You better believe it, and I'm taking you with me, Stan. You and me, buddy—a wham-o combo. Death in the infield—five to three. It's Hendrick to Hendrick."

The magician had just pulled a long silk scarf from a small tubelike wand and this scarf pulled out another and yet another and all of them the same intense blue as the boots of the student who is driving him to lunch. Though Hendrick couldn't swear it to be the same color, for this might be just another of those associations he was always making, one more instance of his mixing colors for a particular effect and sometimes, some critics said, only for the effect.

On the other hand, the young woman behind the wheel could have been part of the magician's act, one of those comely assistants who stand to one side of the magic and, with a flourish, call attention to the incomprehensible. A second skin of black tights limned the slim legs that rose from the blue boots, and a loose sort of doublet in brown velvet with full sleeves was fastened high around her throat. Actually, she was more like one of those androgynous players in *Twelfth Night* who pass through different sexual possibilities with a lyrical ease.

"I have to stop at my motel on the way to the restaurant," Hendrick says suddenly.

"I'm . . . I'd rather not," she says, and leans over the wheel. Serious driving in progress.

"Is it out of the way?"

"No, it's not that. I have a boyfriend." She blushes.

"Oh," Hendrick says after a bit. She wears a wool scarf of sienna and, all at once, he knows of the care with which she selected it that morning, how she prepared for her assignment.

Perhaps, she borrowed the rebozo from a roommate. "That's not it," he says finally. "I need to make a phone call. That's all. You can wait for me in the parking lot."

"You never know what to expect these days," she says airily, and guides the car into the right lane, rounds a corner. His motel is just ahead.

"I guess not. I'm sorry," he says, though why he apologizes he does not know.

"Who are you calling?" He can tell she's not so much interested in the answer as in the fact that he has an answer. Smart girl.

"I've been trying to get hold of my son, but I haven't been able to reach him." Hendrick reads the billboards along the highway. All these advertisements for comfortable nights and colorful food—crooked strings of steamy flavor rise above huge round plates—all these pictorials don't attract a pilgrim so much as they announce his lack of choice.

Turn in here, the billboards say, *it's all the same*, and she does turn into the parking lot of his motel. Though it is not the same in Arizona, where a person might still camp out, away from all messages, however delivered, or even in California, where the phone continues to ring and ring, unanswered. Hendrick tries the number again. He may have mispunched the long series of digits his particular phone service requires. Down in the parking lot, the young woman waits for him. He watches her through the window. She leans against the car's right fender, a smoking cigarette in one hand, her elegant booted legs crossed at the ankle. Even more, she resembles a player waiting her cue to go onstage.

How long would she wait, Hendrick wonders? Could he keep her there indefinitely, holding that pose? He pulls the telephone line out from the baseboard, pulls it taut, half expecting to see a vibration along one of the lines on the pole outside by the highway, all those lines going west toward St. Louis and then beyond, across the prairies, then over the mountains and to California and then the vibration coming back again, to hold the girl in the parking lot at the end of it, smoking by the car, as he is also held in place waiting for the sound to return. On silver skates, he thinks, and then he hears a voice, but not in his ear. "Get back to the story. Where did the balloon go?" the voice had asked.

The green balloon rose higher and higher until it came to a small, soft planet that was gently nudged round on its axis by all the lost balloons ever let loose; their forlorn strings, some of them with useless knots still tied at the ends, dangled in space, and all of them had slipped away from the sunny carelessness of children who believed they could bring them back if they only reached high enough. That was the fantasy he had autographed all morning, the invention that had given him a little fame, and he was sorry for that.

The burr of the phone signal drills his ear. He hangs up the phone and the line goes slack. The young woman stamps out her cigarette and makes a slow, graceful pirouette in the parking lot. She turns and turns, as if delighted with her sudden freedom, and Hendrick is pleased also as he closes the door and comes down the steps to join her.

"How about those Numero Unos?" she asks.

"How about them," he says.

He had watched the last balloon rise into the evening sky just as the local symphony orchestra tuned up for the fair's final event, a concert in the ballfield. He had looked up as the violins and horns sounded the A natural together, and the eloquent sound was pulled aloft into the vast silence by a swift rising yellow balloon. Just then he felt his father's arm go around his shoulders. "It's all right," he said. "It doesn't matter."

Blues for Solitaire

Dad is here, I say, and then you answer something like—
Oh, I'm happy you are having this time together—though just
a minute before you were saying you had this problem you hoped
I could take care of, thinking your words were daring, dirty-boy
talk that went along with clapping erasers together in the sixth
grade outside of Horace Mann in Blue Springs—Hey, Emily, we
got problems with our homework. Give us a hand with it?

"What's that, Dad?"

He is saying that he has to use the last four digits of his
Social Security number as a code to get into this new apartment
complex he's moved to from Blue Springs. He is sitting at the
kitchen table, playing solitaire, and I can see his neck has gotten
thin; the cords pull out and up into his skull like cables pulling
the rest of him up, holding the rest of him up by his ears it seems
like, because they have gotten much larger.

"It's a damn nuisance," he says, and lays down a black
seven neatly on top of a red eight.

"What's that, Dad?"

"Memorizing those damn numbers. You have to punch
them into this panel by the mailboxes and then run across the
foyer to the door to grab it while it's still buzzing."

"I guess it must be for your security, though," I say.

"I never had to remember my Social Security number before," he says. "Never." He gets an ace free.

You'll have to get that cleaned off, Momma would say. I'm serving dinner in ten minutes. Hold your horses, he'd say. I almost got this worked out. Why don't you give me a hand and I'll get done faster.

So, you all talk like that no matter what age, whether it's playing cards or whatever. Just last week, this director of consumer relations leans across the crudités and says he would like to pin the subject down, open it up and see what it is made of, and so I pass him the olive that has all these toothpicks sticking up in the air and he looks at them for a second and then says no thanks.

Sometimes I must remind myself that I am a woman with a boy-child who is almost half your age, like tonight, when I heard your voice on the phone, saying those dumb shit things, and I'm going along with it—I reach up to my hair and expect to find rollers—and then I turn around and there's Dad with his cards all laid out and stuck on the fridge door is that card Billy gave me—"Happy Birthday to Mom, the Apple of My Eye."

Your eyes have a way of rolling up sometimes so you look like Our Savior on the cross, I mean those statues I used to pray to, look up to from my knees and catch just a glimmer of whites as He bore His blessed agony. "I didn't know feminists went in for this sort of thing," you said the other afternoon, and then I saw your eyes slip back into your skull, though I expect your agony was not all that unbearable. All this shocks me a little, mixing all these things up together, but not the language or the various activities. Just the mix of them.

"Playing those drums noon and night," Dad is saying. "They must be students from Africa who have rented the apartments below me. I've spoken to the people in the front office about it. But they're a whole new crew down there—bunch of young girls who don't care about anything but fixing up their faces and going out to lunch. Meanwhile, it's boom-la, boom-la, boom-la—BOOM." The four of hearts cracks down and a whole run is precipitated. He might win this game.

"Did you talk to the students about the noise, Dad?"

"That does no good. They won't listen to me."

Is that true about ears getting bigger as you get older? Dad's ears seem to stick out a lot more than I remember. I think of one fall afternoon, tramping through the woods back of our house, trying to keep up with him, wanting to snuggle into his broad red-and-black plaid back against the autumn chill, and his shoulders large, and his neck just right and his ears neat—tucked into his Minnesota Vikings cap. He walked so fast.

You told me the ears keep growing. Too bad for you, you said, that all the other parts stop, and I laughed so you wouldn't be embarrassed by the silly-ass purity of your remark—your humor is sometimes like black socks, if you know what I mean—nor give you any idea that I might have been offended. All these names you give things, all the parts have to be called something—it's a nomenclature I find gratuitous, but the names don't bother me. They bother you, I think. You say them sometimes just to bother yourself. The language is almost enough for you, which brings me back to the ears business. I was laughing, even threw a pillow at you if I remember rightly, so as to keep you busy while I had time for my real thoughts. If the ears get larger we should hear better, we should be able to listen to each other. Better.

"It's terrible," Dad says. "You can't hear yourself think."

"I get the feeling," I say, "that you don't like where you're living." And that stops him. He has to think about that for a while. He pats the cards, pats them straight.

Let me get back to being shocked. It's not what you think. You might think I am having trouble keeping my different selves apart—the old naming of the parts again. But why is it you have to separate everything; I guess putting a tag on something is to claim it? But to identify is not to understand anything. One is subjective, comes from the imagination of the beholder, and the second is a given—the basic rose, you might say.

Last week, I glanced in the mirror on the way to the bathroom and I saw Billy's Mom, the Apple of His Eye, and just then you said my ass looked like a peach. I am an orchard, is that it—a one-tree orchard and all of you perched on different limbs, enjoying different fruit, but one tree? You understand? I don't think you do. Listen to this.

Tuesday, I had gone to bed early to work on some reports and the door opens and here comes Billy to climb under the covers and lie against me, all barely five feet of him from toe to hip to shoulder lined up against me. So, I shift from vice-president of the credit bureau to Mom and then I think of Billy's father—because that's why the boy's in bed with me, he's lonesome for his father and I'm only a substitute—then the phone rings and I know it's you. Remember, you were calling from a bar in Germantown? Want to come out and play? you were saying, like you had just discovered sandboxes, and you were cute, right enough, and I admit to a little burn even with Billy lying close beside me and these market analyses in my lap.

"There, Dad," I say. I reach over his shoulder and point to the nine of hearts.

"I see it," he says. "I was just looking for a better play."

But he hadn't seen it and he has no better play and his voice had that edge to it that Momma used to laugh at and turn back to the kitchen after she had wondered out loud if it wasn't a good idea to call the plumbers about the leak instead of him trying to patch it himself so as to save his good clothes for Sunday. And I would agree with his labeling of her, with the sound in his voice right then that said she didn't know what she was talking about—oh, I wish we could run things backwards like a movie, so Momma would come backwards out of the kitchen, turn around just after Dad had snapped at her, so I can say—look here, Momma, he can't even spot the nine of hearts, can't see that card exposed right here under his nose. But the reason I said nothing then is the same reason I put up with your dumb shit talk—I was waiting right then for him to come out and push me in that swing he had rigged up in a big oak in the side yard. Oh, he would push me so high that I'd leave my breath up there in the leaves. You push me high like that sometimes, but I know better to trust your opinion about plumbing. Do you follow me?

So, we've made some gains, maybe—but it's still swing time; and I'm the tree. That story you told me the other night about that girl changing into a tree to escape Apollo, was it? You like those corny plots, old-time gods chasing girls into trees, and you recite them to me as if they prove something about us—you almost get teary with the telling of it. How romantic, how wonderfully sad it was that the gods felt sorry for the girl and changed her into this tree so as to escape Apollo and it was a laurel tree—that's right, a laurel tree—so all the heroes got to wear her leaves around their heads ever after. But why did she have to become a tree at all? Why didn't Apollo leave her alone in the first place? Why didn't the gods change him into something— say, a rock or a stump?

Dad is here to help me move my furniture. The new suite arrived on Friday. He doesn't so much move as be a pivot. Billy's away with his wilderness group and don't be hurt that I didn't call you to give me a hand—I thought of it, believe me—but Dad needs some activity, some rolling-up the sleeves to look things over. —What do you call that? he said yesterday. —That's a lamp, I said. —But before that, he went on. —Well, I guess it was one of those Russian samovars, I replied. To make tea in. And he steps back to squint at it.

It's the most he can do these days—that stepping back for a second, incredulous look—to evaluate my way of doing things. He took the divorce harder than I or even Billy has. When I divorced David, I deprived Dad of a companion in disbelief, a fellowship in shirtsleeves—the two of them turning to each other and saying, Just what in hell is she up to now? United Chums and I'm something from the Third World to shake their heads over. What's the offer? Sovereignty? Is that it? My own flag and certain trade rights?

"Boom-la!" Dad says. He's just uncovered the king of hearts that he's needed for several hands. Now he shifts the queen of clubs over and that uncovers the ace of diamonds, the last bullet.

"You're going to win it, Dad." I'm losing you—tell me the truth. I can smell it on you like rain coming. You're telling me right now about your week's schedule, you're telling me about this problem you have—but all by telephone. You used to appear on my doorstep with your problem, like the paper boy—in fact, you bear some resemblance to the paper boy, or maybe I think of you bringing me the bad news along with the good. I'm always saying or doing things that shock you and I guess that's my appeal, because you feel free to do and say what you had always wanted to say back in the sixth grade, and it tickles you that I know all those words, and that it's okay to say them to someone who looks like me; a mom and a vice-president.

But it's the words beyond those I want to use, and that bothers all of you; that would make it all come out right, card for card. Maybe I don't like where I'm living either, and I have a whole bunch of numbers to memorize just to get through doors that ought to be open to me around the clock—but that's the way you like to do things for my security, you say, but is it for mine or yours? Just to walk through the same door, even together, is not the limit of my aspiration. But, I prefer it to being given my own door on the other side. Sovereignty is no guarantee of equality.

"It's not the same thing," I tell Dad. I just caught him shuffling the last of his playing cards. "You have to play them as they come out."

He needs one card to clear the board, win the game, and it's the ten of hearts—he can see it in the pack and he's started to shuffle the cards to get it to come up on top. I've ruined it for him, handed back to him the rules of solitaire he taught me, and I can see he's a little angry to be caught out.

"Damn it, look at that," he says. He's gone through the same set of cards several times, and the red ten stays in the same place—one card from the top, one card away from freeing up the rest of them.

"I'm sorry, Dad," I say as you're saying these things to me across the wire that stretches taut from the wall when I lean across his shoulder. Tenderloin black and blue. A bottle of 1978 Bordeaux. And this problem of yours that is getting bigger by the minute. Yes, I am tempted. But I'm tantalized by something else, which is what I've been trying to say to you all along.

"Do it again, Dad. Try a new game." He's been grimly obeying the rule I have reminded him of. The ten of hearts just stays where it is in the pack, to be seen but never played out. It never gets clear between us either even though we keep turning it over and over and you think these highs you push me to are the solution—that I like them so much somehow puts us on the same level, or I'll go along with the rest. Like I'm on your side.

But as the lady said, *I find this frenzy insufficient reason / For conversation when next we meet.* Can you imagine Edna St. Vincent Millay being changed into a tree? Not on your tintype— nor me either. But all the time, I see something that's never played out if we go by the rules. I keep seeing it just under the top card—always there, teasing me to turn the same ones over, time and again, which is why I'm more than willing to play with you, because I hope one of these games will come out right sometime; that red ten will come free—will set us both free.

But not tonight. And I don't know when, either. Maybe never. You don't like to hear that. You say you love me, but that scares me a little. But a lady can change her mind. That's one of those rules the United Chums have passed for the benefit of us in the Third World to make us feel equal. It comes with our sovereignty—we're allowed to change our minds. It's expected of us. Like some of the other natives being slow in the sun.

"Those are the rules you taught me, Dad," I say. He mumbles something under his breath but slowly scoops all the cards up, starts to shuffle the whole deck together. He was only about nine or ten cards from winning. I'm hanging up now. Enjoy your steak and the St. Émilion. I'm getting out the other deck of cards and we'll see how we do doubled up. Maybe it will come out right. Thanks for calling.

Ohm's Law

for Fay Fay

"I have a plan," my mother says. Papers and letters wash over her feet, and just then I feel the floor swell beneath my chair. We are together and alone.

That's not a bad association, Olivia would say, and go back to her literary criticism. Round, large reading glasses relay the smooth curve of her brow and define the sharp angle of her chin. I mean the reference to water, for the papers and letters strewn about the floor of this small cottage have to do with my father, and he had been a hydroelectric engineer; in fact, one of the architects of the Hoover Dam in Nevada.

"This is the last bunch I have to deal with," my mother is saying. "Once I get these organized and sent off to Kansas, I can do something for myself. Close this place up and go somewhere. I can't stand another winter in this place. You don't know how hard it is for me to live here."

"Here" is a small town in northern New Jersey where, she says, the winters are too cold for her, the library is too small, and the intellectual interests of the general population too far beneath her. In fact, whenever I have visited her, she has always stood in the middle of the floor, like now, as if ready to walk out

138

the door, walk south in her inexorable arthritic rhythm toward a more hospitable clime, where the weather and the intellectual stimulation will thaw all the potentials frozen within her.

But it is also more comfortable for her to stand; moreover, with an old letter in one hand, she projects a little of that authority which used to propel my father about his last years, answer his mail and minister to his needs. "Ah, there it is," she says, and slips the letter into a spilled sheaf of documents as if she were filling the suit of a tumbled deck of cards. "You don't know how glad I will be to be done with this. I've done nothing else since he died. I have been tied to these papers and nothing else."

But in truth, there would be nothing else if not these papers, which are the last threads of a personal history, the major portion already part of the archives of my father's alma mater. He had been the attention of her life when living, her occupation in death. So, these secondary materials, not just on the floor but also overflowing file cabinets in the small anteroom, have made up a kind of loom over which my mother passes, back and forth and year after year, not in anticipation of her husband's return but to unravel the threat of his complete disappearance.

"For instance," I once told Olivia, "if I look under a certain Victorian armchair in the corner, one with old lace on its arms and back, there will be the same pile of letters that has been there for years, with the same letter sticking out from the bunch with the letterhead—'The White House, The Office of the President,' et cetera, et cetera, et cetera. 'The President has asked me to convey to you his personal congratulations on the occasion of' et cetera, et cetera, et cetera and so forth. The same letter has been in the same place for years. She can't finish the job. She won't finish."

"Your letters overwhelm me," Olivia said during one of those desultory telephone conversations we dawdled through late at night just before we broke up. Rather, it was late at night at my end of the wire, for the continent separated us—all along the enormous territory between us had been there, an impossible logistic we would never acknowledge but that separated us at last.

"What do you mean?"

"I mean you write me such wonderful letters all the time and I never answer them. I want to write you but I don't. But I do phone you. I phoned you tonight. Hello, darling."

"You grew up using the telephone. I was from a different generation, we wrote letters."

"There you go again. Topic A again."

"I didn't mean that," I said, though I wasn't sure.

"You never listen to what I say. You only hear your own words, your own concerns. I said 'overwhelm.' You write me these wonderful letters, full of persuasion. Your letters persuade me and they overwhelm me. I find myself waiting for them. Doing nothing else, thinking about nothing else. It makes me angry sometimes."

"Then they're not so wonderful."

"You don't understand." Olivia's voice had become furtive, like a small animal that has carelessly shown itself and now scurries back into its burrow.

There was a considerable age difference between my mother and father also, so that when he died in his eighties, my mother was yet a vigorous woman in good health and with all the faculties and means to enjoy a complete second life. At the time, I remember nurturing the idea that it had been one of my father's droll ways of giving gifts—his death a cover for the gift of her freedom with all the means to enjoy it. One Christmas he gave me gold cufflinks, but they had been secreted in the toes of a pair of his oldest and smelliest sneakers. After the years of the restraint his degeneration had imposed upon her, I had thought she would make some radical change in her life, but she stayed in New Jersey and began the endless catalog of letters of confirmation, thank-you notes and files of carbon copies—not only originals were saved—of recommendations he had written for generations of technicians.

* * *

"But what could I do?" my mother is saying. She holds up another sheaf of papers as if the answer was not to be found even in their contents. "Your father's things were in terrible shape. He was a brilliant man but not very practical—small matters escaped him. When he died, his name was no longer included in the history. I'll never forget the biography of Westinghouse that little twerp of a professor wrote, which never mentioned your father."

It is a familiar subject, more like an obsession—his enshrinement in the pantheon of electrical wizards when, actually, he had been only one of several young protégés taken up by George Westinghouse. Then came his clever manipulation of Ohm's law into several patents that have insulated us both from the variant currents of need.

But that isn't the only subject that concerns her. "I've discovered a new place for lunch," she says. "It's an old water mill that's been made into a restaurant. You can hear about my plan on the way over."

"But what else could she do?" Olivia asked. She looked worried. We were staying in a small resort near her university and close to a ski area. I had just returned from skiing with a picture still in my head of my mother standing in the middle of her living room, slowly coming apart, piece by piece, like the papers scattered around her. It had ruined my morning.

I am a very good skier, and that particular morning the snow had been superb. Usually, the sport has a way of clearing my head, and I had been enjoying my speed and weightlessness in open fields of feathery powder, rather pleased with my style and amused by a group of much younger skiers who were keeping me company or, at least, trying to keep up with me as I came down the mountain. We had paused on the lip of a bowl, the Rocky Mountains around us as clear and as close as starlight, and just then my mother's constant complaint crackled in my head like the errant distress call put out by a disaster from another history: There's a fire in the library and Caesar has turned off the pumps. So the day had been ruined for me.

"What else could she do?" Olivia repeated the question

calmly. She had every reason to be upset with me. I had promised her the whole day alone to read and grade papers, and here it was only midafternoon and there I was sitting on the edge of the bed, pulling off my insulated clothing, to interrupt her with a tiresome monologue that she already knew by heart.

"She could have done anything she wanted. She was only in her mid-fifties when he died." I made a quick calculation. "Yes, she was just fifty-four when he died." Olivia had recapped her fountain pen and looked amused by something. Outside the window, a magpie perched on a bare tree limb, scouted the terrain and flew off.

"You know, the baths here are historic," I told her. "There's a plaque in the lobby that says all sorts of famous people took the waters. Walt Whitman and Frank and Jesse James took baths here."

"Not together, I hope." She laughed. "That would have changed the course of American poetry."

"Or American bank robbery." As always the shift of her good moods flattered me, because she had closed up her books and taken a robe from the closet. The garment was tailored and with white piping around its lapels, something a parent might have given her when she left home.

The baths at this inn are cut out of the red rock beneath the building's foundation, and their waters bubble up through the ground naturally hot and redolent with minerals. Just to breathe the atmosphere is an act of restoration. Our private grotto glistened darkly and my eyes, still a little blind from the morning's snow fields, had almost adjusted to the subterranean gloom when Olivia dropped her robe and the whole process had to commence again.

"My brother and I used to take baths together when we were children," she said, stepping daintily down the slippery steps and into the simmering water. "Those were happy times for both of us."

"To be laved and loved."

"Something like that. Are they the same root, loved and laved?"

"Quite different. 'To love' comes out of the Old English

word for pleasing, I think. 'Lave' has a Latin family, has always meant washing.''

Olivia's eyes had become cobalt blue as she studied me, almost recorded my explanation; a quick change from a woman to a student that presented me with a familiar dilemma: Which of those roles did I prefer? Only later, remembering this moment in Colorado, would I understand she had been weighing a similar choice. But then she rose from the hot waters and sank down once again up to her breasts.

The volumes of a woman's body have always amazed me by their concentration and their impossible suspension, which at the same time suspends all belief in the ordinary laws of physics. Yet the vision of Olivia rising, then disappearing into the water was no dream. "Hello, darling. Hello," she said, and draped her arms around my neck and kissed me.

The image of her brother and her bathing together slipped into my mind like a cold draft from beneath the door of our private cave. I kissed her back. Amphibious sprites, not fully formed or barely sexed; I placed their childish bodies within the basin of my own history. "Perhaps we will dissolve if we stay here long enough," I told her. "Become one solution."

"That's no solution," Olivia said, and moved to the other side of the bath. She stretched her arms out along the rock ledge. "I already melt when I'm around you."

"You said you liked that."

"That's the problem. But I melt to nothing. Your worry about us—Topic A—that's not my worry. I wish this water could change me into what I want without . . . ''

"Without what? What?" She had stopped suddenly, but her look continued the thought. Her mouth had buckled into a moue of profound sorrow. "Tell me?" I was alarmed.

"Oh, come here and tell me something," she said quickly. She wriggled with anticipation and the waters lapped richly about her shoulders.

"What do you want to hear about?" She floated within my arms.

"Ohm's Law. Tell me about Ohm's Law."

Georg Simon Ohm was born in Bavaria, the city of Erlangen, on March 16, 1787—the same year our constitution was being written and things were beginning to heat up in France. His father was a locksmith. After three years at the local university, the senior Ohm forced his son to withdraw because Georg was wasting his time dancing, ice skating and shooting billiards. He finished his schooling later and became a professor of mathematics at a Jesuit college in Cologne.

"Shooting billiards!" Olivia giggled.

It was there, after several papers of little interest, that he published his famous theory in 1827, the year Beethoven died. Byron had already coughed up his last quatrain three years before. However, Ohm's theory about measuring electrical current was so simple that no one took it seriously, and this poor reception disheartened him, so that he resigned his post in Cologne and made a living doing odd jobs of scholarship and research. Finally, he received an appointment to the University of Nuremberg and about this time (we're talking about 1842—the same year Nathaniel Hawthorne married Sophia Peabody) his discovery was recognized for what it was and he received many honors. He died in 1854, just as the Crimean War got under way.

Ohm's Law cites the relationship of the electrical current between two poles in terms of the conductor's resistance and the original voltage. The law can be expressed by the simple formula

$$I = E/R$$

where I represents the strength of the current, E stands for the initial electrical force and R is the length of the conductor or the size of the wire or its composition—or all three. The longer the wire, the more resistance and a proportional reduction in current between points. Or some conductors, their kind of material—say, copper—give less or more resistance than others and therefore affect the original charge (I) that is put through the conductor. Simple. Why hadn't anyone thought about that before? We accept this idea as commonplace now. But Ohm was ignored, treated badly by the academy of his day until only a couple of years before he died, without marrying. Alone.

"Your father was a very clever man," my mother is saying. This part of the state is very beautiful and quite unknown, apparently, to those wits on *The New York Times* who write about the ravishment of New Jersey on the op-ed page. We are headed west, toward the Pennsylvania border, on a two-lane highway that rises and falls on the serene tide of a landscape that had its tumultuous origin in the last ice age. "The universities were all after him to do his research on their campuses. Tulane offered him a chair. But he went his own way. He was his own man."

"But he had you," I reminded her, steering around a graceful curve.

"Well, my work on conduction had been getting a little notice. I'll never forget that reception your father brought me to—we hadn't married yet, and he was still living in Princeton—and he met me at the station and said, "I hope you've brought something classy to wear."

This is an old story, part of a dog-eared anthology she keeps thumbing through when I'm around, though I wonder if she goes over the collection when she is alone, as she arranges and rearranges the papers on the floor, polishing and rubbing each anecdote so that it might illuminate these incidents, perhaps cast them in a different light.

" . . . and before your father could finish pronouncing my name, Professor Einstein took my hand in both of his—both of his hands—and said, 'This is the little lady who has done that most interesting monograph on Lorentz. Thank you for that.' Imagine, Einstein thanking me.''

"What did you wear?"

"What?"

"To the reception—what did you wear? Something classy?"

"Oh, dear, I can't remember." She looks out the window. We are passing a farm. A long laundry line is stretched between the house and the barn, and several generations of clothes flutter in the clear light. "I had a pretty, wine-dark velvet dress with mauve inserts down the skirt. But maybe not that—it might have been too warm that time of the year. It was spring, I remember." Our car rolls along, up over a crest and down into a hollow and then up again. My mother looks ahead and through the windshield but with a blankness that registers nothing of the countryside, and this annoys me a little for I had gone to some effort to give her this outing.

"If only," she says.

"What?" The car hums along; I scarcely feel that I am steering it at all. "If only what?"

"I could do with a nice bowl of soup," she says.

"What's this plan you have?"

"Let's wait until we get to the restaurant and have a drink."

"What are you wearing?"

"The robe you gave me. It's beautiful, thank you. Everywhere I look I see the lovely things you have given me." Olivia's voice pulls away; the phone seems to tug at my ear, and I imagine her turning to look about her small apartment, to assess its contents. A pair of brass candlesticks. Boxes of lacquer. Porcelain figurines. A very large teddy bear. Of course, all of her books.

"Are you alone?" I had heard china scrape.

"I'm just having some coffee and a doughnut."

"You seem tired."

"A lot of interviews today."

"How did they go?"

"All right. The job at Stanford looks fairly certain."

146

"That's even farther away." I was sorry it had slipped out, for this old debate fell heavily upon our fragile conversation. I could see her waiting patiently for all the pieces to come to rest, to be fitted back together one more time. She had probably bent low in the chair, her face at her knees and the phone pressed to one side of her face.

"I love you," she said finally.

"But . . . "

"What would I do?"

"Anything you want."

"That's the same answer." A cup was set down on a saucer. It would be past ten on her end, for it was after midnight on my clock. "Not anything I want."

"Is that your supper—a doughnut?"

"You see, I would get fat with you. You would feed me too much."

"You're changing the subject."

"Don't be hurt by this, but if you are, I can't help it. You think I'm resisting you, that I am saying no to you."

"It amounts to the same thing."

"Not from here." Her voice caressed my ear so intimately that I turned quickly toward the empty pillow. Outside my bedroom window, the lights of Pittsburgh's skyline burned unattended, insulated by a darkness that deepened as I looked upon them just as the hush in my ear flew farther away into space. I listened for Olivia's voice to come along some edge of it. Her words slowly rounded a distant point and began their track down toward earth. They arrived, one at a time, in my ear. "I cannot *be* with you."

"Being with your father," my mother is saying, "was all that I wanted. Was more than enough for me."

"You never thought of remarrying? Ever?"

"Absolutely not," she says defiantly, as if the subject were dishonorable. She is on her second daiquiri and her eyes shine. The large water wheel has been saved as part of the restaurant's renovation, and several millstones are set about the dining room

147

on pedestals to make serving tables. The waitresses are in gingham and look cheerful. "But here's what I want to tell you."

I listen to my mother's plan, which is no different from the one she had last year or the year before that. That is to say, she has no plan. Outside, the old mill stream roars down the channel cut for it by the early settlers, pushing ahead in its strong current all the debris and yellowed ice that had been caught up by winter and now has been loosened by a sudden jolt of spring. My mother's talk goes on, and I notice that I am leaning forward as she talks of letters that must be saved, secreted; documents crackling with such awesome revelations that they must never be read by anyone for hundreds of years. Except by us, of course, and that is where her plan is different from the others, for I am to make the difference.

"This will all be yours to deal with," she says. "I am getting this ready to hand over to you." We give our order to a waitress and then I listen carefully to everything my mother has to say.

The Moving Finger

One time, changing planes at O'Hare, he yields to an impulse. More than once, on other trips, he had looked up her number, had split the thick slab of the Chicago phone directory apart and traced down the long columns of Joneses to what might be her number; but he had never made the call, and spent the time until his next flight prowling the vast terminal.

Jones, C. W. Cynthia Jones. Cindy. He could not remember if her middle name began with a *W* or even if she had a middle name, and so he was not sure if this was the same woman whose long legs and large brown eyes had been among the more comprehensive studies of his senior year. He remembered her forthright manner and the style with which she would enter his off-campus apartment, spill her books in the kitchen and slip out of her clothes in the bedroom where they raised gentle conspiracies against the era.

Jones, C. W. He had heard several years ago that she had been through a bad marriage, had lived in Europe and then returned, divorced, and took back her maiden name. But the use of initials stumped him, as they were probably meant to discourage obscene phone calls or maybe the calls of old lovers passing through, which might be the same thing, and this idea made him pause every time, every time close up the heavy directory and start his semi-serious inspection of the terminal building.

Something else had kept him from dropping money into the pay phone. Generally, a few hours before his wife would have driven him to the small country town that was still graced with a train into New York City. It would be early in the morning and she would have his barn coat over her nightgown, a pair of his boots on her feet. Her mouth would be warm as they kissed in the parking lot as the train arrived. Hours later, in the filtered, impersonal air of O'Hare Air Terminal, he could call up the feel of her lips, her aroma rising from the open throat of her gown, half woman's flesh, half warm bed. It seemed to him that a phone call to someone in the distant smoke that was Chicago, a person who would be no closer afterwards, would somehow abuse the sense of separation from his wife that he valued and enjoyed.

So, the questionable Jones, C. W.—looked up every time he passed through—was always smothered in the pages of the phone book, and he spent the time looking for the flaw a colleague had told him about, a remote wing of the terminal where the enormous windows faced a blank wall.

But it is different this time; a little more than a year has passed since his last layover in Chicago. The weather is rather balmy in Chicago when he gets off the plane, his second flight since nine o'clock, and he has about an hour's wait before his flight to Los Angeles. His final destination is Hong Kong. But it had been cold at home this morning, and after three days of rain, the station wagon would not start. He had reminded his wife the last time he left to get a new distributor cap, but the car had not been taken to the garage.

Also, one of the boys was in bed with his foot bandaged and shot full of tetanus serum because he had stepped on a broken bottle while playing around the trash burner. All bottles and cans were supposed to have been separated and taken to the town recycling center, and never thrown in with paper and other burnables. He had asked that all of this be done. Finally, while shaving, he had gagged on the disgusting odor that rose from the sink drain; danger signals sent up by the old cesspool, from its unknown location. None of the natives could remember where the old farmer who had sold them the house had dug it—somewhere in the front acreage, but never found.

But what really had him going through his change in Chicago was the cool, almost impertinent manner with which his wife had handled these problems. Or if not able to immediately solve them, as with the misplaced cesspool, she seemed to face them with a bemused transcendence, to fit them into a point scale fixed in her mind, but strange to him.

As he made his way toward a bank of telephone booths, he remembered how calmly she had picked up the phone in their kitchen to call the farmer who rented their pastures. Well, she had answered his remarks, the station wagon would not start, there were no taxis, and he *did* have to catch the train in Green River because he *did* have to go to Hong Kong. Besides, she added with a maddening assurance, they charged the farmer too little rent for their pasture and he'd be happy to do something like this for them. So, a few minutes later, he was bouncing on the seat of a pickup truck as the farmer, a man about his own father's age, hemmed and hawed agreeably to talk of weather, cracked distributor caps and backed-up cesspools.

Jones. Jones. Jones. He has a half-hour before he must board the plane for L.A. Perhaps in the past year she has moved, maybe even remarried. Or she might not be in—it's eleven in the morning in Chicago. If she were working, what would she be doing? He tried to remember what her major was, what her interests were. Jones, C. W. In a different location on the page of this year's directory, but there it is.

"Hello?" Miraculously, it is her voice, no question about it. He can hear the sound, the same inflection as when she had called him late at night from the women's dormitory. "Hello?" He almost hangs up without speaking, but that would make him another heavy breather on the line, one more reason for her anonymous entry. "Oh, hi," she says after he announces himself. Her nonchalance demolishes all the years since their last conversation. "What are you doing in Chicago?"

"I'm between planes at O'Hare and thought I'd call to say hello."

"That's nice," she says. He can hear a small dog barking in the background, an urgent sound.

"How did you know I live here?"

"A while back, I ran into Skip Butterfield . . ."

"Skip who?"

"Skip Butterfield—a roommate you may not remember—and he said that he had heard that you were back in Chicago. And, well, I just thought I'd give you a call, that it would be fun to say hello. I'm between planes."

"Where are you going?"

"Hong Kong."

"Wow, Hong Kong!"

"Well, it's on business."

"I see," she says. "You were going to be an architect, weren't you?" It sounds as if she has just pulled his card from the file.

"Yeah, that's right." He feels suddenly elated that she should remember this detail; then his elation turns his head away. Businessmen are browsing among magazines in the newsstand.

"Are you building stuff in Hong Kong?"

"No, actually I went into urban planning. I guess my ideas for buildings, houses, were too wild for people. But we were lucky bidding on a job for the Hong Kong government and I'm going over to lay the groundwork."

"That's nice," she says. "You must be very successful."

"Well, it's a living," he says. His face becomes warm again. The booth is flooded with sunlight. "What . . . what are you doing these days, Cindy?"

"Oh, a little of this and a little of that. My mother died. Then I got married. We lived in Majorca. But he was a jerk. So I came back here and went back to my painting."

"Oh, good," he says, not remembering when she had left it.

"You live in New York City," she says and speaks off the phone to the dog.

"No, we live upstate, about a hundred miles from the city.

It's just an old farmhouse we bought three years ago with a little land around it.''

"So the city life got too much for you and you moved to the suburbs.''

"Well, maybe.'' He returns a little of her laughter. "But actually it's not the suburbs nor is it all that simple. We're—''

"I find all this curious,'' her voice interrupts. It has become solemn, a flat register, and he recalls the way her eyes would narrow when she became serious about something.

"What . . . what is curious?''

"Well, how you can justify planning urban environments for people when you have opted for a rural setting?'' Just then, the coins drop and an operator signals his time has elapsed. "Just a minute.'' Cindy's voice becomes even more firm. "This raises certain ethical points that need to be discussed. What's your number there? I'll call you back.''

Wonderingly, he finds himself carefully reading off the pay phone's number, then hanging up the receiver and waiting. She was always discussing ethical points, come to think of it. Late at night when all he wanted to do was go to sleep, she would sit up—full of energy and resolve—and raise ethical points.

Perhaps she has not taken the number down correctly. Or maybe there is some difficulty with the dog, or a delivery man has rung the doorbell. Why should he wait, anyway? He ought to get to his gate. Then something else occurs to him. Wasn't Cindy the one? He's almost certain that she had been the coed with a seemingly endless supply of Kahlil Gibran quotations. Almost always, he now remembers, she would recite a line or two from *The Prophet* before she slipped into bed.

The phone rings. He could walk away, turn his back on the ringing, and suffer nothing more than the suspicions of the men standing around the newsstand. They would look at him over the tops of the magazines, and think he was trying to clip the phone company. The phone continues to ring, and he imagines her standing patiently in the remote pall of the city, waiting confidently for him to pick up the receiver. If he doesn't, perhaps the phone will still be ringing on his return trip.

"I don't suppose you even try to do anything with all that

land you own." She starts talking immediately when he holds the instrument to his ear.

"Well, there's not much of it, but we do rent the pasture to a local dairy farmer, actually a neighbor. In fact, this morning, he gave me—"

"So you make a profit on the land as a nonproductive land-owner?"

"Well, the term 'rent' is really an euphemism," he answers. "The actual money changing hands is—"

"So you sit up there in your Taliesin like some kind of a Count Tolstoy and tell people how to live in the ghetto."

"Now wait a minute, Cindy. Cindy? First, it's just an old farm, falling down when we bought it. Why . . ." And he almost tells her about the cesspool, but starts to laugh.

"I find very little funny about this," she tells him. Then, "Shush," to the dog. "My ex-husband would be attracted to what you're doing, that life you're living. All he wanted, I guess, was my money, so he could retire as a gentleman farmer. He never wanted to be involved, never wanted to make a commitment."

"That's too bad," he says, looking at his watch.

"Bobby Kennedy, Martin Luther King—he couldn't take what I'd been saying all along. So he split. He couldn't stand my being right."

"Right about what, Cindy?"

"About King's murder being a signal to knock off Bobby."

"I don't get it." He was pretty sure she was the one with all the Kahlil Gibran.

"Where have you been?" Her tone was amused. "Don't they get the newspapers up there on your estate? No TV signals get over the Catskills?" She pauses to speak to the dog once again, because the animal has become more insistent. When she resumes, the interruption has calmed her down.

"I'm referring to the whole miserable plot," she says. "First it was Evers, you remember. Then Jack Kennedy. Next it was King and then Bobby. Right? Think of it in pairs? It's so obvious. Black man, white man. Black man, white man. That was no accident. No accident. Will you be quiet!" she shouts at the dog.

"Those were terrible coincidences," he says. "What would be the reason for any of that? Who would organize such a plot?"

"Well, it has something to do with oil, baby. It's how we got into the mess we are in today. You have heard of the Persian Gulf, haven't you?"

"I just don't get it, Cindy." The browsers have replaced the magazines and left for their planes. Only the dark-skinned proprietor leans against the digital register. "What's the connection?"

"It's no accident," she says evenly, "that Sirhan is from the oil-rich Middle East. Nor is it any accident that Oswald tried to get a job in the oil fields in Mexico. And where, may I ask you, was King's assassin captured?"

"Ah . . . Portugal?" he suggests.

"No, no. He had been to Portugal. He was caught in England with a ticket for the Middle East."

"I don't remember reading that detail."

"Obviously," she says in a little-girl voice. He knows she's about to make another point. "You don't read the right things. I bet you're still hung up with all the news that fits. You ought to start reading some of the news that doesn't fit, that's unfit."

"Cindy, I'm sorry. I'm really sorry . . . What's happened, I'm sorry. I wish to hell we had more time. I mean not just a phone conversation but to sit down together and talk these things over. Like old times."

"Sure you do," she answers. "Mr. Big Shot on his way to Hong Kong calls up the old girlfriend just to show what a big success he is." The dog has continued to bark, a hollow sound as if he were in a room without rugs or furniture.

"That's not what—"

"Just zipping through town, changing planes, so there's no danger of a real meeting, a real commitment with just a phone call. Right?" Her voice has become hard though not completely firm. "I remember that's just like you, claim to want to do something in circumstances that prohibit its doing. You know how long it takes to get from O'Hare to where I am? Sometimes two hours. Fat chance, sitting down to talk things over between planes on your way to big deals. But let's give the old girl a call, cop a feel by way of Ma Bell. What am I, one of those sex-talk numbers?''

"Oh, please, please, Cindy. It's not that. That's not the reason I called, believe me.'' He hears his voice and knows he is sincere.

"Oh, yeah,'' she comes back dryly. "Why did you call me, then?''

"Well, I don't really know,'' he admits wearily, trying to be honest with himself, trying to remember what his reason had been. Then, inspiration struck. "Let's just say, 'The moving finger writes, and having writ, moves on.' ''

"The moving what?'' Her laughter screams painfully in his ear. "The moving finger? Say, you're the one that needs help, baby. You know what you can do with your moving finger!'' There's a crash in his ear and the line goes dead.

Over the sparkling Pacific, still following the sun, he figures he had been looking for some kind of fulcrum in Chicago on which to balance all his travels. He would have to look for it elsewhere, perhaps in a place so familiar that the location is temporarily out of mind.

Face in the Window

Each couple looked out on the landscape with perpetual delight, a molded expectancy that the feast would continue; some of them, half-reclining on elbows, even held out cups for the wine yet to be pressed from hillside vineyards across the way, beyond their reach. Just out of reach. Professor Cantwell turned the jest over in his mind, a lozenge of an allusion—or was that illusion—to taste the flavor of something shared with the terra-cotta couples atop their funeral urns.

Dozens of them, and dozens more in the exhibits within, but in this outside room of the museum, the figures of men and women seemed to rise from their hard ceramic divans with a joyous abandon that must have had something to do with the light that came through the glass wall of the room. A light, he further contemplated, composed of the same combinations of minerals and elements, of earth and sky, that yielded the sharp, uncomplicated quality of Tuscan wines.

Two days ago, in Arezzo, he had tried to explain this crystallike illumination to his group as they stood before Piero della Francesca's frescoes. "A light exploited," he could remember saying, "as if it were invading the earth." And he had looked over their bland disinterest to find her, to see if the idea might have penetrated that sober expression which set her apart from the rest. Cantwell looked around the museum now, wondering if the peculiar telepathy that had just passed between him and the Etruscan statues had also echoed in her mind, like a footfall in the distant passageway of a shopping mall—one of those in Miami, where this student group had come from.

"Per favore, signorina—non toccare." The museum guard had located her for him. Her pose was ambiguous and Cantwell could not tell whether she actually had tried to pick up the ancient alabaster comb or had only got too close to the exhibit. The fingers of one hand were extended but her face had wrinkled; a sure indication that the comb would just not do anyway, would not set right in the thick coils of her blond hair. Not for the first time, he noted her nails bitten down to the quick. He could do something about that, too, he thought.

Only last night he had begun another kind of restoration. As · he prepared a light supper for himself in the small apartment of the villa, his tongue had curled around the syllables of her name, giving each its proper sound and flow. Virginia Ponte-fi-Ore. Bridge of flowers. Ponte-fi-Ore. He had arranged some prosciutto, some Pecorino, a slice of melon on a plate and uncorked the half-full bottle of the villa's Chianti to pour a generous amount into a heavy tumbler. Ponte-fi-Ore. It was almost a toast launched into the night air outside the window, but his whisper bounced back loudly and mangled.

"Pontifore. Let's go, Pontee-four!" her companions called. The village of Radda was a short walk, and two bars offered a minimal nightlife. Several this morning had boasted of getting "sloshed" the night before. "Get your pants on, Pontee-four, and let's go." Cantwell leaned far out from the window, expecting to see the nimbus of her hair, but the garden below was pitch-dark. Across the valley, steep vineyards were yet caught in the brilliance of the western light. The chiaroscuro effect of the scene struck him: the darkness of the villa's garden beneath the diamond-hard light on the distant hillsides. He had tried to share a similar revelation the day before in the Uffizi, even suggest a significance to those who called to her in the garden. They had feigned attention when he talked of the master's technique with light and shade, and, when he had turned to the Caravaggio to make a point, he could hear the rustle of their boredom.

Actually, none of them knew how to pronounce their names correctly. Cantwell assumed part of his job was to remove their American corruptions and to return them to the pure Italian. Miss Mo-*li*-no, for example had just put one arm around Ponte-fi-Ore's waist as the two young women walked out to the museum's balcony, unconsciously taking the same comradely pose as that fixed into the fired clay pieces around them two thousand years ago.

The blonde's trim midriff was exposed between the top of her designer cutoff jeans and the man's shirt tied off beneath her breasts. The two students went on tiptoe at the balcony's parapet to look down on the plain where Sulla's armies were held at bay for nearly two years in 80 B.C. It was a view not without charm for Cantwell, this ancient Villanovan landscape, and it seemed equally appreciated by the thick-necked young man who played the fool for Virginia Pontefiore and her court of sub-debs.

"Look here, Professor," this boy had said to him during their visit to Siena. "My name is John Bargello—not Bargie-jello or whatever." They had gathered in the Campo, near the Palazza Pubblico. Some of them giggled, but Cantwell gratefully noted the blonde's serious expression. "And this here is Patty Mollino and not—"

"But your parents have sent you over here, Mr. Bargello—paid good money to put you in touch with your heritage. How you pronounce your name in Florida is one thing, but yesterday in Firenze, didn't it do something to you to see that whole museum with your family name on it? Museo de Bargello. Didn't that give you a bit of a kick?" The young man had reddened and looked down at the pigeons strutting about their feet. An easy win, Cantwell thought, but keeping Virginia in his side vision, he continued. "In fact, even here in Siena, just up there on the left, is a street with your name—Chiasso del Bargello. You're part of this history. All of you are."

The idea had braked the derision coasting through them

and put an odd thoughtfulness on their faces, though Cantwell suspected that what he saw might also be the sudden recognition of a betrayal—this summer trip abroad promised by their parents was turning out to be more like school, something worthwhile that had to be studied and on which they were to be graded. But after all, Semester Abroad was properly accredited and hired people like him, an established authority with books in the collection of the Library of Congress and a regular contributor to journals—even a piece once in *The New York Times*—so what were they to expect?

"So what does it mean, his name? Does it mean something in English?" Her level voice carried the quiet assurance of the group's leader. She stood front center, flanked as always by Mo-*li*-no on one side and, on the other, by a student named Capi-*tell*-li who wore much too much eye shadow. Pontefiore's blond fall of hair coiled over her right shoulder as her head took that peculiar crook so favored by Botticelli. "What does it mean?" she repeated.

"It could be roughly translated as 'sheriff,' for which there is no real Italian." He spoke quickly against their laughter. "Sheriff comes from the Arabic, brought back from the Crusades, so this is not the sheriff we know from John Wayne movies, but a kind of warden." He sketched the power divisions of the late medieval era. A few of them on the fringe began to bargain with an African street vendor. Their attention was melting like newsprint in the rain, so he spoke directly to her, spoke into the intensity of the gray eyes fixed upon him. He wondered if she were myopic, if she could really see him or only a vague outline of him. If he could just get through to her, the group would be his.

Meanwhile, young Bargello seemed ready to burst the knitted confines of his Lacoste shirt, and a companion thumped the solid mass of his back. "What time does the next stage leave, Sheriff?" The explosion of laughter spooked the pigeons, and they rose as one in a chandelle above the towers of the old city hall. Cantwell's imagination was similarly transferred: a bird's-eye view of them all standing in the saucer of the Campo, Bargello in the center and singled out by the sudden and unsuspected significance of his name. He felt a little sorry for the boy; on the other hand, it had been a handy demonstration of the power of language. Cantwell sought out Pontefiore and was a little taken aback by her serious, flat gaze. Her pose had not altered, but he saw a shift of something in the gray eyes, like light moving under a cloud, and it was an effect he was hesitant to interpret.

Their return from Volterra was seeming to take longer than the morning's drive over, which had also included a lunch stop at a country trattoria where Cantwell had been surprised by the unabashed vigor of a Montecarlo *bianco*. This slower pace back to the villa was because the bus driver's attention was distracted by a couple of the women students who talked to him from the front seats. He could not take the bends and curves in the road with the same swinging elan as before, because they plied him with endless questions on the nature and function of the different switches that stuck out from the instrument panel. "Hey, Raphie-jello . . . *como dice* this? . . . *Como usaro* that? . . . *Permesso*, Raphie, impusho that? . . . *Spingi*, like this . . . *Spingi, spingi?*"

The play of their lacquered voices accompanied the diesel hum of the bus nicely, and Professor Cantwell relaxed into a pleasant reverie. Someone in the rear played with alabaster eggs, always a feature of the Volterra tourist shops, and their soft collisions sounded the depth of his satisfaction. The young women's persistent teasing of the bus driver would have amused Henry James, he reflected; a sort of revenge on behalf of Daisy Miller, one might say. Cantwell often thought this sturdy generation of American women, if not heiresses, at least possessed riches that could yet dazzle the European sensibility, and, curiously, most had sprung from the common ground of an immigrant ancestry, fully armed though sometimes vulgarly arrayed. But this last matter could be easily corrected with a few deft insights, a provocative preface or two.

Virginia Pontefiore sat in the aisle seat just ahead and across from him, so he could only see the shell of one ear set within blond curls and down the bare length of her left leg. She and her brace of companions apparently had also fallen asleep. Cantwell mused on the possible meaning that had filtered through those gray eyes that afternoon in Siena, the light that had warmed their usual impartial stare.

Then, today, at the museum in Volterra, she had turned away from her friends as they leaned over the balcony and had looked through the glass wall, back into the exhibit room as if she might be trying to locate him among the terra-cotta couples. Casually, and perhaps using the glass wall as a mirror, she undid the shirttails at her waist and then looped them together again, pulled them tighter and higher and more snug.

Moreover, the tortelloni at lunch had been of a splendid texture—the whole day had been *moltissimo soddisfacente*—and he settled more comfortably into his seat. He let the twists and turns of each kilometer refine his sense of well-being, but then his thoughts were jolted by the image of Ms. Randall, like a sudden pothole in the road. She had brought this batch of students up from Rome, and her intrusion into his comfortable reverie, if nothing more, was like the appearance of one of those dual divinities that represented both good and evil. An idea originating in Asia, wasn't it, even found in the Mayan cultures of Central America who had come from Asia, and weren't the Etruscans supposed to have come from Asia Minor?

In any event, Ms. Randall introduced herself as the assistant director of the institute. Cantwell never bothered with titles; moreover, the references she made to her own degrees were not all that impressive. Nevertheless, he had shared the last of his Campari with her in the villa's garden as the students unpacked and boisterously explored the fourteenth-century farm building that had been made into a dormitory.

"I heard this was quite a setup," she said, and looked out at the view. On the peaks of the surrounding hills, rosy tile roofs of villages much like Radda softened in the warm light of late afternoon. The cross-stitched pattern of the Chianti vineyards turned the panorama into a large quilt, flattened out and almost childlike in execution, but strangely complex too.

"My own pet theory," he leaned forward to share his observation, "is that Simone Martini and Ambrogio Lorenzetti and the rest of that gang were only painting what they saw. They knew about perspective but they painted the landscape the way it looks. Just like that." The ice in his drink subtly scored the point his gesture made. He had watched her to monitor her response, then he tried saying it differently. "I mean they weren't so primitive as we may think, but actually were realists." The small joke had gone over her head, floated out over the ageless contours of Tuscany and disappeared into the azure of an unblemished sky.

"We've had a few complaints," she said.

"Complaints?"

"Well, not exactly complaints." She looked worriedly at him and then went on. "Some parents have written that you're too . . . " She paused once more as if to flip through some portable thesaurus in her head. "Well, I guess the word for it is—too intellectual."

"Too intellectual?" Cantwell was flabbergasted. The woman did have the good grace to join his indignant amusement.

"I know it's crazy, Ben—if I may call you that. The program has been especially proud to have you on its staff. You're an authority. You're famous. Your name really means something on all our brochures and literature, but we have to remember that the families that fund these programs—whether they be Italian, German or even of French ancestry—are rather conventional people. True-blue Americans, you know?" This time she leaned forward. "Most of them send their kids over here just to get them out of the way for a summer. They're not looking for anything uplifting. You see the kind of students they are. Did you ever have people like this where you taught at the university?"

"That was quite different," Cantwell replied, and looked into his drink. Her casual usage of the past tense had riled him a bit. After all he had been offered an adjunct position and could still be a part of that faculty. But he had chosen the institute's offer, and at some cost. One more division, his son had said; but this time the distance of Europe to go along with the rest.

"But here's the picture, Ben." Again, she leaned forward

like a coach explaining a play during a time-out. "You can imagine the kind of school reports the parents of these kids get during the year. Pretty depressing, you know? So, they hope for something a little more cheerful, maybe even a little optimistic, from Semester Abroad. And then your grade sheets come in with some extra remarks on the side, and it's all very disappointing for them. So, they think twice about the next time around. . . . Our profile research indicates they have 3.5 kids per household. Do you follow me?"

Cantwell did indeed follow her, to the end of something that had been very pleasant, the ideal solution to his early retirement from the university, and an alternative to the ordinary domain of family visits, the obligatory Thanksgiving turkey dinner. He sipped his Campari, tasting its bitterness.

"Hey!" A shout came from the dormitory on the other side of the hedge. "Where's the nearest Pizza Hut?" It had been a spoiled surly voice that he would come to know all too well.

"Hey, Professor." This same voice pulled him up through the drone of the tour bus. Like a balloon blown up to its limit, the fat, smooth face of John Bargello lifted above the seat before him. "You were saying back there that these Etruscans were bird watchers?"

"That's what we think." His answer snapped out a little too smartly. He took a breath. "We know very little about the Etruscans. Their language has yet to be deciphered. As I remember saying at the museum," the pause made apology for the repetition, "we think they were from Asia Minor—so said Livy, anyway—and these civilizations went in for animism and so forth. Yes, they observed birds to divine the future."

The young man's expression had become strangely concentrated, a peculiar seriousness that alarmed Cantwell. He feared the swing and sway of the bus had nauseated the boy and he was about to throw up on him. But like a computer screen clicking on, Bargello blinked and smiled. "Hey, how about that statue we saw at the museum named after me—that one with the lady doing it with the bird?"

"Johnnie . . . " his unseen seat companion scolded, and

snickered. Cantwell recognized the nasal tones of Patty Molino.

" 'Leda and the Swan,' you mean?"

"Yeah, that one with the swan. I guess she was doing some kind of di-vi-nation."

"You could say that," Cantwell replied. He had to smile over the crude epiphany.

Encouraged by this insight, Bargello leaned farther over the seat back. "And that painter you showed us in Florence—this Uccello guy. That also means bird in Italian. Right, Professor?"

"Yes, *uccello* is also the word for bird."

"Yeah, bird, that's right."

"Johnnie . . . !" Molino cautioned once more, and this time apparently punched his side, for Bargello twisted away and looked down.

"Cool it, Moo-*lee*-no, the professor and I are having a discussion. So, *uccello* means bird." His breath was sweet and sour all at once. "Does it mean anything else?"

"Johnnie!" the girl pleaded, and smothered her laugh.

"You know, like *fica*?"

"You mean fig? *Fico*?"

"No, I mean *fica* as in—" A scarlet-taloned hand appeared to close the boy's mouth and pull him down and out of sight like a puppet. Cantwell turned a deaf ear to the choking laughter from the seats in front and looked at the student sitting next to him. She was sleeping, as most of the rest seemed to be doing save for whoever still chucked the alabaster eggs together in the rear. The sound made a curious asymmetrical measurement of the moment.

Then Virginia Pontefiore abruptly sat up and turned around to face him. Her arms raised as her hands sought, found and repinned a miscreant lock of her hair. Cantwell recognized the pose as one that had beguiled painters and sculptors since time began. The student's eyes rested upon him, took him in with an ageless discernment. A clear message was being sent, he felt, to convey her distinction from her companions as surely as her sleep had been feigned to set her apart from Bargello's clumsy attempt to provoke him. For she had heard everything, Cantwell was convinced.

165

"Hey, Virginia," the young man rasped. "We've been talking about *uccellos* and *ficas*. Divine stuff, you know?"

On the return to the villa, Cantwell found the mail slipped under the door of his apartment, and included in it was the elegantly scripted invitation, in Italian, from Professore Leonardi to join him in the garden before dinner for an *aperitivo*. This austere academic from the University of Bologna, hired to teach the language of Dante and Petrarch to these American students, often expressed his scorn for their shallow interests and lack of seriousness. In his present mood, to share a Punt-E-Mes with the man suited Cantwell to a T.

The two teachers spoke Italian as they lounged in an arbored recess of the *fattoria*'s formal garden. Cantwell laughed from time to time as he vainly attempted to match his colleague's rhetorical fancies, which seemed inspired this evening by the exotic topiary of the manicured hedges and shrubbery that surrounded them. The design of the garden was so elaborate, so intricately mazed, that there were parts of it Cantwell had not been in and, moreover, was just a little wary of exploring. From time to time, both their conversation and the enclosing vegetation were assaulted by the sudden blasts of rock music from somewhere beyond their retreat. Finally, he shrugged and looked with apology toward his colleague, and tried to remember a line from Virgil about youth's wasteful clamor, but the line wouldn't come whole to him, so he said nothing.

To be fair, Cantwell often took the adversarial role in these discussions, if only to give them a liveliness and semblance of dialogue, but his attempts to explain the free-wheeling attitudes of American students only brought a Savonarola scorn to the other's face. *"Volgarità si mostra,"* Leonardi proclaimed and pointed his long nose into the vesper air. The rant became more complex, a discourse that touched all the lines of its classical model and that Cantwell could only follow in a general way.

He sought a little relief by making an inventory of the trellised roses, the groves of cypress that paralleled the garden walks, and then the Tuscan landscape beyond. He still held the unopened letter from his son, which he had hoped to read in the serenity of this setting, but Leonardi had been waiting for him, his aristocratic ire idling at fast throttle. The limestone balustrade around the top of the old manor house basked in the roseate fall of evening and the carved stone amphorae set along the rail looked ready to spill their stored refinements. Just below, on the top floor, the three windows of his apartment stood open. How often in past years had he loafed in one of them to watch the coverlet of dawn be pulled over a chilled landscape? He had never really looked at his windows from this side, this view, and he half-expected a face to poke out of one of them, not his face of course, but one of those curious witnesses that often appear in Renaissance paintings—a disinterested observer who might verify his presence in this place at sunset. But the windows remained empty and blank.

How foolish it had been to think he had tenure in this small paradise. Wasn't it the cruel nature of near-perfection to always hold itself away, to portion itself out? Surely, Ms. Randall had been sent from the gods to punish him for his hubris. It would be hard to give up such borrowed luxury, to put away the apparel of youth he had put on every summer, daring to think it was his to wear throughout the year, forever.

This villa the institute had chosen for a base was a working *fattoria* that produced one of the best Chianti classico of the region. A small rack of different vintages sat in his apartment, generously stocked by the vineyard's manager. The farm staff and their wives did double duty as gardeners and housekeepers for the institute, but the surly way they slopped down bowls of overcooked pasta on the long refectory tables made him wonder if they were paid extra. But they were Sardinians, not known for their generous natures or, for that matter, for the purity of their Italian, which only added to Professore Leonardi's frustrations. The American students could not employ at lunch even the simplest phrase he had drilled into them that morning, and the Sardinians became more darkly disturbed when shouted at and made to feel stupid by the ingenious sign language often created just under their noses. How Leonardi spoke to the help, Cantwell never figured out, but he guessed the man's classical precision somehow cowed them into comprehension. Indeed, his

167

fluency was self-sufficient, was its own auditor as now, and required ony an occasional nod from Cantwell, a *sì* or the more emphatic *veramente*, at clearly appointed intervals.

"*Certamente, mio collèga.*" Cantwell shifted in the iron chair and tried to raise a point, but made the mistake of pausing in order to find the correct form, "*ma non pensa . . .*" Leonardi was already clucking, like the mechanism of an old record player as a fresh roll of criticism started up.

Virginia Pontefiore and her two companions, Molino and Capitelli, had just appeared from an alley of high hedges. They paused by a huge marble birdbath and at this distance—out of earshot, that is—Cantwell could imagine them to be a fetching overture for a masque about to commence. Enter the Three Graces. Then, the two friends ran back into the maze, perhaps on Virginia's command, leaving her to gaze pensively at her own reflection in the marble saucer of water. Her head turned aside as if modesty forced her to disclaim the image she saw, and the gesture almost demanded Cantwell try once more with his colleague.

"*Ma non tutti, non tutti, mi amico. Alcuni studenti americani sono differente.*" Leonardi was unconvinced and cited some recent examples of New World stupidity.

Meanwhile Molino and Capitelli had returned, each pulling by a hand the not entirely reluctant figure of Ricardo, the son of the *fattoria*'s manager. Cantwell had seen his little white convertible pulled up under the olive trees outside the villa's walls when they returned from Volterra. The father often boasted of his son's success in business college, and the young man drove up from Florence on some weekends, often bringing a friend or two with him. Over the years, Cantwell had watched the boy grow, becoming taller and more a copy of his father's rough physique as his visits became even more dutiful during the summer months of the institute's session. At the moment, Ricardo was smiling somewhat fatuously in his captivity.

He was the focus of a curious procession, like an ancient frieze unfolding as more and more of the students ambled from behind the hedgerow, composing a happy disorder behind the captive Ricardo, while surrounding and making prisoners of his two friends. All were led by Virginia Pontefiore, and they paraded around the paths, doubling back from culs-de-sac and on into the cinquecènto intrigue of the garden's labyrinth. As Cantwell watched this spectacle, he became even more impatient with his colleague's remarks. The celebrants marked a rite of some sort; he had no doubt of it. Perhaps, they had left their childhoods on the other side of the hedge in a simpler garden not so artfully shaped and groomed as the park they enlivened now, and, as if a token had been needed for such a passage, one or two carried the kind of flashlights they must have used in camp only a year or two before. He was strangely moved to see that young Bargello skylarked with one of these.

Cantwell rolled the last of the Punt-E-Mes around in his mouth and let its sweetness seep through him. The procession disappeared behind the rose arbor, and its good-humored roistering became more and more faint. The light had gone to magenta and even Professore Leonardi seemed affected by the scene, for he had stilled his oration. *"Ma certamente,"* Cantwell raised one last defense. *"Certamente, alcuni studenti sono interessante. Per esèmpio, la signorina Pontefiore è una studentessa seria."*

"Chi?" Leonardi's profile cut the affluent air. His expression registered surprise, doubt and disbelief in that darkening order.

"Signorina Pontefiore," Cantwell repeated. *"La bionda."*

"Ah, sì, Pontefiore," the other replied. He paused as if to reassess the student. *"Sì, molto seria,"* he agreed, and his two hands cupped the air before his chest. *"Molto seria."*

The next day Cantwell waited for lunch, rereading his son's letter in a place near the edge of the garden that was isolated from the rest by a thick wall of privet. It was his favorite spot, for no one else came there, probably because of the deep shade cast on the lounge chairs by the hedge that rose up behind them. He had read the sentences of the letter carefully and then read some of them once again, hoping to come across something surprising in their straight, declarative composition—even a spot of humor. But the prose ran on evenly like a suburban lawn; flat and neat and with nothing untoward left carelessly in the context.

Things have been going well. The Rotary has seen
fit to entrust me with their destiny next year. Susan
is taking some accounting courses now that little
Ben is in nursery school. We had Mom over for a
cookout on Mother's Day. She seems in good spirits
and even brought a date. I hear Florence can be
damp and cold at Christmas. Any chance of seeing
you then?

A question at last, Cantwell thought, and refolded the letter
just as a fast-changing pattern of swifts flew over. If there had
been anything to be divined in the birds' flight he had lost the
knack of reading that as well, laughing at the idea, but then Ms.
Randall's omen had made all prophecies unintelligible. Too intellectual. Did he dare inquire about his future—even next
Christmas? He had made a career of making amusing allusions
and odd facts relevant to ordinary lives, trading curiosa and
pleasantries for his room and board. He was aware that this new
breed of student had little patience with his manner; the endur-
ance to receive any kind of knowledge had been somehow bred
out to leave them sleek and well groomed.

But the letter in his hand confounded him even more. How
had he failed this decent mind, this sensibility that hung up
commonplaces with all the neat success of a coiled garden hose
in a two-car garage? All these years he had been speaking in a
language no one understood, when only the simplest expression,
a conviction unqualified by any wit, would have been sufficient.
A breeze pushed through the close ranks of cypress and Cantwell
shivered a little. Perhaps he deserved to end his days communing
with statues in museums or stuck in the final circle—just to
chance one more reference—of Professore Leonardi's frigid discourse.

In fact, the man's students were just escaping his morning's
conjugations and, as they swarmed into the austere habitat of
the garden, their cries fed greedily on their own excitement. No
classes were scheduled on Saturday afternoons, so the Americans
could poke around the village on their own. But most would lie
about the villa's pool, working on their tans. Cantwell had been

170

thinking he'd drive over to Certaldo, where Boccaccio had lived, and where a respectable *pappardelle con lèpre* could be had at a thirteenth-century inn. But now he wasn't so sure. He might first write a letter to his son, a simple letter, and that might take the whole afternoon.

Voices startled him. They came from the other side of the thick hedge behind him and he was about to turn, to try to peer through the impenetrable screen of foliage when he recognized the offhand register of Virginia Pontefiore. "Hey, Ricardo . . . *come va?*"

"*Ciao*, Virginia." Some sleight of sound put the young man's voice directly into his ear, and Cantwell nearly jumped.

"Go ahead and ask him?" That was Molino speaking, he recognized the head tones.

"Ask him, Pontefor," a second voice urged. The trinity formed in Cantwell's imagination. "It was your idea."

"Ricardo . . . ?"

"*Sì, Virginia.*"

"*Desidiamo te do-man-dare . . .*"

". . . Ask me some-theeeng."

"*Sì . . .* ask your *o-pin-i-one . . .*"

"*Mi opinione . . .*"

"*D'acora . . .* Which of us has the nicest—*come se dice*—tits?"

"Tits?" The Italian was mystified.

"Virginia!" squealed Molino.

"Well, what's the word for them?" Pontefiore asked. "What do you call them in Italian?"

"Try . . . try *mama-mellones*," Capitelli suggested, and laughed.

"Tits?" the young Italian asked again. His puzzlement was almost heartbreaking, Cantwell thought.

"*Sì . . .* tits . . . *regardo.*" Clothing rustled. Breaths were caught. "*Queste*, Ricardo."

Cantwell strained to hear, pushed his ears to visualize the moment. A pine sighed above them. How long, he wondered, did it take the youth to make an identification? "Ah . . . *mammele . . . tettone.*"

"Okay, so it's *tettone*," Pontefiore responded flatly. "We want you to choose—which of us has the best? C'mon, you two, show the *tettones*."

A single bird darted over Cantwell's head and then over the hedge, so swift in its flight as to be blind to everything. In the profound stillness, he looked down at his sandaled feet and counted his toes. He had always been secretly proud of his feet; they had a kind of gnarled patrician quality that would have been appropriate to the stones of ancient Rome.

"*Fantastico!*" the young Italian finally exclaimed. "*Meraviglioso.*"

"*Regardo* Capitelli," Pontefiore directed. "*Regardo la luce* on hers."

"*La luce?*"

"*Sì* . . . the light." The girl's tone, her loft of delivery sounded familiar. "Regard the chiaroscuro effect here . . . and here. The modeling, as old Cantwell would say." Her laughter was abrupt and harsh. She had been always so solemn. "Now, observe, Mo-*li*-no, Ricardo . . . see the massing of the dynamic forms in the foreground. Now you must choose. Who's got the best? Il migliore."

Carefully, Cantwell put his feet onto the ground and raised himself from the lounge chair. He dared not wait for Ricardo's decision, which might be the wrong choice. It could mean war. He smiled at the idea—one last reference—and looked up at the three windows of his room, which looked blankly down at him and this landscape that had inspired so many visions and desires. All along, he had been a common witness and nothing more: one more face in a window.

The Sound of Pines

after Chekhov

A thick mist obscures the road as a black sedan with very heavy tires rounds the curve. Its headlights are burning. It is impossible to tell the time of day; whether it is afternoon or evening, or if the night has only just surrendered to the dawn. The two-lane road becomes straight and flat. The heavy fog hides billboards, fence posts, utility poles; anything that might give the car's occupants a sense of their journey. Only the regular *clump-clump* of the car's tires over the pavement's divisions suggests they are moving somewhere.

The man behind the wheel never speaks. All of his concentration may be required to keep the car on the narrow lane of cement that reveals itself, bit by bit, to the headlights just as wheels roll over it. The driver's torso is long and spare, and he bends over the steering wheel as if to present his sharp, large nose to the windshield.

The man beside him is quite different. He sits casually slouched against the front door of the car; the round ball of his head is placed on the plump column of his neck; even the nose, the ears, the mouth are formed as if drawn by a child's devotion to the concentric. He is the sort who always looks amused by something that has yet to happen; yet to be said. When he speaks, his voice bubbles with a raspy enthusiasm, sometimes talking to the driver but, for the most part, twisting sideways in his seat, confident in the driver's skill, in order to speak to the man in the backseat. A heavy metal grille separates them.

The man in the backseat is a prisoner as well as a passenger. The steel mesh converts the backseat into a cell, for there are no handles on the inside panel of the rear doors. The windows are sealed. The passenger is an ambiguous figure. Man or youth, it is difficult to tell. Student, soldier or vagrant; something of each makes his appearance. Pale hair falls around a small grayish face and, as he pulls at a scraggly beard with one hand, the manacles around his wrists click together.

He looks very frail within the thick material of the army overcoat, a contrast to its great bulk, and he wears large, high-topped shoes. No knapsack, no parcel or belongings rest beside him on the seat, and he has just managed to pull a package of cigarettes from one of the overcoat's pockets. With both hands, he shakes one out to fit it between his lips and, because of the handcuffs, he lights the cigarette with an almost comical difficulty.

"I guess we don't mind if you smoke, do we?" the round-faced officer asks the driver, who makes no response. "I gave it up a few years back, and his nibs here . . . well, he's a challenge. But I don't remember you asking, Slim," the policeman continues gaily, "but hell, go ahead." He twists to press his face to the window. "It's too bad you can't see this country we're passing through. Best damn dairy land in the state. Prime dairy land. Beautiful barns; great big beautiful barns and neat fences. And the cows? Why they're treated like movie stars. Mostly Holsteins. You know, the black-and-white ones. Their milk's not as rich as some others but they sure pour it out." He turns to his partner and laughs. "That's what I'm going to do when I retire. I'm going to get me a little milking herd."

The car becomes silent but for the measured thumps of its passage. The jolly officer looks back through the steel mesh slowly, as if some wonderful idea is coming to him. "It's just too damn bad you can't see those farms out there in the fog. Talk about beautiful. Course, farmers around here get more for their milk than in the Connecticut milkshed, across the border. Just over there. Never did understand how that works, that market business." He carefully inserts the tip of a small finger into one ear, twists and withdraws the finger and inspects it closely.

He looks as if he is waiting for the prisoner to speak, to comment on dairy prices. But the man remains silent, inhales the smoke from the cigarette and stares at the opaque surface of the window. His lips barely mark his pale face, like an after-thought hurriedly sketched in because it is normal to have a mouth there.

"Aw, c'mon," the round man continues with a soft intimacy, "tell us who you are. Won't you tell us who you are?" The gentle nature of the request brings a smile to the young man's lips and he laughs soundlessly. "You know once we get to town," the policeman continues, "all we got to do is put your prints on the computer and we'll find out everything. What? No prints? Can you believe that?" the plump officer asked his partner. "He says he's got no prints on file. Hell, everybody's got prints on file somewhere. Even the two of us are on file, ain't we?" He chuckles.

The driver does not respond but grasps the wheel as if to flex his muscles to better propel the black sedan through the mist and toward an evasive point in the road ahead, a point made by the two lines laid down by his eyes and a third from the long blade of his nose.

"Well, don't worry about it," the round officer continues cheerfully. He tips back the gray fedora to show a pink baldness. "We got all kinds of machines. You'd be surprised at the equipment we got these days. Those farmers out there with all their tractors and fancy milking machines; they got nothing on us, believe me. Why, we got one device, it takes your picture and sends it out on the telephone, all in a minute. Every department in the country will have your picture in a minute. New York City. Providence. Hartford. Poughkeepsie." He has paused after each city's name, intoned them like an old-fashioned train conductor announcing destinations or departures, and looked at the man in the backseat as if expecting him to claim one of them.

175

"Anywhere and everywhere. They all wire back, prints or no prints, that it's you, Slim. They'll tell us, all in a minute, who you are.

"After all, what the hell do we care, eh?" His face is fixed in amiability. "We can hold you for a long time, long enough until something turns up. Maybe a little rest will help the old memory, eh? 'Cause there's more than just the vagrancy count and the hitchhiking, you understand? That's just minor stuff. Misdemeanors. Right? They'd get you a warm cell and a good hot meal. Sure, that's nothing. But that corncob pipe we took off of you; now that could be serious. That might mean real trouble for you, Slim. Some might misconstrue that for possession of an instrument, don't you know?" He pauses to look at his partner for confirmation, then looks back through the steel grille. He winks. "Also, we've had a lot of summer cabins broke into around here. Rich folks come up from the city on weekends and they find their little hideaways broke into. We have to look after them. Taxpayers, you know? Put that together with one or two fires of suspicious origin and you're just in a whole lot of trouble, Slim. Well, it all takes time to investigate. You understand?" His manner is at ease, his voice familiar. Then he turns to his partner. "What's up?"

The car has begun to slow down; the monotonous hum of their journey has changed. Without speaking, the driver uncurls one index finger from the steering wheel and points it toward a yellowish glow in the mist ahead. The outline of a gas station slowly materializes.

"Good idea," the round man says. "I could stretch my legs a bit and I guess we could all use some coffee." With only a slight turn of the wheel, as if he has steered the car with his nose, the driver eases the black sedan off the highway, over a small shoulder and into the station's service bay. The station is either closed or abandoned. The attendant may have gone home for supper or lunch, perhaps has not come to work yet. The car pulls up before a metal unit the size and shape of a large filing cabinet. HIGHWAY CANTEEN. The letters are lit from within and are of plastic the color of cheap mustard.

The car's front doors open and the two policemen get out

slowly. It is a languid, almost practiced motion, as if they were actors stepping onto a rehearsal stage before cameras hidden in the heavy mist. They hesitate, look at each other across the top of the black sedan, and the taller one, the driver, shrugs and walks toward the refreshment stand. The round one opens the rear door of the car and reaches inside.

"Come on out and stretch your legs, Slim," he says. The prisoner is pulled out by the chain that links his wrists together. When he puts one foot on the pavement the other one catches inside the door frame, and he stumbles. The officer holds him up by the handcuffs, and they resemble a circus act: a trainer holding up an animal that is not accustomed to walking on its hind legs.

The young man is very tall, even taller than the driver, but the olive-green overcoat is far too large for him in the shoulders, and the belt has been tied around the waist rather than buckled. A small blond head emerges from the exaggerated shoulders, and the huge bulky shoes stick out like small satchels from beneath the coat's hem. He staggers slightly on the pavement, the movement of a carnival clown diverting an audience while the center ring is being prepared for the main attraction.

"Okay, Slim, it's my treat," says the round-faced officer. His partner already holds a steaming cup of something beneath the long, pointed nose, and the man's eyes now focus on the prisoner. "Let's see what we got here," the jolly officer says, jiggling the change in his pocket. "Hey, they got pound cake. Not like home, but it's okay. You hungry, Slim? How about crackers and cheese? No? Well, I can't blame you for that. Pretty stale, I'd guess. Something to drink? Coffee. Hot chocolate. Tea?"

"Orange juice," the prisoner says.

"Orange juice it is," the officer replies casually, and inserts the coins. He showed no surprise when the prisoner spoke, and the young man's request seemed to be part of a long conversation the two have been having. But the tall policeman lowers his eyes and looks away into the mist. "Of course, you know, it's not real orange juice," the plump officer apologizes. He carries the full cup of colored liquid and serves it carefully to the prisoner, fits it between the man's manacled hands, and watches him raise it to his lips and drink as if curious to see how the trick is to be performed. Then he returns to the machine, puts in more coins and punches out some coffee for himself.

"No, sir," he talks to his partner. "It's almost impossible to get real orange juice nowadays. Except from someplace like Florida. Or a place like California. Or maybe Florida. Now you take California. Way out west. I guess you were headed that way, Slim? Sure, I thought so." The prisoner has nodded, then quickly sips from the cup held in both hands. He resembles a giant squirrel feeding.

"Boy, that's the life," the round officer continues. "All the way to Cal-i-for-nee-aye with a banjo on my knee. Except you don't have a banjo, Slim. You got nothing but that corncob pipe. You're the first one we've picked up without a banjo or a guitar. Hell, not even a harmonica. How come? Well, no matter. Go West, young man—go West. Right? That's what old Mark Twain said."

"Horace Greeley," the prisoner says.

"Horace what?"

"Horace Greeley was supposed to have said that," the young man says. "That's what I think, Horace Greeley."

"Well, here I thought it was Mark Twain. I guess you've read all the books and so you're probably right." The officer sips his coffee. No traffic sounds in any direction, nor can the far side of the highway be seen. Some mechanical apparatus within the station turns over briefly, then clicks off, as if it monitors the scene on the ramp outside.

"Say you get there, to California, all in one piece, Slim," the man continues amiably. "What were you going to do out there? What can you do, Slim?" The circles of the man's face have hardened, about to change into more angular shapes. But his voice remains calm and relaxed. "What were you going to do? How were you going to live?"

"Plant trees," the prisoner replies. He has raised his chalky face in a gesture that is nearly defiant. The skin around his eyes has tightened; he looks ready to flinch from a blow yet to be struck.

178

"Plant trees?" the round officer says with genuine amazement. His face is soft once again. His eyes gleam like those of a popular salesman about to hear an old joke for the tenth time.

"Sure," the prisoner says, finishing his drink. He walks to the over-full trash barrel and carefully places his empty cup onto the peak of the garbage. "A bunch of people I know are already there. There's these old mining camps that nobody wants. Nobody's lived in them for years. There's houses and old store buildings and everything just standing around empty. They're kind of falling down, but they can be fixed up. The land's too rocky for farming, but you can plant trees."

"And where do these trees come from that you plant, Slim?"

"From the government." Now he seems unable to stop talking. "The state government sells them to you cheap. Only a few bucks per thousand. Then, the state gives you a long-term lease on the land, if you plant the trees—sometimes as long as ninety-nine years." He has run out of breath, laughs eagerly, then continues. "Ninety-nine years. Think of that. That's more than enough time. And it's almost like you get the trees for nothing, too. Just a few bucks per thousand."

"Now that's California for you," the round officer tells his partner. "They sell you trees for just a few bucks per thousand."

"Well, they're actually not trees," the youth says. "They're just—"

"Just a minute. You said they were trees." The policeman's voice is flat, matter of fact. "Didn't he say they were trees?" he asks his partner. "You heard him too? Yeah, I thought that's what I heard. You said they were trees, Slim. A few bucks per thousand, you said. Are they trees or not?"

"Trees. They're trees," the prisoner replies, and he holds out his manacled hands. "But they're little trees. Very little trees. Seedlings. Like this . . ." And he bends over, nearly doubles, to measure off a small height from the paved bay.

"Well, what are you going to eat? You can't eat those trees, no matter what size they are." The man chuckles and scuffs his heels against the cement.

"Oh, all kinds of stuff that we raise. You can plant gardens, even corn. All sorts of greens, cabbages. Tomatoes. Yes, cabbages and tomatoes."

"It's hard to get a good tomato these days," the officer says. His partner has tipped his cup for a last swallow of coffee. "I remember the old tomatoes you'd get, the juice would leave acid tracks down your cheeks."

"Like that. Like that," the youth continues. "That's what we'd eat. Then, there's the mountain streams. They were used for the mines, to pan the gold, but now they're full of fish. Trout. Salmon. Bass." He looks at them both as if expecting a response. The portly officer looks interested.

"Lots of fish," he says finally.

"Oh, just a lot of fish," the prisoner says, and nods. "More than you can catch. I hear you just put down a line, put down a line with several hooks and every one of them comes up with a rainbow trout on it. You don't even need bait, they say."

"Just drop the line in the stream and pull it out," the policeman says.

"Yes, just like that," the prisoner agrees. "That's what I've heard."

"Think of it," the officer says, "and all the time, these trees keep growing. All those pine trees you've planted." He pauses and cocks his head as if he's just heard something in the mist, some sound so soft it cannot be caught up. It could be almost anything. "What a life," he says seriously. "Mountain air. Fresh vegetables from your own garden. Real tomatoes and maybe some turnips too. It's good to have fresh turnips by Labor Day." He closes his eyes and takes a deep breath. "Trout just out of the water and frying in the pan. I bet they would jump into the pan by themselves. All you have to do is wake up, start a fire and just hold your frying pan out. Plop, here they come." He runs his tongue over his lips. "And the water in those streams: clear and pure. Cool. You can drink it right as it runs, it's so clean. All the while those trees are growing and growing." He sighs. "Then, you'd keep a couple of cows too."

"Goats," the youth replies. "The pasture's only good for goats."

The mechanism inside the station turns on again and then

off. "What was that?" the officer said. "Goats? You said goats?" His eyes blink as if he's waking from a dream. He looks at his prisoner.

"Sure," the youth says, and tries to smile.

"Well, that just about hangs it up," the policeman says. "That really just hangs it up. Here we are in the prime dairy land of the state, generations of blue-ribbon Holsteins, and this yo-yo talks about goats."

"Wait . . . wait a minute." The prisoner's gesture is doubled by the manacles on his wrists but it is no more effective. "It's not that I don't like cows. I like cows. It's just that the land, you see, is not so good . . . can only—" But he doesn't get a chance to finish before he is hurried back to the car, bent double and shoved into the backseat. The fat policeman slams the car door shut.

"Goats," he says, and shakes his head as if this were the confession the police had been waiting for, the offense for which the prisoner can be charged.

The driver has already taken up his oblique position behind the wheel. The key is turned and the engine starts, and he grips the wheel as his shoulders take up their sharp angle to the front of the car. The round officer slips into the seat next to him, shuts the door and looks squarely ahead.

"What a lot of crap," the driver says as the car pulls away. The engine picks up speed, and the heavy tires whisper to the gray pavement. The transmission passes smoothly through the gear ratios but the car seems to make no progress down the highway, almost suspended in the mist. Then, it is gone.

The Catch

The day's catch had been put down, nose to tail across the entire floor of the foyer—on newspapers, Williams was quick to note, so that he and his wife had to step carefully around and between the fish like hikers who had come to a peculiar ford of a stream. What looked to be the glistening surfaces of rocks turned out to be the soft sides of salmon and trout.

"What on earth!" Janice Williams exclaimed.

"On earth is right," Williams replied. "How is all this to be cooked?"

From the far side of the room, in the alcove of the reception, the director of the lodge waved to them. "Come ahead. Step through, step through," the man cried gaily. "They won't bite, in fact—"

"—they've already bitten," Rick Williams finished the joke under his breath and his wife nudged him. The inn manager's manner had rubbed him the wrong way from the day of their arrival in Leenane. "Looking up the old connections, are you?" the man had said to Williams as they registered. Nothing in the name Richard Williams sounded Irish; yet the manager's question had neatly caught the purpose of their visit to this small village on Killary Bay in Galway. What's more, he was to advise his wife later, the guy wasn't even Irish but had one of those tricked-up English accents like an actor in an old movie, someone playing a butler. This was always the case, he told her, the English had done well here.

"The gentlemen have had some little success," this butler-turned-hotel-manager was saying. A peal of fellowship sounded in the tap room and glasses knocked cozily against solid wood.

"But what's to become of all this?" They were looking back now on the expanse of dead fish they had just traversed. Something biblical about it, Williams thought. "You can't possibly serve up all of this for dinner."

"Oh my, no." Their host laughed lightly. "We'll send most over to the hospital and nursing home at the Cross. Give much of it away to the natives here. Did you have a good day? Find any relatives?"

"I'm going up for a bath," Janice Williams said quickly.

"Wouldn't you like to have a drink?" Another gust of laughter blew in from the tap room.

"No, I think not," Williams replied, and took their room key from Mr. Gibbons. Williams enjoyed leaving the expectant look on the man's face, leaving his questions unaddressed and ignored. He knew his wife had wanted some time to herself, to be without him for just a little, but he had felt awkward all day, out of place where he had hoped a part of him would fit, and the fraternal order of fishermen holding forth in the bar would surely define this sense of strangeness even more.

So, when they reached their room, he went to the large window set into a recess that overlooked the road and the head of the estuary. He would be out of her way. Yet, as he looked down the long stretch of water that was Killary Bay, he was able to monitor the subtle sounds of her undressing, the discreet movements from bed to closet and back to traveling case, and then the click of a metal clasp. He tried to associate each sound with some interval in her bath preparation, visualize how she might look at each interval, for unlike most men at this stage of a marriage, or so he thought, he still took great pleasure, even pride, in his wife's appearance. She worked hard at it, he would give her that, so even with three children and the dents of middle age, she had somehow preserved the girl-athlete quality that had first appealed to him from across the net at her parents' place on Cape Cod.

"That was sort of interesting today, wasn't it?" He heard her shoes being arranged on the closet floor. He pictured the sensible walking brogues lined up even-toed in much the same way they had been positioned earlier in the day on the crude planks of the cottage floor.

"Yes." Her voice came back breathily from the chore. "And I wonder why you think it strange that people see you as Irish. Every man in that place today looked like you."

"Do you think so?" he asked, only to make up the dialogue, because he had to agree. If not like him, certainly like his grandfather, his mother's father. Every one of the old men who had passed through the large single room of the farmhouse had turned toward him the same large ears that had been his grandfather's, as if to bring him into focus, if not see him better. Was this Petey John O'Brean's grandson, to be sure? Surely, he has the O'Brean eye to him.

"Ah, Dickie-boy," his grandfather would say. "The salmon come out of the waters in Leenane with the knife and fork already in them, ready to go. You'll never see water so clean and so pure as the streams come down with. As a boy, I would catch a trout for supper on my way home from school. Then, I'd have a swim in the bay, cold as it was. We never lacked for anything, what little the English left us, that is." The old voice, even older in his memory, spoke to him as he and his wife sat by the high, open hearth of the cottage in the upper part of the village. Tea and some very hard scones had been given them. A large hound, gnawing cold potatoes, lay on the apron of a fireplace that smoked with burning turf. The aroma of the peat was rather pleasant, and, for a couple of hours, men and women came through the open door to meet and talk to him with a stiff formality, like people in the early hours of a wake. Even their clothes looked stiff, as if just unbent from boxes that kept them for these occasions. Many referred him to nephews or cousins in Buffalo or St. Louis or Brooklyn, and Williams dutifully took down names and addresses in the small notebook he carried. "No finer people," the old voice continued in his head, "deceived and as betrayed as we have been."

Also, the whole interlude had gone pleasantly, largely due to the direct, offhand way Janice always had with strangers, which quickly made her a part of any group. At once, she had started to chat with these Irish country women as if they had been her old classmates from Sarah Lawrence. He could hear them, as he answered questions about his grandfather and about the Kennedy brothers, talking of their children, the prices of things and the value of a good cup of tea. In her ensemble of tweed and cashmere, a hint of gold about her, she looked dressed for a scene in a play by Philip Barrie rather than Synge; yet her tasteful attire seemed to stimulate this instant intimacy, as if the casual elegance she had brought into this smoky, low-ceilinged room was something these farm wives were meant to share, at least momentarily.

Through the open doorway of the farmhouse—he couldn't remember seeing a door on hinges—he could sight the length of the bay as it came up from the North Atlantic. Steep hills came down to the shoreline on both sides to make the estuary look even more severe. The Vikings had rowed their long ships up this narrow waterway, his grandfather had told him, and next came weary Spaniards from the wrecked Armada. "The English had been there for some time," the old man would say. "We never really had it to ourselves, you know. Not even a front door on the place to keep the wind out. Not even a front door," the ancient voice repeated. Or had he been making that last part up as he sat there, a harangue that became almost comical?

From their room window, Killary Bay offered a more gentle nature, the view athwart its headwaters, as the hazy light of the oncoming evening softened the bare sides of the hills on the far shoreline. The hard definitions of the whitewashed stone of the farmhouses, like the one they had visited, became blurred, while their thatched roofs merged with the landscape, going back to the vegetation from which they had been made.

A small car had just pulled off to the water side of the road that passed before the lodge. Three men got out and stood for a moment, looking down the bay. Williams idly fancied they might be reviewing the history as he had been doing, maybe telling the same stories that had been told over and over on that back porch in Ohio. One was older than the other two, who were alike in youth and the dark fall of hair over pale foreheads. A father and his sons, Williams figured, pausing to admire the vista and to recount the glorious defeats of Ireland that he had heard of so many times, and—come to think of it—at just this time of day. Then all three began to remove their clothes; vests, jackets, shirts, trousers; all were pulled off in a companionable scramble beside the car, with joshing and jostle, like three brothers, he thought, rather than a father and sons.

"I was hoping we'd hear from ol' Steverino," he said. His wife said nothing. A clothes hanger scraped across the closet rod. "I mean, he has our itinerary. I expected something from him in Dublin."

"You must simply get off the boy's back." Her voice sounded a little distracted, as if she might be looking for some last item to take with her into the bathroom. "He'll write when he has something to say." She padded behind him on bare feet. "To write to us about nothing only increases his embarrassment."

"Why should he feel embarrassed?" Outside, the men were down to their underwear and were removing shoes and socks. Long white shorts came down to their knees, and they looked ready for a sport no longer played. "Embarrassed just to say hello, how's it going?"

"Because, dear heart"—her voice rounded the tile walls of the bathroom—"he has these high standards set for him by his father."

"But I never—"

"No, of course not. You don't have to. It's just there." Now she sounded angry, though it might have been the bathwater, which gushed furiously. "Must we go through all this again? Right now? Go down and have a drink and let me have a quiet soak."

The three men walked abreast down the small slope to the water's edge and, with no hesitation, plunged into the water like boys playing hookey. "Go on, now, Rick. Wait for me downstairs. You'll be more comfortable." His preference for being with her was only another example of what she had just called getting off their backs. He never wanted to interfere with any of them, though he had come to understand that this yen to be in their company often had the same effect.

The long hallway outside their room was heavily timbered and the slanted floor creaked beneath his feet so he could imagine that he was walking down a companionway of one of Philip II's ill-fated galleons. But then the character of the interior abruptly changed at the top of the stairs into that of an English country house, newels and banisters as solid and as noble as the empire. Coming down to the mid-landing, he was astonished to see that the fish had all disappeared. Another biblical miracle, perhaps. Not even a remnant odor was left behind to suggest their presence, and when he reached the bottom step, the aromas of malt and grain wafted out from the tap room with a heavy sensuality.

He was also surprised, as well as relieved, to find the place not as crowded as he had feared. Only a few sportsmen still held court at one part of the dark bar. The room was a polished composition of woods, glass and old metals—it must be pictured somewhere in a travel magazine—and the paneled ceiling was redolent with tobacco and whiskey smells and the dank odor like damp velvet produced by two centuries or more of fires in the manteled fireplace. To this mixture, the pungency of perfumes was added, spiced by the tinkle of jewelry and laughter from about a dozen women who sat around a mahogany table near the open French doors that faced the road. Williams had paused just inside the doorway.

Behind the bar, and obviously master of these revels, stood Mr. Gibbons. The manager had changed his costume to a mustard-colored vest, a crisp white shirt and a tartan bow tie. Even his face looked refurbished, perhaps thrust back into its original mold while he had changed clothes so that its ever-bright expression had been sharpened up. He raised his eyebrows and invited Williams to a place at the end of the bar.

"Ah, now, Mr. Williams. What may I get for you?"

"I guess some whiskey, thank you."

"Something from Cork?"

"That will do."

"Give a man his *dew.*" Mr. Gibbons returned the slogan of a particular whiskey. He looked like the boy in class who had just spelled "idiosyncratic" but who wasn't. Yet, Williams was grateful for the way he had deftly settled him away from the camaraderie and boastful exchanges at the bar's center. This professional host was at least trained to recognize the differences in his guests, who would mix with whom, and he seemed eager to please them all. Williams was a little chagrined by his own arrogance, which had misread the man's good intentions.

"This is your high season?" he asked when Mr. Gibbons returned with a whiskey neat, without ice, and a small pitcher of water on the side.

"It is that," the manager replied. He looked carefully at his guest, trying to judge whether Williams wanted to talk or was merely being polite. "When the salmon run, we have to quick-march and fetch. Some of our guests go back for generations, you know. It's the place to come for the salmon."

"All from England, I suppose."

"You can say that," Mr. Gibbons said and shifted his head slightly to indicate the men behind him. "Most book their rooms year in and out—the same reservations, year after year."

"I know," Williams replied. "The travel agent said we were lucky to get a room."

"Sir Harold Fitzhugh canceled out. Some sortie with the Common Market, I'm afraid, ruined the fishing for him. He's on that, you know," Mr. Gibbons confided amiably as he wiped a cloth over the lustrous finish of the bar, then refolded the napkin and patted it down on one side, ready for another go, another time. "But I'm pleased we had the place for you and Mrs. Williams. It's fishing of a different sort for you, and just as important, I dare say."

Williams had sipped the whiskey, enjoying the smooth burn it made down his throat and the oaky flavor curling around his tongue, so he had been unable to reply immediately. The man's attitude had nicked him again; yet, he could see no mockery in the upturned alertness. So, he said, "Yes, we had a very interesting afternoon. Strange to come on so many cousins all at once."

"They're fine people around here," Mr. Gibbons assured him. "Poor, of course, and a few too many mouths to feed for their own good because of their way of looking at things. It's their business, of course. But fine people all the same. But—not to include yours, now"—he leaned over the bar—"you have to keep an eye on them, you know." He winked. "If they're working for you, I mean." He had cocked a bright eye at a busboy who had just left the room with a tray of dirty glasses.

One of the gregarious anglers called Mr. Gibbons, and the manager quickly answered the summons, leaving Williams with a hard sourness in his belly. Probably the whiskey, which he wasn't used to drinking straight and without ice, though this was the only way to enjoy the local vintage. But wasn't it what the man had said, his sniggery spread of the same old calumnies that had fueled the vain rages on that back porch in Ohio? So Williams's words had come up to answer the manager, but they had been stoppered by the whiskey going down, slipping to the pit of his stomach to turn in the acid of their own fury. Ulcers started that way, he reminded himself, and not for the first time.

He had been touched by the distance between the busboy's wrist and the sleeve cuff of his mustard-colored jacket, and by the raw exposure of that pink flesh that had unknowingly made its way through the dark tunnel of material to emerge innocently and under suspicion all at once. Something about that young Irish boy's bone and tendons that called up his grandfather's neck when it stretched up above the starched white collar to make a point of exclamation to his anger: " . . . so I walked the whole distance back to the quartermaster and returned the part of the pay that wasn't mine, and I was *still* passed over for promotion." The laughter had been dry and knowing.

But his children would look at him. "So what," they would say—not all at once, but each at their different times would say that—and they would shrug and look away. Williams believed an inarticulate void within him always absorbed the words, the right words he knew to be there, which would make sense to them, quell their impatience with the stories of betrayals and denials and a curious honor so that they would have to sit down with the sagas' significance. Often, he would picture the moment, how it might happen in a corner of their library-den or by the small pond in back of the house, and how the young face would suddenly grow serious, look deeply for the first time into something not visible to ordinary vision.

But then, one of them—or all of them—would say, "But look at you. You're a success; this has nothing to do with you," and they would laugh at him, for they were proud of him and his success—or so his wife would assure him in the same tone of appeasement she used when talking to them. "You must listen to your father," she would say, which sometimes sounded—he wondered about this—as if she were granting them liberty not to listen. Lately, it had occurred to him that her role as a moderator had actually kept them apart, like a referee stepping between fighters, rather than permitting them to settle their differences, speak directly to each other.

Just then, laughter from the nearby table disturbed his own thoughts. Most of the fishermen had left the tap room to dress for dinner, but two had lagged behind to joke and flirt with the women. Their voices reflected the English upper class, or what always sounds like upper class to an American. Williams fancied the women to be sirens and impervious to the lures being played about them. Indeed, could not any one of them become the mortal clutch of a passionate angler? Their outfits suggested an abandonment of London shops for the ateliers of Paris and Milan, and his speculation turned to other betrayals. What, after all, did these women do while their husbands fished for the big one? How did they employ their time here in the lodge while the men kept their footing in treacherous currents?

Wasn't there a wonderful story about just this sort of thing? He tried to remember the author's name as he signaled Mr. Gibbons for a refill. It came to him as the manager brought over the Three Swallow and poured a generous dollop. William Humphrey had written about a fishing lodge on a river in Scotland, a place where salmon spawned and where, the humorous narrative implied, the sportsmen's consorts performed their own leaps against the current while their men were away. He couldn't remember all the details, who the rogue fisherman in the tale was, but to round out his fancy he wondered who might be baiting the hook here on the banks of Killary Bay.

"There you go, Mr. Williams," Mr. Gibbons said pleasantly. The man's whippet attentiveness made Williams smile. "Fine whiskey, it is," he announced and returned to other duties.

The road outside had become strangely busy. Pedestrians passed quickly before the open French doors. Their country dress of caps, thick jackets and dark wool stockings on the women was of such a startling contrast to the smartly dressed wives in the tap room that Williams felt he might be watching a film, that the open doorways were actually screens upon which an old film was being projected. But this was no entertainment being provided by Mr. Gibbons for his guests. Confusion edged the man's sharp profile, and he came around the bar to pass through one of the doors and to look down the road in the direction the townspeople were headed. Then he joined the rush.

"Something's up," one of the women said, and pushed back her chair.

"Let's see," another said, and joined her, and they were all on their feet and out the door with a clink and whisk of jewelry and silk. Several took their drinks.

Williams left his whiskey on the bar when he followed them. The crowd had collected around the small car at the side of the road, and by the time he reached the spot, two men were taking turns trying to revive the man on the ground. He lay belly up, and the flesh was very pale, perhaps never meant to be seen this way, turned over. The face had a bluish-green cast to it, as if bruised by a rough landing. The long white undershorts wrapped wetly around his loins, and he looked like a long-distance runner who had collapsed at the finish line, out of breath.

"Oh, Da, oh, Da, oh," one of the man's sons lamented, while the other countered his grief by shouting fierce directions at the two working over their father.

"Give it to him, lads. There now, don't you be shy with him. Get into it, man. Can't you do better than that?"

The dead man was not a stranger to the villagers, and they

spoke of him. He was from a small place in County Mayo, just up the road. He was a farmer. He and his sons had been to market below Leenane and had decided to have a swim on the way home. It was a common thing and done for generations; Williams knew that well enough. He encountered the women from the lodge as they moved gracefully through the crowd, the ice in their drinks hardly making a sound. "Poor man," one of them said to another, and turned her head aside to check an earring. Now a priest had crouched over the man.

"Ah, no, Da . . . no . . ." the one youth implored. His brother embraced him and they both looked down on the priest giving the Last Rites, looked expectantly, as if this practice would succeed where the earlier one had failed. The two men who had been doing CPR stood within the circle of onlookers, sleeves rolled up and chests bared like fighters who had come to a draw. A villager pounded one of them on the back and the fellow looked away modestly. Suddenly, like a brightly feathered land bird lighting among gulls, Mr. Gibbons was everywhere, managing and directing.

"Here now, we can put him into the boat house until his people come for him," he said. "That's the ticket, lift him gently, boys." He led the way, pushing back the crowd to create a small avenue for the corpse to be carried through and then across the road and into a whitewashed building, completely open in front. Inside, several fishing boats were stored upside down, and the dead man was laid onto the lapstraked hull of one of these. Meanwhile, the crowd had begun to disperse. Williams saw that his fellow guests were already halfway back to the lodge, stepping carefully over the unevenness of the gravel road. Some walked arm in arm and, just as they reached the inn, his wife came through one of the French doors.

One of the dead man's sons had got into the car, and a couple of locals gave it a push to get it started. He hunched over the steering wheel, looking straight ahead, as the car jerked into life. The other brother sat on a keg in the opening before the boat house, his head in his hands. Someone handed him his clothes, and he looked at them as if he might not claim them, then slowly pulled on the pants. Williams realized right then that the other brother had driven off in his underwear.

"Someone drowned?" Janice Williams said as she came up.

"More like a heart attack," he told her. They walked slowly back to the lodge. The light had slipped deeper into an eerie quality, like that of an eclipse, and the meager color of the landscape, the flat gray of the bay, had been all but filtered out. She reached for and took his hand, and he felt strangely comforted. "It's a terribly cold body of water," he heard himself say in a voice that sounded like another's. "I expect the shock of it might have kicked him off."

"What a tragedy," she said. "Coming in the middle of . . ." and she fell silent. After a few more steps she said, "You mustn't let this upset you."

Her consolation surprised him a little, as though there was a need to console him or that she had come upon that need. He pulled his hand away and searched through some change in his pants pocket. "Why should I be upset? The guy knew what he was doing." The glow from the tap room spilled out through the French doors. Some of the fishermen, a few in regimental pinks with ribbons on their chests, had joined their wives and were being told of the event. Before stepping through the door, Williams looked back. He could barely make out the shape of the boat house, but a lantern had been lit and placed on the ground by the young man on watch to mark the spot.

A second whiskey had been placed beside the one he had left on the bar, and Mr. Gibbons, accompanied by a barman and a waiter, was making the rounds of his guests, taking orders for drinks. "On the house," he invited eagerly. "On the house."

"It's like a plane having trouble," Janice Williams said. "You remember that time I was coming back from Nelly's and there was some problem with the flaps and the plane had to circle and circle until they fixed it? We were all loaded by the time we got on the ground; they kept pouring free drinks into us."

"I do remember," he said, and put his arm around her. The funny incident with its core of terror had refreshed their affection for each other then, as the remembrance of it did just now.

193

"I'd like to call Nelly tomorrow. Maybe we could get her to join us in Rome."

"Just like that?" She looked at him with amusement. "Leave her job and her friends and join the old folks on holiday?"

"Well, of course not." She had caught him out once again and he felt himself blush. "I just feel sometimes that there should be more chances given out—not time, but chances. You know, chances." His words came up against the familiar impasse, so he looked at her directly.

"I'll have a sherry, Mr. Gibbons, thank you very much," she told the manager.

The dining room on the other side of the foyer also had similar French doors that fronted the road, and they had been seated at a table before one of these. Several tables of sportsmen and their ladies were in the center of the room, and Mr. Gibbons moved around and through this boisterous group, pausing to lift a bottle of wine from its cooler, stopping to pass a pleasantry or bestow a discreet pat upon a uniformed shoulder. Williams had to admire the man's finesse: a great performance, and the noisy scene did resemble something out of a Regency drama or a print by Rowlandson. A thick-legged waitress set down a tray near them. The busboy with the short-sleeved jacket assisted her as she served them. Thick slabs of salmon were daubed by a heavy white sauce that made a quick reference to dill. Several boiled potatoes lolled to one side, their ramble halted by a pile of greenish vegetable.

"Well, we know the fish will be fresh," Janice Williams said as she scraped the sauce off to one side.

"And the potatoes," he said. "I remember my grandfather talking about their taste over here, and he was right. They're different, aren't they?"

"Yes," she said, taking a bite, but her voice had gone flat. She handled her knife and fork methodically and in the European fashion. Williams shifted his fork from left to right hand and lifted some potato to his mouth. Then some salmon.

It was Sir Francis Drake who brought the potato to Ireland

194

from Peru, his grandfather had told him. "They seeded the whole country with it," the old voice went on. Even in this dining room, with the cool night air blowing upon him, Williams could feel the heat of the porch steps coming through his clothes. "They were a cheap food supply to keep us going while the English took the sheep and the cattle for themselves. When the blight hit the potato, we had nothing. We starved. My people had the fish, at least."

"Are you enjoying the salmon?" Their turn with Mr. Gibbons had come. "Some of today's catch, and you can't beat a fresh piece of fish. I hope the unpleasantness down at the water has not spoiled your stay with us, Mr. and Mrs.— ah, Williams." The pause was not so much to remember the name but to turn it over again in his curiosity, to match it up with how its bearer looked. "My apologies for this awkward occurrence. Bad timing, for sure." He had checked their bottle and refilled their wineglasses as he spoke. "Can I close the windows for you?"

"No, thank you," Janice Williams said. "The night air is lovely."

"It is indeed," the manager replied. "As long as you're not disturbed by the gathering."

Only then did they notice the figures moving on the road in the darkness outside. The squarish outline of what must have been a hearse had just rolled by silently, as though pushed by the line of four or five people walking behind it. Then another line, all abreast, and then another. The relatives and villagers had come to claim the farmer's body. They could hear no sounds of weeping and barely the shuffle of feet upon the gravel road, and once again Williams felt he was watching an old movie with the sound off, or perhaps a film so ancient as to be a silent record of a tragic history. And wasn't this typical? he thought. The peasants parading their dead for the amusement of the English gentry dining on fine china? Most of the fishermen bent over their plates or threw back their heads with uproarious pleasure. Outside, the quiet procession continued. Perhaps the sounds of grief would come later, when the stunned senses regained their articulation.

Then the road was empty as well as dark. The last party of

mourners moved away on a curve around the bay and into the night. Williams looked into the blackness, trying to make out the figures as they became phantoms. Sea birds put out a last few cries. He could not be sure if the shapes moved only in his imagination, if only the sense of their passage now drew the images from him as it pulled at something else. A part of him wanted to run after, to join their procession to the graveyard. There, he might return all the old stories in his head to their source—just give them back—perhaps then the angry gift of them would be eased from his grasp, no longer catch at his words.

"What are you doing out there?" His wife's voice startled him. He had been standing outside the French window, holding his napkin in one hand. She looked amused but a little worried. "Are you all right?"

"They've gone, I guess," he answered. "I'm okay." The night had become freshly abundant, and he laughed in his embarrassment, being caught out once more, but maybe for the last time. Maybe the illusion had at last disappeared with the evening light, which had already given stone and reed back to the earth.

How the Indians Buried Their Dead

When the conference adjourns, the men relax and their talk turns to personal matters. Some swivel their chairs to face the large window, a vault of glass that keeps the city's skyline. Clouds, the color of gunmetal and perhaps as heavy, hang below the top of the skyscraper, their edges traced in gold by the weak afternoon sun.

On second thought, the clouds remind him of thick puddings baked in an unregulated oven so the tops become a toasty brown as the rest remains gray and lumpish. He has not been out of the tall building since he arrived for the meeting; all living, entertainment as well as the business, was conducted inside it. However, he knows what it would be like outside this large window, down there in the city. He can feel and smell the heat out there, like the memory of an old blanket in a summer attic.

"But that's interesting, that you were born here," the man at his elbow replies. "Remarkable to come back here like this and overlook the old home town from up here. Haven't been back since you left? And when was that?"

No, he will say, he doesn't remember exactly when he left, though he remembers the sort of day it was, what time it was and

197

other similar details. It was many years ago. In fact, he now recalls, he had been sent to visit relatives while his parents disposed of the house and packed their possessions. They had moved to another city and he had been sent away to visit someone to ease the shock. The details of that leavetaking he remembers, not when it happened. The man beside him accepts a cup of tea and a small sandwich from a uniformed steward.

And what had happened to that old man who had lived with them? A distant relative of some sort? Or maybe he was a boarder? He remembers the shoebox full of ribbons and medals the old man would bring down from the closet's top shelf for bedtime stories; star-shaped and crinkly to the touch, in browns and purples and yellows. A particular story went with each device; stories of hardships and deprivation and courage in the face of impossible odds, and of an old-fashioned sort of honor. Some tales were of killings, both just and unjust.

"He had a huge saber in a steel scabbard. It had a brass basket guard with brass wire wound around the grip and it stood in the corner of his closet. He'd let me play with it at bedtime while he told these tall stories. The sword was twice my size."

"What happened to it?" his companion says, peering into his cup, then drinking the last of the tea. "Swords like that are very rare these days. You could probably get a lot for it." The man looks around for a place to put down the cup and saucer, but they are by the window and no flat surfaces are close by. Courtesy, mixed with a little deference, keeps him standing there, holding the empty cup and saucer.

"He had these marvelous stories also about the Indians, of how they lived and buried their dead. He had a hat box also full of items found in their burial mounds. Trinkets and clay fragments, pieces of fabric. Arrow points and the heads of small hatchets. He loved the Indians, even though his duty was to kill some of them."

"Will you excuse me?" his colleague says. "I'm taking the evening flight out. You're not leaving until morning, are you? Until next time, then, and a pleasant journey." He leaves him by the window. The clouds have moved in across the city, have cooled and turned to lead.

Had the old man died that summer? Perhaps that was the reason they had moved away, or maybe they had moved to get away from the old man, to put distance between them and his boxes of faded ornaments, the clank of the saber in the corner of a closet. Perhaps he had ended his days in an old soldiers' home, talking of the prairies, the way of a horse, and about the Indians. In such a place, his medals would not be extraordinary; there would be many shoeboxes with similar contents, and a saber would be no novelty.

In the short distance between the building's main door and the taxi stand, he is able to take several breaths of the heavy, supercharged atmosphere. By contrast, it makes the purified air he has been breathing seem pallid, like the drinking water, manufactured from the sea, that is wet enough and cool enough, yet strangely unsatisfying to the thirst.

The address comes to his lips as if pinned to his memory, as it had been to his shirt pocket when he walked to school. But he must repeat the address, for the cab driver has turned about to look at him quizzically.

"I heard you the first time," the driver says. "That's a long way across town and it will be dark soon."

"And?" he asks the cabbie, who studies him closely now. Then the man shrugs and turns back to the wheel, puts the car in motion.

A store here, the curve of an avenue, a monument; each landmark fits into the different gaps of his remembrance. Much to the driver's mirror-reflected annoyance, he opens the windows to let the hot wind caress his face. The car's air-conditioning is quickly exchanged with the atmosphere outside, a mixture of fumes and odors that seem on the point of fusion.

Farther on, the streets broaden and there are more trees, the stores are less pretentious. An old motion-picture theater has become a garage, but the yarn store is still in business on the opposite corner. His mother would look over the colored bundles of wool, compare swatches of material for an hour at a time. The cab swerves around a sharp curve in the boulevard. Here trolley wheels had grated against the polished tracks and, coming home from downtown at night, he had pressed his face against the glass window, hands as blinders, to see the sparks.

The tracks have been removed, but it's remarkable how few other changes have occurred in the general outline of the area, and when they near the old neighborhood, his pulse quickens. He has a curious apprehension that the taxi may pass a corner where something or someone will be standing that will be too awful to see.

At last, the cab turns on to the large avenue that traverses the street where he had lived. The large town houses that line this thoroughfare are set back deep in the gloom of their dilapidation, but they were old even when he lived here and some of them had already been cut up into rooming houses. Built of sandstone or of brick, they are three and four stories high with great parabolae of porches, and bay windows of curved glass; curious open balconies too small for anyone to stand upon and for which there were no entrances from inside, anyway. Side by side in the dark waste of the neighborhood, they resemble the tall, rococo sterns of Spanish galleons marooned in a Sargasso sea.

"This is as far as I go," the driver has been saying. He has stopped at the curb. "You'll have to walk in from here, whatever your business is, so make it quick. That's my advice. Get out before it gets really dark."

The driver's tone is curt but not unfriendly. He thanks him for the warning and pays the fare. The cab makes a U-turn in the empty boulevard and drives away, and he starts to walk toward the head of the old, familiar street. Shadows rustle near him; sighs, sudden bursts of laughter and music. From one of the darkened houses comes a heavy version of a saraband. One of the clouds he had watched from the skyscraper's penthouse has just drifted over the neighborhood like a lid, sealing out the last light of day and compressing the atmosphere.

Suddenly, his leather shoes are stiff and awkward against the sidewalk, so he thinks of the pleasure of this same walk when he took it as a boy, barefoot in summer. This route lay between his house and the corner drugstore, apparently a dry cleaner's now, and almost every summer's night, the old man—

200

the boarder—would fetch some change from his pocket and send him running for a double scoop of ice cream. On the way back, he would sometimes take a shortcut between two of the old mansions and through a vacant lot. He would not go that way tonight.

He recognizes the corner of his block. An apartment building's dim outline rises from a raised terrace that has become a bald knob of clay. The building had been new in his day, its residents envied by his parents, but now it seems abandoned, windows and doors open and blank. Lights are in a few windows and the remains of an automobile sprawl at the curb. The car has been salvaged on the spot and still smells of the fire that finally took it. He turns down the street.

One, two houses, then past a fourth, a vacant lot, a row of garages, a few more desolate yards and he comes to the end of the block. He has walked past the place without recognizing it, or maybe it's been torn down and has become one of the vacant lots. He retraces his steps, past the street lamp that had been the safe-home of hide-and-seek games. It is the third house from the end. He has not recognized it for its smallness. He traces the roof line, the eaves and the walls, the front porch and steep stoop, and the building's shape gradually develops to match the larger image he has kept of it in his memory. Yes, this is the house.

Perhaps they had moved because the house had become too small for them, though he cannot remember any successive place being larger. Another consideration: Perhaps this house had not belonged to them at all but had been owned by the old man. Perhaps his parents had been the boarders. Maybe they had been asked to move.

The one light within the house burns in what he remembers as the kitchen. The people inside would be at supper now, and he recalls the old man sitting down to the kitchen table at supper, carefully peeling a boiled potato impaled on his fork. He always wore his hat at meals, a shapeless fedora, and wide suspenders stained with perspiration. The old man's room had been on the second floor, rear, and could not be seen from the street. His parents' room was in the front, and he slept in a small alcove off the bathroom, almost like a window seat. The living room was directly beneath, and on hot, muggy nights mattresses would be dragged downstairs and placed upon the bare floors to bring them closer to the cool, musty basement below. The old man never left his bedroom.

The basement was reached by stairs from the kitchen, and the three rooms down there were given over to storage, a workshop and furnace with some evidence of a summer kitchen and pantry. These basement rooms were where he played in bad weather. So many recesses and corners, so many perfect hiding places. He often forgot where he secreted a favorite toy, and the discovery of it would make it new. Perhaps, behind a molding or in a cobwebbed niche, a model car or a favorite top might still be hidden; there, after all these years.

The steps up to the porch crunch beneath his feet, the masonry rotted out, but the porch itself seems sound. However, he notes two wires poke through the mullion where a large brass bell plate had been, and he is amused to wonder what would happen if he joined the bare wires together. Perhaps the house, if not the whole neighborhood, might explode. He knocks on the screen door. The living room is very dark; only a faint gleam comes from the kitchen in the rear. No sound comes through the screen door.

He smells cooking oil and something he associates with old clothes and damp upholstery. In sultry weather, a dampness would waft up from the basement that had been as welcome as a sea breeze. He knocks again. Someone must be home; the screen door seems unlatched. The evening meal occupies them. They are carefully cutting meat and methodically peeling the skin from boiled potatoes. Then, without his knowing when it happened, someone is standing on the other side of the screen door.

"I beg your pardon." He speaks into the dark screen where he imagines a face might be. "I'm sorry to disturb you. I'm a visitor, just passing through, but I used to live in this house, and since I was just passing through it seemed a good chance to visit the old neighborhood. To see this house. I was only a child then and it was long ago. Maybe only seven years old. Right here." No sound comes from the other side of the screen, and his eyes ache from their concentration. He cannot see anything that even resembles the white of an eye.

"The old neighborhood hasn't changed much," he continues. "Same old street lamp down there. That string of garages. Some of us had a clubhouse in one of them. Well, it does seem quieter. Maybe not so many children on the block now. You wouldn't believe the sound we all made coming down the sidewalk on roller skates. Quite a bunch. Well, the house looks in good shape." He looks away from the naked wires by the door. "It's been kept up well. I guess it would be too much to ask— I don't suppose it would be possible for me to come in and look around."

"No, I don't think so."

The answer stuns him; not the negative, which was to be expected, but the tone of the voice. It was neutral, inflectionless and carried no emotion. "No, I don't think so." A calm statement of a position, a little bored by the necessity to express it, as if people continually came to this door, day after night, asking for admittance, and the person within patiently denied the requests, night after day.

"No, of course not, and I quite understand," he says, catching his breath. "After all, it's your house now, and I'm only passing through, only a visitor. Actually, I lived here just a few years, not even the minimum residency most childhoods could claim. But tell me"—he moves closer to the screen—"if I may try your patience just a bit longer, is there still that peculiar grass in the backyard?"

"There's no grass in the backyard," the voice says tonelessly.

"Really? I would have thought it impossible to kill off. You see, an old gentleman lived here with us, or we with him, and he had been a world traveler with many stories to tell and many mementos. He had brought back from South America this peculiar grass. Two large clumps of it that made marvelous hiding places because there was a small space within each clump where you could squat down and not be found for hours. But you had to be careful handling the stuff. If you ran your fingers the wrong way, backwards, along the strands, it would cut you, actually draw blood. He said it was used in South America to cut ticks off cattle as they moved through the pampas. Pampas grass. Very tough stuff. I remember my parents tried to burn it out because I was always getting cut up by it. But it grew right back. Now it's gone. Amazing.''

"Yes, gone,'' the voice says. A foot is shifted, a sigh— sounds of forbearance in the dark.

"This is one of the reasons I became so bold, almost was impelled to ask if I could come into the house. So many things about the old man I never knew, never understood. He had strange things in boxes. Nothing really valuable, of course''—he looks frankly into the blackness—"but trinkets, odd bits of stuff. Old campaign ribbons and medals. He had been a soldier too. Yellowed newspaper clippings and photographs and different manuals for the operation and maintenance of weapons that were obsolete even then. Yes, even then they were old-fashioned, out of date. But for a child my age, you can imagine— fascinating.'' A siren wails far in the distance.

"I just thought I might be able to locate a few things, find stuff in places you may not know about. Old, worthless things really, but something he might have left behind. This house has so many nooks and crannies to it. He might have left something behind. I don't suppose you found anything like that when you moved in?''

"No. Nothing.''

"No, of course not. He kept all of it in a shoebox and then he had another box with things he had taken from . . . well, no matter. One thing he had, maybe you've come across, because it was made of steel. It was his old saber.''

"What's that?''

"A saber? A saber is a long sword with a curved blade. It's one of those old-fashioned weapons that was used by the cavalry, soldiers on horseback in the old days. It must have been four, five feet long in its metal case.''

"No sword like that here,'' the voice says with some anxiousness, maybe hostility. "Nothing like that here. Nothing like that ever here.''

"Oh, but there was, I clearly remember—''

204

"I'm telling you there's no sword here."

"Well, maybe not when you moved in, of course, but in the old days when I was—"

"You better go," the voice says calmly. "It's late. You shouldn't be here now. It is not safe for you to be here like this."

"Yes, yes. You're right," he replies, backing away. "I'm sorry to have bothered you. I'm sorry," he says from the top of the steps. "I'm very sorry. Truly sorry."

"Go," says the voice out of the dark.

A few scattered giggles and snorts pursue him up the street to the boulevard, where they fall away, diluted by the grand, illuminated width of the old parkway. Here, louder cries echo within the stone verandas, and the crash of a heavy door cuts short a scream.

At the corner, a modern street lamp with a damaged filament peoples the empty intersection with sporadic, jerky shadows. It is not yet completely nightfall, but he sees the dancing illumination of flames several blocks away, as if a large fire were silently at work and being ignored.

He turns toward the center of the city, following the scars of the old trolley tracks that have risen through the layers of macadam that had covered them over. To his right is a playground, surrounded by a high fence of heavy mesh steel welded to substantial posts. Inside is the full-scale replica of a gingerbread house, though its peppermint candy shingles are blackened and its chimney has toppled into the hole made by the fire that had gutted the playhouse. "An inside job," he thinks, and laughs a little.

At last, just as it goes completely dark, he comes to a rise and sees the glittering prospect of the downtown skyline, dominated by the huge skyscraper he had left earlier. The tall building is illuminated by searchlights that set it aglow, inflaming the clouds that surround the top floors so it looks as if it were on fire, too. But then, the building appears like a great rocket ship preparing to ignite its engines, preparing to pull itself up through the heavy clouds and leave all this behind. He would have to hurry.